SEEKER 4

Invasion of the Pirates

VOYAGES OF THE SEEKER

CLINT HOLLINGSWORTH

For Warren E. Stewart.
I'll see you on the other side, my friend.

1

Our sister ship, the *E.S.S. Wanderer*, was missing.

The term sister ship had even more desperate meaning to me. My own sister, Valiel Voss, was on that ship. And we were *so* far away.

Traveling through Nth space is an experience best taken in small doses. The continued overuse of the *Seeker*'s Jump Drive had everyone's nerves on edge.

The roiling blues and azures that lined the "tunnel" of our jump path, normally considered beautiful by the crew, had become almost painful. The forward lounge, usually quite well occupied, had very few other people in it, from any of the species onboard.

This was the longest Nth space jump that our explorer ship, the *E.S.S. Seeker* had ever taken since I'd been brought on board as a cadet for her maiden voyage. Such a journey was generally broken up into multiple jumps to prevent wear and tear on the ship's systems and on the mental state of the crew.

"Tanner, love," Ensign Emily Darkfeather said, "you're making yourself sick. You've literally worn a rough patch in the carpeting in that spot, and the carpet's made of Duralon." Emily, formerly my superior officer and now my lover, had been sitting with me for the last hour. She'd been trying to talk me 'off the ledge' without much luck.

"I've been trying to keep it together, Em," I replied. "But then my mind starts running through awful scenarios. Val's body drifting through space, or spread out amongst the wreckage of a planetary crash. Then, the anxiety spiral starts up again."

"Val's lucky to have a brother who cares so much, Tanner."

"It's always been Valiel and I against the world, even before we were put in cryo-sleep for a hundred and fifty years. No one else on Earth knew that we were alien-human hybrids, it was our secret. It made us super close, maybe more than most siblings because we..."

"Ensign Tanner Voss report to the bridge," Lt. Sedgewick's voice came over the ship's speaker system. The same message emerged from my belt-mounted padd's speakers and my sub-dermal transponder.

Emily rose from her seat too. Being a bridge officer, she could access the bridge even when she was off shift and I knew she was going with me simply to offer moral support. Emily and I had developed a bond that was stronger every day, and I thanked whoever was in charge of the universe for her.

"We must be close to emergence," she said. "We've been jumping for fifty-two hours now, and that's near what was calculated to get to the farthest point out *Wanderer* could've reached on her exploratory route."

"Hopefully we can get some answers now," I replied, dodging around other crew people in the ship-long central corridor. We entered Primary Lift Number One and Emily hit the key for *Seeker's* bridge.

"Hopefully, *Wanderer's* radio silence is a malfunction issue. Best case, we'll find them and they'll ask us for a tow home."

"That'd be one hell of a malfunction, Emily. Think of all the redundancy the *Seeker* has. *Wanderer* was built on the same specs. If there was a big ship-wide malfunction, one of their Remora probes would've been able to make the multiple jumps back to Earth, even at their farthest planned point away from home."

Before Emily could reply, the lift doors opened onto the bridge and we emerged into the hustle and bustle of a ship about to emerge into real space.

"Mr. Voss," First Officer M'Buku said from the Captain's chair, "since you're not on duty, take a side seat. You too Darkfeather. We're about to emerge and the Captain said to have you here as a courtesy." He looked at the ceiling, "You too, Dora. Feel free to join us."

A blue-tinted hologram of a female junior officer appeared next to the commander, wearing the face of my artificial intelligence mother. "Thank you, Commander," She said. It was a show of solidarity from M'Buku, perhaps a show of respect. He well knew that Dora, being linked in to all *Seeker's* systems was ever-present.

She was just as worried about Valiel as I was. We were both worried about my dad Evan, also. Evan, like Dora, was a Laldoralin AI who'd cared for Val and I when we were kids. Both had stowed away digitally on our respective ships to keep an eye on us.

I'd never known my biological mother, a famous astronaut who'd died on the first mars mission. Val and I had been born from her stored ova, but Dora was the only mother we'd ever known.

"Five seconds to emergence," Lieutenant Kolara said from the helm station. "Navigation puts us emerging from our target point with a divergence of less than five-hundred fifty miles."

"Still, that's a bit of a ways off," M'Buku replied. He touched the intercom panel on the command chair. "Captain, we're emerging right about... *now*."

The forward view screen abruptly changed from the strange spinning glow of jump space to the vastness of normal space. Ahead I saw several stars, a smallish nebula and beyond that, in varying degrees of brightness, a seemingly infinite number of glowing galaxies, all digitally enhanced.

For all that we could see of celestial bodies that were visible, the area nearby was relatively empty. These coordinates were at a point just beyond the limit of what the *Wanderer* could've reached in the time that's passed since our missions started. We'd follow her assigned path backwards in our attempt to find her.

"Captain on the bridge!" Emily called out.

"As you were," Captain Megumi Yamashita said before her people could stand to attention. She'd tried to curtail that particular military behavior, saying it was counter-productive, but ingrained academy habits are hard to break. "Have we launched Remoras yet?"

"Not yet, Captain, but we're primed to do so on your order," Commander M'Buku told her.

"Permission to deploy in Remora Two, Captain," Dora said. "I'm eager to join the search, and Organizer of Armadas has asked permission to twin to Remora Three to aid in our quest."

"So our guest alien AI wants to help? Is he good to go on this, Dora?"

"Reminding the Captain that I also am an 'alien' AI, I have coached Organizer on how to compress his processes to fit in one of our second generation Remoras. Commander Truvall has also retrofitted Remora Three with extra storage for scanning data. I believe this will be a good test, and Organizer is oh so eager to be a help to us. To be one of our crew."

"If you think he's ready, then you are green to go. Commander, deploy probes." The Captain looked over at Emily and me.

I felt hopeful. *Oh, please give us something to do, I mentally pleaded. I'm going crazy just sitting around.*

"Tanner, I'm betting you're going crazy just sitting around," she said. "You and Emily report to the Alt Bridge and help Lt. Commander Sharma with analysis when the probes start sending back data. Dismissed."

I glanced at Dora and breathed a sigh of relief.

"Aye Captain," We said simultaneously and left the main bridge.

———

The Alternate Bridge on our ship was designed to be, first and foremost, an emergency replacement in case the main bridge was rendered inoperable. It also worked well as a data processing center, having the exact layout as its primary counterpart. I'd spent a lot of time here before being promoted to acting Ensign.

The *Seeker*'s second officer, Lt. Commander Parul Sharma, was often here when she wasn't commanding the night shift on the main bridge. As Emily and I entered, I could see, as per regulations, this secondary control center was also manned by junior officers and crew members. Now that we had finished our journey, half of them were getting ready to leave for their regular duty stations.

"Ensigns Darkfeather and Voss reporting, Commander," Emily said. "Captain Yamashita felt we could help you with the incoming probe data."

Sharma, a slender dark-haired twenty-something woman

from Earth's India, looked at me knowingly, "I'd be glad for the help, Ensigns. I imagine Tanner would like to get right to it."

"I would indeed, Ma'am. Not knowing what's happened to *Wanderer* and her crew has been weighing on me pretty heavily."

"Tanner, it's okay to admit that you're concerned about your sister."

"And his dad," Emily said.

"Your father is on that ship?" Sharma asked. "I thought your father was a very high-ranking Laldoralin official. How'd he get on..."

"Krizon is my genetic father, Ma'am, and honestly he's not a part of my life. Evan, however is my real dad. He's an AI, just like my mom. She stowed away on *Seeker* to watch over me, and he did the same on *Wanderer* to watch over my sister, Valiel."

"The AIs were the ones who did the actual parenting before you and Valiel were put in cryo-sleep, weren't they?" Emily asked.

"Yeah. Krizon was there in his underground science lair, but Evan and Dora were the ones who raised us and gave us emotional support. Quite frankly, I don't think Krizon was capable of that."

"Your life has been anything but mundane hasn't it, Tanner?" Sharma noted. "I understand about distant fathers though, believe me. Anyway, if each of you could take a station and configure it for data processing, I'll take all the help I can get. These slackers are all deserting me." Several of the departing crew grinned as they left for their regular non-jump stations throughout the ship.

Emily and I logged onto adjoining duty stations and made the proper requests to the bridge for data access. A few moments later, information being relayed from the Remora probes began to scroll across our screens.

"Looks like the captain has deployed the Remoras in an offset box," Emily said. "Maximum coverage of the areas we pass through, but shorter range on our path of travel."

"*Wanderer* has a pre-planned exploration route," Sharma said. "I find it hard to believe that they would've deviated from that course to an extent that our advanced probes couldn't at least pick up a trace."

"And a trace is all the Remoras need to track them," Emily said.

2

Three days later, three days of nothing-burger results, the Captain and Dora decided to change search tactics.

"The problem is, of course, the pure vastness of the area we're searching," Dora said as she 'stood' next to the command chair. "*Wanderer's* flight path entailed jumping from planetary system to planetary system. The problem, however, is that even the best laid plans of mice and starships can go awry."

"If our sister ship had a major unfixable Jump Drive failure," Captain Yamashita replied, "which is an unlikely event, she could be in what we quaintly call 'the spaces in between.' She'd be lost in the emptiness between solar systems."

"The distance from one end of a planetary system to the other end is an impressive distance, but it pales in comparison to the amount of 'empty' space between star systems." Science officer Torvald interjected. "At least in a system, there would be asteroids for *Wanderer* to mine for materials needed for the replication printers, and probably gas giants to mine fuel resources."

Sitting at the tactical station, I thought about what

Commander Torvald was saying. With those printers and enough of the proper materials, you could replace almost any component of Earth's explorer ships.

But the basic hard fact was that we had to scan every astronomical unit on the general line of *Wanderer's* flight path. That was several light year's worth of astronomical units between each system. There are about 180 AUs in Earth's solar system. A light year is about 64,500 times the size of an AU. It was a Herculean haystack we were trying to find our interstellar needle in.

"This is taking too long," the captain said. "Time for a new strategy. Here's what I want to do. *Seeker* will jump into a new search grid and begin scanning. Then, the Remora's, divided into two flights of two, can leap frog past the ship into the next two grids, rotating around their flight path for maximum scanning area. With the ship and two probe flights jumping along over each other, we'll increased our scanning distance and speed considerably."

It would speed us up, but it wouldn't make the waiting any easier. It also strengthened the possibility that we might miss something by stretching our probes over a larger area of space.

Fortunately, our Remora's are some of the most impressive information-gathering devices ever created by man, and two of ours were doubly enhanced by technology provided by the AI controllers of one our new colony worlds.

The Melpin and the Kulpin had provided us with leaps ahead in shield tech, weaponry and sensor improvements far beyond any other earth ship. Add to all that new technology, Remoras Two and Three were controlled by Dora and Organizer of Armadas, and there was very little chance that anything would escape our notice.

It was some of these enhancements which allowed us to make our first discovery.

"Contact!" Emily yelled, her single long black braid whipping about as she swung around to report to the captain.

"Report!," Captain Yamashita said. "Is it *Wanderer?*" Yamashita had been sitting, drumming her fingers on her command chair off and on for the last two hours. Her normally stoic expression was replaced by one of fierce interest.

"It's definitely a ship, Ma'am. Getting more details now. Remora Two has jumped to the contact's position and...." Emily looked up from her screen, disappointment on her face, "It is not *Wanderer*, Captain."

The entire bridge crew had perked up at the word 'contact' and we all visibly deflated at the clarification.

"Ship is of an unknown design," Emily continued. "Nothing in the Laldoralin database matches."

"Have we finished our scans of this area?" the captain asked, her voice quiet with the disappointment we all felt.

"Ninety-eight percent complete, with no positives," Science Officer Torvald told her.

The captain turned to the helm/navigation station. "Mr. Kolara, plot a jump to Remora Two's location. Let's take a look at this unknown ship."

———

"Definitely not any Hegemony design." Lieutenant Commander Torvald looked up from the data scrolling across his workstation monitor. The tall, lanky Norwegian science officer looked up at the hulk slowly tumbling on the main view screen. "It's a sturdy design, perhaps made for high-FTL speeds. Unfortunately, there are no life signs at all."

The Laldoralin Hegemony, which Earth was a member of,

had numerous divergent species, some of which were members of our own crew. Since none of the Hegemony members had ever designed a ship like this, we were making first contact with a new species.

Unfortunately, there was no one on the slowly-spinning vessel to shake appendages with. The alien ship was dead, with only a flicker of power in its various remaining systems.

Note the use of the term "remaining."

"She looks like someone has surgically cut her open and scraped out her guts," I said from the tactical station. "There are huge openings in her aft section that I'm sure were not part of her design." My post at tactical gave me access to the science section's sensor array. I was glad I was on shift when the alien vessel was found.

The other ship consisted of a bulbous saucer in front with long engine pods extending from struts on the top and bottom of the saucer. It reminded me, in the most vague terms, of a video science fiction ship from a show I'd regularly watched back in the twenty-first century.

"Surgically is the right word here," Torvald said. With a few strokes on his touch pad, our science officer highlighted sections of the vessel now taking up most of the forward view screen. "These large sections have been cut away from the hull with precision and inside the ship, at these points, it appears large systems have been removed." He brought up a pointer at a section near the rear of the vessel. "This huge area, with lots of power leads and conduits leading in, is essentially empty of anything important. There are consoles, but most everything there leads to the conclusion that a large piece of technology, and I'm guessing a power plant, has been... pirated. Cut out of the ship and scavenged."

"Dora, can you tell how long she's been drifting to be here in the middle of nowhere?" Captain Yamashita asked, pensively watching the ship slowly tumble end-over-end.

Dora's hologram appeared next to the captain. At this short distance, she could literally be in two places at the same time, resident on Remora Two and in *Seeker's* main computer with no lag between her two selves.

"The alien ship has been dead for some time now." Dora told the captain. "I've been estimating energy degradation on the cuts used to open her up, and my calculations indicate that this vessel has been in this state for roughly fifteen solar years."

"Makes me wonder if we'll find the *Wanderer* in similar shape," Lieutenant Forbes said from the primary tactical station. Forbes, my lead at tactical, tended to 'worst-case scenario' things early on. The thought of my sister's ship drifting dead in space with no survivors made my head swim for a moment. The Captain must have noticed my expression. She glared at Forbes.

"It is far too early to make assumptions like that, Lieutenant," Yamashita said. "*Wanderer* is much more likely stranded somewhere with technical problems than the victim of piracy. Please rein in such speculation until more facts are in evidence."

"Yes, Captain," Forbes replied. He glanced at me then back at his screen, his message clear, *I hope she's right, but I don't think she is.* I felt sick to my stomach at the very thought he could be correct.

"Captain," Dora said. "I'm scanning the remains of life-forms. All seem to be the same species except one. Of the second species, I only have a few blood stains. One odd thing, though."

"Which is?" Yamashita said to Mom's hologram.

"This ship, while foreign in design is still laid out upon recognizable principles. The majority of the dead are humanoid in nature, and from that I can extrapolate on the number of beings needed to crew this vessel. There are far fewer corpses here than are needed to do so."

"So what are you saying?" Commander M'Buku, sitting in the first officer's chair, asked as he ran his hand over his shaved head. "They were spaced?"

"At the speed this ship is drifting," Dora replied, "I can calculate fairly closely where it was attacked. Moving at the relatively slow speed that it is passing though space, the point of attack is well within the range of our scanners. For added veracity, I have just instructed Remora One to jump to those coordinates." Dora said. She stood still for what seemed like a full minute then continued. "There are debris in the general area matching this craft's metallurgy. There are no organic signs there, or even on any possible drift trajectories. Unless the missing crew were accelerated to a speed of near .5 light speed, there is no chance they'd be outside of scanning range."

"The bottom line, if you please, Dora," Captain Yamashita said.

"They were either very thoroughly vaporized, or the more likely answer, they were abducted."

"To what purpose?" Torvald asked.

"I regret, commander," Dora replied, "my powers of extrapolation do not extend that far."

3

We spent a full day scanning the derelict. After that, the Remoras were sent farther ahead on *Wanderer's* search path. After scanning the dead ship thoroughly, *Seeker* jumped out in front of our probes to resume our part of the search grids.

I was temporarily reassigned to my original position on our ship in the robotics engineering department. We were running the Remoras 24/7 and all hands trained on their maintenance were needed to keep them in top shape.

Remora Three had just returned from deep space and Organizer of Armadas, the alien AI resident therein, was giving me his impressions of the search while Crewman N'Tar and I worked on his probe body.

"Are you experiencing anything not showing on your diagnostics, Organizer?" N'Tar, a female humanoid from the planet Kapa asked the AI. N'tar looked almost human, with the exception of lavender-ish skin and a smaller second pair of multi-jointed arms sprouting from near her armpits. She was one of several Laldoralin Hegemony volunteers on the *Seeker*.

"I am functioning at optimal levels, N'Tar Crew-person.

However, I am experiencing an emotion that I do not have a great deal of experience with."

"What emotion is that?" I asked, remembering that this AI had been trapped, all alone on a dying Blah-Veht battleship for centuries. "Do you feel it's compromising your performance?"

"Negative. The emotion, while unfamiliar to me is almost humorous. I am feeling what I believe is... envy."

"Really?" N'Tar said, looking at me with a surprised expression. "What is the cause of this?"

Organizer paused a moment, as if coming to terms with this new feeling, then continued. "I am envious of Dora's transfer rate. We have twin versions of ourselves in both the *Seeker* starship and in Remora probes. We synchronize at regular intervals, but Dora can do so at will, from great distance. I, on the other hand, must be much closer to our ship for complete uploads, and my transfer rate is much slower. When I am transferring, I lose the capability to fulfill several of my main functions, as syncing between ship self and Remora self takes up a great deal of my processing ability. To cloak the situation in human phraseology, I cannot walk and chew bubblegum at the same time. It is vexing."

"In all fairness," I said, "you're transferring an enormous amount of data when you return. Also, working in the probe is a completely different function than what you were designed for."

"I would also point out that your residence in this probe enhances its capabilities by a vast amount," N'Tar said. "Remoras One and Four, neither of which are upgraded, only have human-designed computers. Their processing abilities are far, far inferior to yours and Dora's. No offense intended, Ensign Voss."

"None taken, N'Tar. I'm perfectly willing to admit that Earth's technology is still in its infancy compared to the older races in the Hegemony. And we'd be even further behind if my father's people hadn't been doling out bits of advancement here and there. Another thing though, Organizer is that you are syncing yourself at the same time you are transferring information to *Seeker*'s main computer. That's a big data load."

"For me, Voss Ensign. For your mother, it is child's play."

"Organizer, I know you are transferring your findings on your last grid to our science teams," N'Tar said. "I am merely curious if there is anything you can share those of us who are not on the bridge?"

"I have been finding ion trails, more than I would expect from being, as humans would say, 'in the middle of nowhere.' Though most of these trails, which indicate the passage of ships moving above FTL speeds, have dissipated to the point of faint recognizability. There are, however, a few that are relatively recent."

N'Tar and I looked at each other. When the *Seeker* left Earth, this news might've been thrilling to learn. Now, after all we'd seen on our travels, such news engendered caution.

"Hopefully," I said, "they're not from ships with a strong interest in piracy."

4

After another six days of searching empty space we at last found something.

"Contact!" Emily Darkfeather exclaimed, excitement in her voice, from science station two. I was sitting at the tactical station and like the rest of the bridge crew looked up from what I was doing at the announcement.

I had to stop myself from jumping up to look over Emily's shoulder, but Captain Yamashita would've told me to sit down, possibly in a humiliating fashion.

Please let it be Wanderer!

All eyes on Emily, she continued: "It's a ship of unknown design, about twice our size, moving about three times FTL. Course is approximately 55° port and 12° up from our own. Moving away from us. It ran through Remora Three's scanning zone."

Not Wanderer. Dammit! I had reached the point where new wonders meant nothing until I knew Valiel was safe.

A few days before, Emily had sat me down and given me a lecture on holding it together and being professional, especially on the bridge. She was my lover, but she was also technically senior to me and I'd been a little embarrassed to be called on my inability to hold my frustration in.

"Distance?" Captain Yamashita asked.

"Roughly 450 AUs from us, about 200 AUs from Organizer's Remora. At that distance, our Remoras can get basic exterior details, but nothing beyond that. No shields beyond basic deflectors."

The captain rested her chin on her palm. "Have Organizer halve the distance between them and see if he can get more detail. I wish that Torvald and Solas were farther along with their stealth experiments. That Sallan technology would come in very handy if we wanted to get our probes in close to someone."

Emily sent instructions to Organizer of Armadas. The bridge's main view screen had plots of our position, the positions of our probes, and now an icon representing the unknown star ship.

"Commander M'Buku," The captain said, looking over at our first officer, "Just to be safe, bring us to yellow alert."

"Aye, Captain," he said, touching part of his keypad. Two chimes rang out, and the floor lighting around the ship turned an amber shade. *Seeker*'s crew went to heightened alertness.

The icon for Remora Three disappeared for a moment, then it reappeared much closer to its scanning target. Readouts on the bridge began updating immediately. The tactical station had access to the same readouts as the science stations and I followed along as information came in.

Maybe these sentients have news of Val and her ship.

The strange vessel was shaped like a faceted diamond cut in half lengthwise, the pointed end facing front. The aft end appeared to be one huge drive, pushing the craft at FTL speeds easily exceeding *Seeker*'s best speed using our Faster Than Light engines.

"Captain, I'm not reading any power outputs that would indicate jump technology. They're powering along under FTL drive alone." Emily said.

So they can't translocate. They're just able to go really really fast.

"Hmm. Jump capability seems to be a hit or miss thing out here," Captain Yamashita said. "It looks to me that the speed they're casually cruising at would be maxing out and straining our FTL drive. I wonder how fast they can actually go in a sprint."

It was a mere moment before Captain Yamashita's question was answered. The diamond-shaped ship sped up another 30 percent above the speed it had been traveling, far faster than our top FTL speed, and even farther in advance of Remora Three's FTL capabilities.

This didn't faze Organizer in the least. Without waiting for instructions, he used his Jump Drive to bounce ahead of the fleeing ship and placed himself squarely in their path. He resumed scanning as they rapidly approached his new position.

"Get out of their way, Organizer! NOW! Inserting yourself in front of that fleeing ship could be construed as hostile intent. GET OUT OF THEIR WAY! Do you understand?" Captain Yamashita commanded. "Dammit!" she added, almost under her breath.

"Vampire!" Emily cried out from her science station. "Multiple missile launches at Remora Three."

We watched as four FTL missiles closed in on Organizer's position. Our guest AI jumped immediately and re-emerged into normal space far to the side of the alien vessel. The missiles launched at him passed thorough his former position and seconds later all detonated simultaneously.

"Those detonations had all the earmarks of abort self destruction," Commander M'Buku said. "They destroyed them when there was no longer a target."

"Lieutenant Sedgewick, hail them," Captain Yamashita commanded, irritation dripping from her voice. "Hopefully we haven't screwed this up too bad. Let's see if we can establish meaningful communication. Transmit visual as well."

"Transmitting."

We waited for a few moments. "Captain, they're slowing." Emily said.

"Transmission incoming," Sedgewick said.

The image that appeared on the main viewer was surprising. What appeared to be a large and very ornate wolf spider stared out at us. With the exception of the bright colors and baubles festooning its exterior, it was a dead ringer for Lieutenant Bitt-Nurr, our arachnid computer lead.

"Lieutenant Bitt-nurr. This is the captain, report to the bridge immediately." Yamashita said. "Dora? We'll need your help here."

"Well, this is interesting," Dora said, her hologram appearing next to the captain's chair. "We are a long way from Bitt-Nurr's homeworld, Ang-Doh. I wonder... parallel evolution? Or is there some ancient link as there was with the Dohannen and the Medigin on the planet Derilon?"

The image on the screen let loose with a barrage of clicks, trills and snaps. Having heard Bitt-Nurr speak without my sub-dermal transponder-translator engaged, I knew the alien was trying to communicate, and it sounded very similar to our spidery computer experts vocalizations. Unfortunately, our translators didn't have the proper Rosetta stone for the language we were hearing.

That meant that it wasn't speaking Bitt-Nurr's language either.

A few moments later, our eight-legged officer emerged from the lift, a rather tight space for her. Bitt-Nurr was a large, no-nonsense sentient and seemed a little exasperated with the size limitations of our human-designed star ship.

"Bitt-Nurr reporting as ord..." she pulled up short, her front end raised high, her forward two limbs in a defensive position. Knowing what I did of her, she was experiencing surprise as she noted the image on the view screen. Even more interesting, was the other ship's captain and his or her reaction.

It was an exact mirror of Bitt-Nurr's.

"Lieutenant, we've encountered a new species," Captain Yamashita told Bitt-Nurr, gesturing toward the screen. "They don't seem to be speaking any language in our translation matrix, but for obvious reasons, we were hoping between you and Dora that we might establish basic communication."

"Happy to help am I." Bitt-Nurr moved near the main viewer so that the alien captain could see her more clearly. He seemed as surprised to see her as she had been to see him. He began a new stream of vocalizations accompanied by rapid gesturing with his front two limbs.

"Hello," Bitt-Nurr was also clicking and trilling, but at a much slower pace than the other. I guessed that she wasn't picking up too much of what their captain was saying. Since her words were translated, the rest of us could follow along. She gestured toward herself with her own front limbs. "Bitt-Nurr."

The other Captain noted this and mirrored the gesture. He clicked slowly this time.

"He is Captain Drunor," Dora remarked. "Or whatever the rank of leader might be on his ship, I'm extrapolating a little there. But his name is Drunor."

From there, it became apparent that Captain Drunor wasn't hostile. In fact, his actions seemed quite friendly. I was glad after our first interaction, involving missiles, that we had the possibility of good relations. For the next several hours, Bitt-Nurr and the alien leader slowly began to communicate with each other while Dora built a communication index.

I'm ashamed to say that the novelty wore off after the first hour for me, since I wasn't able to contribute anything of worth to the first contact process. I spent most of my time going over what our scanners had learned of Drunor's ship. As I did so, our equipment told us that Drunor's people were scanning *Seeker* intently as well.

Eventually, a breakthrough was made.

"Ah. I believe I am ready to begin rudimentary translation," Dora told the Captain. "Our friend there has, in his language, similarities to Bitt-Nurr's. Communication will be quite basic for a while, but the longer they speak, the more I can build a translatable language database."

"Freight," Drunor said via the view screen, "we make from to between several (un-intelligible). This is our eat. Is your eat too?"

"We are explorers," Bitt-Nurr replied. "We are from far away, looking for empty worlds to explore."

"Ah. There some of these," Drunor replied. "Space here is dangerous. Kalikak. Dangerous beings eat ships. Take beings away. Leave ship empty dead. We move fast. They do no catch."

"We found a dead ship with no crew."

Drunor seemed to droop slightly at Bitt-Nurr's comment. "Is bad. We not shoot at friendly. Did not know you friendly."

"It is all right," Bitt-Nurr assured him. "Can you tell us more of these... Kalikak? We are seeking a vessel like this one? Like ours. Missing, it is."

"This is bad," Drunor said. "Dead ship you found is what Kalikak do. Was all cut up and emptied?"

"Yes."

"Steal all value. Take beings labor. Slaves. Captured beings slaves. Leave ship drifting. If ship missing, we think Kalikak. No see ship like yours. I travel this area much. More than is safe. Have good ship eyes. Never see ship like yours."

Forbes turned to me and said quietly; "For a ship with "good eyes", they didn't seem to notice us until Remora Three practically dropped onto their front porch." I had to agree. We'd seen Drunor's vessel long before they seemed to see us.

"Can you send us any information on the Kalikak? Anything you know? We must continue our search," Bitt-Nurr told the other captain.

"Yes," Drunor replied. He gestured to one side, and another one of his species was briefly seen. "Must go too. Is not wise to stay sit too long in one area. Kalikak always on hunting."

"Receiving files from the other ship," Lieutenant Commander Torvald told the captain. "A fairly hefty data packet. Though I think I'm going to need Bitt-Nurr and Dora's help into turning it into usable data."

"Lieutenant," Captain Yamashita said to Bitt-Nurr, "thank Captain Drunor and we'll continue our search."

"All right every one, if I may have your attention."

Captain Yamashita stood and moved toward the view screen in the conference room. "This is the best chart we have of the area that we've not yet been able to reach. It's based on old long-range scans by the Laldoralin, and it is in *no* way complete. Our benefactors didn't have much interest beyond Hegemony space in this direction of the spiral arm. It only came important when Earth, and by extension Derilon and Salla, our new colonies, joined their alliance."

She touched her padd and a blue line appeared, passing though several systems. Another touch on the device added a green line coming from the opposite direction.

The captain pointed to the blue line. "This is *Wanderer's* scheduled path, up to the last point she was heard from. The green line represents *Seeker* coming in from the opposite direction on our own flight path. As you can see, we still have a lot of space to cover, and now we have to be on the lookout for these Kalikak pirates."

"Could it be possible that *Wanderer* is hiding from these

jerks?" Emily asked. "I mean it might be they've gone comm-silent for their own safety."

"I hope that's the case," Torvald said, "But from what we've learned from Captain Drunor, this may not be only a search and rescue mission, but a hostage extraction as well."

"Assuming they're all still alive," Lieutenant Forbes said. "If they have run afoul of these beings, there's no guarantee that the Kalikak aren't... carnivores."

"Jesus, sir! That's an awful..." I said, standing up from the table. The very thought of Valiel being eaten was more than I could take. My heart rate spiked through the roof, and I was having trouble breathing. "Why would you even..."

"Ensign Voss, take a seat," The captain said. "Lieutenant Forbes. Really? Do you always need to go to the worst case scenario? If you'll recall, Captain Drunor did mention 'beings taken for labor' which I hope means that if the *Wanderer* has been taken, her crew is still alive. While there is life, there is hope."

"Yes, Captain," Forbes replied, running his hand through his jet-black hair. "I want them all to be safe too. For all we know, Ensign Darkfeather's theory could be true. I can certainly see going into silent mode If faced with a superior threat. But we need to be ready for every contingency."

"If that were only possible," Master Chief Kurakin, our valkyrie-like head of security said. She glanced my way for a moment. "But if this turns into an extraction, Sec-Ops are more than ready to lead the charge."

"Commander Solas," Captain Yamashita addressed *Seeker's* chief engineer, "If we wind up in a fight with the Kalikak, how much more ready would we be than, say... *Wanderer* would be?"

"In a hypothetical battle between us and our sister ship," Solas replied, "it wouldn't even be a contest. We've got the

Sallan magnetic shield overlaying our own Laldoralin-designed shields. We've also enhanced our particle cannons with Sallan tech as well as added in the high-yield Sallan FTL missiles. Even our scanning capabilities have been greatly upgraded. To the best of my knowledge, we'd be a match for a Laldoralin light cruiser. Though to be honest, you never know what the Laldoralin haven't yet shared with us, so that may actually be hubris on my part. But, to the point, we're much better off in both offensive and defensive technology than *Wanderer* would be."

"Any progress on the stealth system?"

"I've been overseeing Lieutenant Commander Danforth and Chief Moreland in their quest to get the Sallan cloaking system onto our Remoras, Captain. They believe that they can now add that technology to our two newer probes. The two remaining original Remoras probably won't be candidates though. They simply don't have the needed power to do the job."

"Nonetheless, that's excellent news!" Science officer Torvald said.

"But..."

"Oh. There's always a but, isn't there?" Commander M'Buku said.

"I'm afraid so, sir," Solas told him. "As I said, Danforth and Moreland don't think that the technology will be useable on the older two Remoras. And it'll take Remora Two and Three being out of service for a day or so while the upgrades and new generators are installed. They'd be out of the search for at least that long."

"Well. Damn," Yamashita said, steepleing her fingers. "All right, here's what I want to do. Dora? Think you can slum around in Remora One for a few days? I'd like to start by taking one of the new Remoras offline and get that stealth system onboard it. Remora Two would be my first choice. When that's done, and the cloaking field has been fully tested we can get Remora Three in and have it "cloaked" as well."

"I can do so, Captain," Dora replied. "Though I will be 'breathlessly' waiting for my return to my newer residence. Pardon my AI humor."

We all stared at her hologram for a moment. Exasperated, Dora elaborated; "Because I don't breathe? Honestly, people..."

"Amusing," Chief Kurakin said in a tone that belied her statement.

"Anyway," Dora said, faking a theatrical sigh, "yes. I can continue in Remora One until Remora Two has been further upgraded."

"Good. I think having Remora Two out of service won't seriously impact our search grid. Commander Solas, please inform Danforth and Moreland that they are to take Remora Two out of rotation for upgrades."

I wasn't sure I agreed with the captain's assessment, but in light of the information about the Kalikak, having stealthed probes would probably be in our long-term best interests. Having an enemy not be able to see our advance information gathering probes might make the difference between facing an unknown opponent or facing one whose information and technical specs we'd stealth scanned. But taking one probe out of the search would also slow us down.

And finding *Wanderer* was my *biggest* priority.

"Sir?" Emily said, turning toward Solas. "Is this 'cloaking' technology scalable? Could it ever be used to hide *Seeker*?" Emily looked embarrassed, as if she surely must be asking a question everyone else had already considered and discarded. But it was obvious from the nervousness in her tone she couldn't risk not making the suggestion. I'd been having similar thoughts as well.

"The Melpin was able to hide entire weapons platforms,"

Solas replied. "And those were almost twice the size of this ship. Believe me, Ensign, a ship-wide cloak is definitely on the drawing board."

We all sat, digesting that, and all the advantages it would offer us. A comm chime interrupted our reveries.

"Captain, this is Sharma. We've got another contact."

"Is it coming toward us, Commander?"

"Negative, Ma'am. It's following our new friend Captain Drunor's ship. Following it like a shark."

6

"Have they seen us?"

"I don't believe so, Captain," Lieutenant Commander Sharma said, stepping down from the command chair. Sharm had her jet-black hair pulled back in a severe bun, as she usually did when she had command of the bridge. It was almost a joke among the crew. *Ears showing, duty calls.* "We have no indication they've noticed us, or our Remoras. They seem very intent on Captain Drunor, though."

The rest of us had left the conference room, replacing our second shift counter parts. I sat at my tactical station to take a look at our new arrival. The recent contact was a ship shaped like a fat missile, with four large streamlined pods sticking out from its aft end. It was a strange thrust configuration, but the pursuing vessel seemed to have no problem moving at five times the speed of light.

"Evidently," Lieutenant Commander Torvald said, "our scanning capabilities are superior, or they're ignoring us. Either way, they're definitely in pursuit of, and catching up to Captain Drunor's ship."

"Or, since Remoras One and Four are between us and

them, they just haven't noticed something as small as our probes," Emily said, pushing a few errant strands of hair away from her eyes. "Are we going to come about, Ma'am?"

"The newcomer does seem to be on a pursuit course, Captain," Lieutenant Forbes said.

"Torvald, have Remoras One and Four trail behind the newcomer, using their jump drives, without getting too close. Keep to the edge of scan range. Helm, bring us about and lay in a pursuit course, but let's not catch up just yet," Captain Yamashita said, her expression fierce and determined. She was always at her best when attempting to save someone else. "I want to make sure I know what's happening before I commit this ship to getting involved."

"We're going to Drunor's aid?" Commander M'Buku asked. My heart jumped with excitement with the first officer's words. I didn't want to be a war hawk, but using my skills at tactical felt like what I was born for.

"Maybe, Bosede," the captain told the commander, "If there's trouble, I may want to jump in on top of them to aid our new friend."

"Forbes," M'Buku said. "Weapons hot, but not free at this time."

"Charging defensive systems," Forbes replied. "If these are the Kalikak Drunor spoke of, we'll show them the error of their ways."

"Let's not get ahead of ourselves, Lieutenant," the captain replied. "We still haven't confirmed whether this is a pursuit or simply a rendezvous."

"I'm guessing pursuit, Ma'am," Torvald told her. "Drunor must've just now seen them. He's kicked his speed up to... holy smokes! He's moving at eight times the FTL threshold! The newcomer is matching speed! We'll never keep up without using our Jump Drive."

"Jump Remoras One, Three and Four to keep them close

enough to observe," Captain Yamashita commanded. "Helm, take us to maximum FTL speed, but spin up the Jump Drive. We'll use it if we have to intercede."

"With respect, Captain," M'Buku said. "I feel I need to remind you that *Seeker* is an explorer, not a purpose-built warship. We have an earth vessel to find."

"You are correct, Bosede," she replied, "But we need to see what we're up against in this sector. And if it's pirates and we have the capability to stop them, we're going to do so."

———

If we hadn't had jump-capable probes, the point would have been moot. *Seeker* was far outmatched when it came to using FTL drives for local travel. Even at our max Faster Than Light speed, we were soon left in the proverbial space dust. Remoras One and Four used their onboard Jump Drives to translocate ahead, keeping pace with the chase. This allowed us to keep up virtually.

Drunor's ship was slowly losing the race to the larger vessel and our probes registered an energy transmission from the pursuer to the prey. It was a blast of energy for which we had no corollary in our databases.

"That was some sort of FTL capable magnetic blast," Torvald noted.

When the blast caught up with his ship, Drunor's diamond-shaped vessel instantly dropped out of FTL speed and fell to sub-light. The larger attacking ship overshot him, but, dropping to sub-light speed as well, it quickly came about and began to again chase Drunor.

"They have an FTL weapon that could outpace Drunor at eight times the speed of light!" Forbes said from the console next to me.

"Damn. That ain't good," I replied. Even the Laldoralin

didn't have that, and they were the most advanced civilization in our corner of the galaxy. Or at least they'd never shown any such capability to the newest members of their Hegemony. "I hope that's the only new trick they have up their sleeves."

"Captain," M'Buku said in a quiet tone that nonetheless carried across the bridge. "Drunor is obviously being attacked. Are we going to involve ourselves? I wish to remind you again, that we are explorers, not a warship. Also, we don't know this enemies full capabilities, offensively, yet."

"Drunor took time out of voyage, a voyage fraught with risk, to help us build a language database so he could tell us what was going on in this neck of the woods," Captain Yamashita replied. "If he'd told us to take a hike when we contacted him, I might be less inclined to get involved. But he didn't. He tried to help us." As she said this, I did wonder for a moment if *Seeker* hadn't been so formidably upgraded during our adventures she would've felt the same way.

Nonetheless, we all looked her way as she stood from the command chair. She looked around the bridge and, pushed a toggle for the all-ship intercom.

"All hands. This is the Captain. Set Condition One. Battle stations!"

7

"Status on the chase, Mr. Torvald."

"Energy weapon fire is being exchanged, Captain. It looks like the newcomer has crippled Drunor's sub-light drive. His ship is losing speed. Attacker is using heavy lasers and some sort of particle cannon. Ah. And missiles."

"Mr. Forbes, what can you tell me about those missiles?" the captain asked, turning to our tactical station. "Better than our new Sallan missiles?"

"No, Ma'am. They are definitely sub-light while ours move faster than light. And... ouch... they just scored a hit on Drunor. They're fairly low yield, probably designed for crippling rather than destruction."

"Doesn't mean they don't have worse ones, ma'am," I interjected. "Drunor's just launched a quad of his own missiles, all moving under FTL speed. Four hits! Annnnd... the newcomer is shielded. No damage to speak of. Drunor doesn't appear to have shields."

My heart sunk as I realized our new friend had a much lower degree of survivability than we did.

"It appears Drunor's ship is relying mostly on ablative armor panels," Forbes said from his station at tactical.

"Torvald, what can we see about the attacker's shielding?" the captain asked.

"Very similar to our Laldoralin shields, ma'am," the science officer replied. "Almost parallel technology. With roughly the same energy needs as far as I can tell."

"Commander M'Buku, tactical assessment?"

"Captain, unless they've got something big hidden away... we can take 'em." M'Buku replied. "We've got laminated shielding, and our Sallan missiles pack a big punch. But it's a risk, nonetheless, and we are a *long* way from home or help."

"Noted. Helm, I want to drop in right behind them," Captain Yamashita said. "Dora, from the what the scans are showing, it looks like most of their shield power is rotated forward to take whatever Drunor throws at them. Can we take out their drive?"

"I would say this is our best bet for quick victory, Captain."

"Ready the jump drive. We'll translocate to their stern. Tactical, I want that ship disabled. As soon as we jump, weapons are free."

"Understood, Captain," Forbes said. "Voss and I are ready."

"Helm, jump us!"

———

There is a difference between emergence from FTL speed and from Jump Space. From FTL it seems like a ship just appears from nowhere, moving at high speed, a colorful plume of energy trailing behind as the vessel bleeds off speed. The bleeding off of speed usually requires flipping the craft and using main sub-light engines to force thrust in the opposite direction of your line of travel.

With Jump Drive translocation emergence, one moment there's nothing there, the next a ship appears, with only the forward momentum the vessel had to enter Nth space. Motion easily controlled by thrusters.

Against someone who's never seen such a thing, that's a pretty damn good advantage. We appeared less than a mile astern of the attacking ship, and Forbes and I lit them up.

First priority was their FTL drive emitters, two massive blue-glowing blocks at the aft end facing toward us. If they'd been incredibly fast on the uptake, the enemy might've dashed into FTL and gotten away to try and jump us later. They weren't, unfortunately for them.

Forbes was shooting the forward particle cannons, concentrating on the FTL emitters, while I used my sixth sense to aim for the danger to us, their aft weapons.

My special "talent" allows me to feel my target, and allows me to hit faraway targets with great precision. The other ship's particle cannons swiveled on long extensions allowing them to shoot in any direction aside from their own vessel. I began surgically removing their cannons at their mountings.

We began taking hits on our shields only a few moments after we began firing.

"Gentlemen," Dora said from just behind us, "I suggest you do this with all due haste. They are attempting to redistribute their shields."

"I've taken out one FTL emitter," Forbes said. "Tanner, how are we doing with their weapons?"

"Two cannons disconnected from the ship at their mounts so far. It's faster to take out the pivots they're attached to than hit the cannons themselves. Two to go, back here, but I can't get a shot at the forward weapons. The curve of their ship is occluding my firing solutions." As I said this, I took out a third aft cannon. "Only one left in the stern."

The words were barely our of my mouth when the attacking ship vanished into FTL space.

"They're running, Captain," Torvald said. "Limping along at a mere two times the speed of light."

"Pursue?" Our helmsman, Lieutenant Kolara asked from the helm.

Captain Yamashita looked at the main viewer for moment. "No. Let them run. Maybe they'll be a little more hesitant to take us on if it comes up in the future. In the meantime, let's recall all the Remoras and post them at points best configured to give us early warning while we attempt to aid Captain Drunor."

I hoped she was right. Letting the pirates escape could also come back to bite us in the butt.

8

While *Seeker* was battering the butt end of the enemy ship, Drunor was taking a battering from the *front* end of the enemy ship.

Drunor's craft, which his records named the *Guzit Zut Zut*, translated as *Web of Dawn*, had numerous holes in her. Missile strikes and beam shots had crippled her engines and destroyed most of her external missile launchers. Most disturbing was a precision cut into the rear hull. While we'd were hitting the attacker from behind, the Kalikak had been trying to cut an opening into Drunor's ship.

We'd interrupted the pirates from getting very far. Our scans showed that the hole that would've been created was directly over *Web of Dawn*'s drive area.

"That particular invasive laser cut tells me we just started hostilities with the same space pirates who left that derelict we encountered earlier," Commander M'Buku said.

"A pretty safe bet, Commander," Captain Yamashita replied. "We have met the Kalikak."

Not only met them, we kicked their ass, I thought. It felt good to have saved Drunor and his ship from complete annihilation. And the Kalikak was no ordinary foe: they were a first-class predator species. I was happy to send them on the run.

"Mr. Forbes, how did our new multi-layer shielding stand up to their return fire?" the captain asked.

"They hit us twelve times before Ensign Voss destroyed, or perhaps I should say surgically removed, the enemy cannons, Captain. Of those twelve hits, the magnetic shield completely diffused and absorbed ten. Two hits made it through to the Laldoralin shields which only had a 5% drop in energy."

"I have to say though," I commented, "Their particle cannons pack a wallop. Even with our Sallan-enhanced beam weapons, the Kalikak cannons are putting out shots with a good 25% stronger beam. Captain, may I make a suggestion?"

"Always ready to hear new ideas, Ensign. What are you thinking?"

"I was careful to take those cannons off at their extended mounts. The actual weapons themselves may still be intact and drifting away."

"And you want to retrieve them for study," Captain Yamashita said, a slight smile on her face. "Lord knows we haven't even managed to incorporate all the tech The Melpin gave us, but... why not? Make it happen, Tanner. You're in charge of retrieval. Make sure you brief Ensign Kinzler on what we've learned when she takes your position at tactical."

As she said it, I sent out a call for Kinzler to take over for me.

"Ma'am," Lieutenant Sedgewick said from the Comm station, "Captain Drunor is hailing us."

"Put him on, Lieutenant." Yamashita replied, "I want Bitt-Nurr on split screen also. Dora, if you'll sit in as well."

"Of course, Captain," Mom said, as her hologram appeared beside the command chair. "Hello Lieutenant," she said to Bitt-Nurr's image, now taking up half the main view screen. Bitt-Nurr raised her second set of arm/legs in a gesture of greetings. A moment later, a disheveled looking Captain Drunor appeared on the other half of the screen. Behind him I could see other giant spiders frantically moving about trying to put out fires and clear debris.

The magnificent colors of Drunor's body were scorched in a few spots, and one of his smaller eight eyes was swathed in what looked like spun spider silk. He had a general feel of dishevelment about him.

"I greet you, Captain Yamashita." Evidently between the early conversation and the record we'd been sent, Dora had jumped forward in her progress of the translation matrix. "And you I thank to the ends of the [untranslated]. Without help from your selves, slaves we might be now."

"Greeting to you, Captain Drunor. What is your status? May we render assistance?"

"Several of my crew are injured, but we have no fatalities. Obviously we are adrift, but my [untranslated] are working on repairs. Problem ourselves have is resources. We have replacement equipment, space journeys being [untranslated], but those are for malfunctions, not ship-wide damage from an attack. There are technological items that we must replace to travel again, but even our spares damaged were."

"I think we can help with that," Yamashita replied. "If you sent over schematics, there is a high likelihood that we can replicate what you need. You may have to send over raw materials of any exotic matter that we are unfamiliar with, though. We may not be able to replicate raw materials."

"Your Laldoralin Hegemony has such abilities?" Drunor stared at us for a moment. "I find that [untranslated]. We have materials printers, but to remake even small parts is a long and energy intensive process. Our abilities extend to small repairs using materials and parts that we've brought with us."

"We can, as you say," the captain responded, "remake items, from elements found in asteroid belts and gas giants if we run out of shipboard materials. Unfortunately, we're some distance from either of those. So hopefully, our on-ship supplies will be enough to get you on your way again, though we may be able to recycle damaged hardware for raw materials." Captain Yamashita turned toward the science station. "Ensign Darkfeather, I want you to be the liaison between Drunor's people and our replication teams. Dora, please get a list of what Captain Drunor will need and relay schematics to both the ensign and engineering."

"Yes, Ma'am," Darkfeather said. "Permission to leave the bridge and go to engineering?"

"Off with you, then," Yamashita said. "Dora?"

"Yes, Captain?"

"Check with Danforth and Solas on the status of the stealth upgrades for Remora Two. Seeing our enemy, and yes, I am designating the Kalikak as enemies, I think having undetectable probes would be a very good thing, indeed."

9

"Frag it to hell!"

Trying to match speeds with a tumbling, disconnected particle cannon in a class two shuttle is not as easy as you might think. And Lieutenant Jim Fowler wasn't helping. Fowler, one of those exceptionally handsome people whom you can't help but compare yourself (usually negatively) was using a hands-off approach to assisting me.

"You're going to have to stop its spin before you'll ever get close enough to grab it, Tanner," he said from the co-pilot's seat. Fowler was a far superior pilot to myself, but Master Chief Kurakin had told him to not help me unless there was a good reason to do so. She'd had been assigned by the captain to oversee my last year of academy studies when I'd been conscripted aboard *Seeker* at the start of my senior year (due to my strange hybrid abilities).

The Chief took her assignment seriously and aside from my academy studies, she delighted in making me perform every task I might conceivably perform on the ship to perfection. She even made me combat train with the *Seeker*'s security force as my physical training.

The only place I'd been a disappointment to my taskmaster (as far as I knew) was in my shuttle piloting. While I'd gotten a *lot* better over the course of the last year, I was still not up to her standard. Consequently, anytime I was in a shuttle, my far more experienced co-pilots were forbidden from doing much more than verbally assisting. Unless there was an emergency.

There was no emergency today, just a lot of frustration.

"With respect, sir, I understand that I need to stop it spinning," I said, keeping my voice as level as my frustration allowed. "But trying to keep the shuttle moving along at this snail's pace *and* work the grappler beam is imposs..." Fowler raised his eyebrow at me. "..is somewhat difficult," I lamely continued.

"Just get in the same track with the target, Tanner," Fowler replied. "Now, trust your ship. Lock in the course." I did so.

"Good," he said. "Now slow to just slightly slower than the target. The Grappler actually has pretty good range. You don't have to be right on top of that cannon to grab it. Just bring the beam's strength up gradually. That should stop the spin."

"Yes, sir." I did as I was told, and was rewarded when the spinning, tumbling and wobbling cannon began to calm the flip down. "Got it! Pulling it in... and we're ready to take this one back to the bots."

"Good job, kid. We'll make a decent pilot out of you yet." He grinned at me over that movie-star chin.

"Hopefully the chief will take note," I said.

"She only rides you to make you the best of the best, Tanner."

"Sometimes I wish she didn't have so much confidence in me."

"Really?"

"No," I replied sheepishly. "I recognize that everything Chief Kurakin puts me through will serve me well, later on. But while it's happening..."

"Yeah, I get it," Fowler replied, laughing. "My uncle Marcus is high-ranking Terran Exploratory Force brass. He's the one who sponsored me into the academy and that little fact had him on my butt most of my academy career. But his chiding and encouragement helped me make it into the Explorer Program and thus onto the *Seeker*. I doubt I need to explain why I'm proud and happy to be here."

"No sir! I'm happy to be here too, even if my start was a little rocky." Fowler knew of what I spoke. A cadet at the academy with a full year to go in his studies should have had zero chance to be aboard the best assignment the Terran Exploratory Force had to offer. I'd been assigned to *Seeker* because of a combination of having a very high-ranking Laldoralin father and because of the strange danger/accuracy sense I possessed as a result of my genetic pairing. Valiel, my sister, had the same talent.

"Yeah, those first few months were a trial, I'm sure, Tanner. But you have more than proven yourself, and those crew members who believed you were here on "silver spoon" duty know it. I'm always glad to have you along when we're doing something dangerous. That's the bottom line."

"Thank you, Lieutenant."

"All right then, Ensign. Let's get this thing back where it can be studied."

———

"It's the focusing mechanism here," Lieutenant Commander Danforth said. Danforth, nominal head of the robotics department, had been co-opted by Chief Engineer Solas into *Seeker*'s unofficial 'new projects' group. "The power generation on this weapon isn't much in excess of our own, but this focusing technology sends the beam with almost no loss of energy!"

The alien particle cannon had been dropped off next to *Seeker* while Fowler and I had gone after the others. While it sat stationary, our K-series float bots grappled with getting the cannons in through the closest cargo bay hatch. Using the designated corridor for the ships small army of floating robots, the bots used anti-gravity floaters to ferry it to science lab four.

Having retrieved the other two cannons, I'd joined the engineering team analyzing our "spoils of war."

"Is this something we can integrate, Lieutenant?" Science Officer Torvald asked. "This, in combination with the Sallan FTL missiles could make *Seeker* pretty damn formidable."

"The FTL missiles are impressive not just for their speed," Danforth said, "but for the incredible yield of their payload. Drunor's missiles, by comparison, while FTL capable, only had an explosive yield roughly a quarter as powerful as the Sallan versions."

"These emitters could indeed be integrated with our current cannons, but, like our current particle beams, they'll only be usable at sub-light speeds," Solas noted. "We'd also need to redesign their power access and design new mounts for the emitters. I'd also be more comfortable in using the concepts of these Kalikak emitters while remaking new ones 'in our image,' so to speak."

"We've got other fish to fry at the moment," Torvald reminded the two engineers. "The captain was pleased that we're going to have stealthed Remoras, or two of them at least, but she keeps telling Commander Solas and myself that she'd like to be able to cloak *Seeker* herself."

"Well, Commander, the Melpin was able to cloak entire weapons platforms, many of them larger than our ship,"

Danforth replied. "Theoretically, it's possible. But we're going to need a lot of tests with the Remoras first before we can get a field stable enough to hide this entire star ship." Danforth said. "Commander Solas has every spare person in engineering trying to figure out how to stealth grid a vessel this large. We don't have anyone left to work on weapon innovation."

Torvald looked at me. "What about him? For the cannon emitters."

"Voss, sir? You mean having him work on the cannons?" Danforth said. The expression on his face did not really express much confidence. "I'll remind you that Tanner, though he is deservedly an acting ensign, is still in the time period where he is also an academy cadet. Combine that with his duties on the bridge and you're stretching a very junior officer pretty thin."

Though technically correct, I felt this was a bit unfair. My class back on Earth would be graduating the Academy in just over a month. I was actually ahead of most of them in my course work. True, I was working in split shifts in both the Robotics division and as a junior tactical officer on the bridge, but I felt I could tackle this while we were essentially stationary in space.

And I was no longer a raw cadet. My experiences on *Seeker* alone made sure of that.

Evidently Lieutenant Commander Torvald didn't share Danforth's reservations. "Danforth, I'd like to give Tanner here the opportunity to design new emitters that will fit our current systems. Pull him from robotics for now. I know he's got a good head on his shoulders. Plus, he can always seek *parental* help, if he gets stuck. Also, I think it'd be best to keep him occupied while we're stuck here helping Drunor."

"Yes, sir," Danforth said, a grin spreading across his face.

"How can you fail when you've got the smartest *mama* in the quadrant?"

"Gawdammit," I said under my breath.

"What was that, Ensign?" Torvald asked.

"Nothing, Sir! I'm grateful for the opportunity to contribute. I'll come up with a design in a timely manner without needing any help from digital personages."

"Then get to it, Ensign. Oh, and Tanner?"

"Sir?"

"Don't let pride keep you from seeking assistance if you need it."

10

It turned out to be a good thing that Torvald had given me a difficult problem to gnaw on.

Getting Drunor's ship in a navigable state took three solar days, days we weren't searching for *Wanderer.* If I hadn't had the knotty problem of redesigning the new particle cannon emitters, I might've gone bonkers.

As I sat at a Robotics Division workstation, designing with holographic software, a familiar voice said from behind me; "That's looking very good, Tanner." Dora's hologram shimmered into existence behind me.

"Hi, Mom," I said. "This has been a little harder than I thought, but I'm almost there. I'm thinking we're missing something here by only intending to install the emitter with the barrel focuser the *Seeker* already uses."

"A quick analysis of what you've accomplished, if installed in our current particle cannons, appears you've improved energy output by at least twenty percent. Tanner, that is no small improvement."

"I know," I replied. "But I just get this feeling that if we changed the focuser that it'd concentrate the beam to a point where it'd punch a smaller area with a lot more energy. The problem is, while I can see what it needs, I'm just not able to figure out how to reconfigure the focuser. Not smart enough, I think."

Dora, as an AI, has millions of subroutines devoted to human expression, left over from her years as a human-appearing android. Her "physical" years were devoted to making sure that Valiel and I had a mother. It wasn't until I'd been in stasis for a hundred and fifty years that I was informed that my 'above ground' parents were actually incredibly advanced computer programs.

She used one of her 'mom' expressions now. Her holographic lips went tight and her eyebrows arched. "Tanner Voss! Don't you dare ever say that you are not smart enough! You are the product of one of the most brilliant males of the Laldoralin people, and your genetic mother was a human astronaut, one of the first people to reach your system's fourth planet. Both highly intelligent sentients, and their children are too."

"Okay, okay, Mom," I said, putting up my hands in surrender and trying not to laugh. "Let me rephrase. I feel like I'm not smart because while I can see what would work, I can't figure out a path to get there. Better?"

"Infinitely. Perhaps the problem here isn't lack of smarts, but lack of inspiration. Or, more precisely, teamwork. Ensign Darkfeather has finished her assignment, and I also see that Chief Zahn has just come off shift in engineering. I've asked if they would be willing to join us here for a little brainstorming."

"Oh. Okay.. Um..."

"I'm sure that Shendra will behave herself, Tanner. Particularly with Emily being in the room. And she is a very skilled engineer. The Kiffallans are quite advanced scientifically and technologically. As well as psychologically. Between you and I, I find that refreshing."

"I'm sure you're right," I said, because you know us humans are..."

"Just fine, Tanner. Humans are a young species and still maturing." A slight smile came over Dora's face. "And besides, she and Emily are still in negotiations for your stud services."

"Mom!"

———

Emily and I were looking at the 3-D model of what I'd accomplished with the emitter when Shendra Zahn walked in.

Like myself, she and her sister Duala (*Seeker*'s 2nd medical officer) are Laldoralin hybrids. In my case, I'm half human, while they're half Kiffallan (Kiffers). Unbeknownst to most of the Hegemony, my father's people (the males) have wholeheartedly embraced the notion of 'conjoining' with other humanoid species. But not because they're galactic-level Don Juans.

What most sentients don't know is that the Laldoralin are going extinct. Their ability to produce offspring amongst themselves has greatly diminished. They can mostly only produce offspring with the 'younger' species. Hence my existence.

"Greeting, Emily. Tanner," Shendra said. "Dora informed me that you have a problem that I might be able to help with." She gave us her ever-present hint of a smile.

The Kiffallans are not an emotional people, though they certainly have emotions. Shendra and Duala both keep incredibly calm in circumstances that would have the average human freaking out. They're very much like the aliens of a twenty-first century science fiction show I used to watch, even down to the upswept eyebrows and stoic demeanor. Things diverge a little at the almost glowing gold eyes and reddish bronze-tinted skin, but I think in Shendra's case some of that comes from her Laldoralin father.

"Hi, Chief," I said. "I sure hope so. As I was explaining to Emily, I've been working on adapting the particle cannon emitters from the alien ship that attacked Drunor, and I'm pretty sure this will work, improving our firepower. The thing is, I feel like there could be more. With better focusers, I think we could make a beam that could punch through a standard shield, albeit in a very concentrated contact point."

"Even a small hole in a star ship is a cause for... concern." Shendra said.

"With enough concentrated energy," Emily said, intently looking at the new emitter, "you could do more than put a hole in the hull. If you could get targeting scanners to a more precise level, you might be able to surgically take out complete systems on an attacking ship without having to batter down its shields first."

"Theoretically," I said.

"If we could indeed make this work," Shendra replied, "and knowing something of your particular extra-sensory abilities with targeting, Tanner, this system would seem tailor-made for you to use."

"Yes," Emily said, looking at me with a tilt to your head. "Are you designing your own personalized weapon systems now, Acting Ensign?"

"Not on purpose," I replied. But looking at it, I saw their point. One of the reasons I was on this vessel was a set of skills that bordered on paranormal. Part of that was I was able to sense incoming danger with an uncanny success rate. The other side of the coin was the ability to hit what ever I aimed at over tiny or vast distances. Valiel, my sister, has the same abilities.

"Anyway," I continued, "my engineering abilities are at the 'grasp exceeding reach' stage. I know what might work, but I'm having trouble figuring out how to make it work."

We spent the next hour with me bringing Emily and Shendra up to speed on what I'd accomplished, and what I generally wanted to accomplish. After they'd both considered for a while, Shendra gave me her take on my efforts.

"You've done a good job of adapting the Kalikak emitter, Tanner, but what you are wanting with the focuser is basically designing a complete new methodology." She spun the 3-D image of the emitter with one finger, and looked at the rough notes we'd all been writing on the virtual chalkboard. "With everything we've gotten from Sallan tech and implemented on *Seeker*, we've had concrete examples to adapt from. I'd like to take all this and throw it in front of my engineering team. They're Earth's best and brightest in engineering, and a completely new problem is something they can really sink their teeth into."

"And I'd like to get Commander Torvald involved too," Emily said. "There are also a couple of the civilian scientists that might be interested in this problem."

"Thing is, Torvald threw this to me basically because everyone else had something more important to work on," I replied.

"Hey! Wait." Emily snapped her fingers as she looked at the hologram. "Dora?"

"Yes, Emily?" Mom said, her hologram reappearing.

"You're a fancy-pants Laldoralin AI. Can't you design this for us?"

"No." Dora told her, a slight smile on her translucent face.

"No, you can't?" I asked.

"No, I won't."

We all stared at her hologram. She stared right back.

"But mom..." I started.

"But nothing. I won't steal this from you, my flesh and blood darlings. You are very capable sentients, more than able to overcome this hurdle. I follow my maker's philosophy. Too much given and not earned engenders weakness and laziness. How much better your accomplishments will be if you don't cheat."

Us "flesh and bloods" could only look at her, nonplussed. Shendra finally broke the silence. "Thank you, Dora. You're right. We can and will achieve this without... cheating."

I wasn't convinced. We were in space with hostile parties who may have already attacked the *Wanderer*. If it'd been a new design in food replication I might've conceded her point, but we were talking about improving our weapons array.

I didn't get a chance to say it though. Dora tilted her head slightly, as if listening, then said: "We are leaving. Captain Yamashita has decided to accompany Captain Drunor to that sentient's next safe haven. Ensigns Darkfeather and Voss report to the bridge."

11

"We're flying escort for Drunor?" I said, moving quickly down *Seeker*'s central corridor while trying to keep my frustration from bursting out of my chest. "What about the search for the *Wanderer*?"

Speaking through my sub-dermal transponder, Dora said, "Drunor has convinced the captain that they'd be sitting ducks moving at the speed that *Web of Dawn* is currently capable of. At best, they'll only be able to proceed at three times the speed of light, considerably slower than their normal ten times c. The captain has agreed to help."

"*Seeker* can only do about three times FTL speed on her best day," Emily said. "And prolonged travel at that speed is going to be hard on the FTL engines."

"We are going to leapfrog *Web of Dawn* with the Jump Drive," Dora replied, "using our translocation abilities to stay within striking distance should trouble arise."

"And how long is that going to take?" I asked, giving up on trying to keep the exasperation out of my voice. "We're kind of on an important mission here."

"I do not give the orders, Tanner. I just recite them,"

Dora said. "The captain has made a decision, and though that decision might frustrate you and I, it is not open for debate. So I suggest you master yourself before you step onto that bridge, young man."

I took a deep breath as I stepped into the lift leading to the bridge. "All right, I'm cool. I'm calm. I have myself together." Emily looked at me with no small amount of skepticism.

"Good. Now, to answer your question," Dora continued, "we are heading to a heavily protected space station. Evidently every world, every orbital, every system with intelligent life in this sector is heavily invested in defensive orbital weaponry. This speaks to how great the threat from our enemies is. Open space in the area is simply something to get through as quickly as possible."

"Hence the high-speed FTL designs," Emily said. "Evidently our translocation drive is unknown around here. So how long until we reach this station?"

"Not too long. Roughly two solar days at Drunor's top available speed."

We were interrupted by the opening of the lift doors onto the main bridge. There was much hustle bustle as we prepared to get under way, and Dora was already 'standing' next to Captain Yamashita. Looking at the main view screen, I saw Drunor's ship accelerating away from us. It was quickly out of visual range, and the screen switched to a tactical display showing the arachnid captain's ship heading away, gaining speed. Its icon turned from white to blue when Drunor achieved light speed.

I took my seat at the tactical station and Emily sat next to Lieutenant Commander Torvald at science. I checked all weapons systems and all were green, though not at full combat mode.

"Commander Torvald," Captain Yamashita said, "deploy

Remoras One and Four ahead of us. Organizer of Armadas, do you read?"

"Yes, Yamashita Captain. I am here. Here being resident in Remora Three, of course."

"Good. I want you to stay within fifty-thousand miles of *Seeker*. Full scanning suite. I don't want anyone sneaking up on us."

"Understood. I will mirror *Seeker's* movements and provide overwatch."

"Excellent," Yamashita said. "Helm, lay in coordinates to our first jump."

"Laid in, Captain."

"Jump us."

The jump took us five light years ahead of Drunor. When *Seeker* had left Earth, this sort of staggered translocating wouldn't have been feasible. Since we'd been on mission, our engineers had finally solved the problem of jump alignment. Earlier, each jump had taken a toll on the human crew, originally resulting in serious "hangovers" after each jump. Through long-term tinkering with the jump alignment, Solas and his people had managed to bring the problem down to a few moments of mild discomfort.

Now, the human cost of making multiple short jumps was negligible. Everything we'd accomplished and learned about jump drive enhancement had been sent back to Earth in the form of our logs and records. Hopefully our homeworld was taking advantage of all the improvements we were sending them.

———

"Final jump, Captain. Translocation drive is ready," Lieutenant Kolara said, having completed our fourth jump. "On your command."

"Do it," the captain said.

We'd let Drunor pass and get ahead of us on the last leg. With the situation being what it was in this sector, Captain Yamashita had decided that jumping in ahead of *Web of Dawn* might not get a good reaction from the orbital defenses of the station we were approaching.

A few moments later, we emerged less than 10,000 miles from Drunor. The Arachnid captain had dropped to sub-light and was making for a huge structure that was surrounded by a variety of space going vessels.

"Wow," Torvald said from the science station. "That is a *big* outpost. You could fit twenty *Seekers* inside of it."

"With impressive defensive measures," Torvald said, as he perused the data coming in from the Remoras. "Particle cannons, heavy lasers, rail guns and rotating high-speed missile launchers."

The station was a huge sphere surrounded by an even larger ring on its equator. The ring had a dozen spires radiating out from it and most of these had space craft of various designs docked to the spires. Numerous other ships orbited the structure in a discernible pattern. Huge doors in part of the sphere hinted at internal ship repair yards.

"Organizer, do you recognize any of these ship configurations?" Captain Yamashita asked.

"Affirmative. Aside from Drunor's vessel, of which I see at least three similar ships, there are also vessels of the Wulkin and Yakar. Both of these species were encountered by my people on our intergalactic journey to this arm of our galaxy. They are trader species which the Blah-Veht did business with, trading for essential materials. Since Dora has all my files, if I'm not mistaken, she has already worked out translation matrices for them in her spare time."

"You translated two alien languages on the off chance we

might run across these species in the vastness of space?" the captain asked Dora, surprise written across her face.

"Actually, I've worked out translation matrices for forty-seven different species that Organizer of Armada's people ran across in their travels. Many were encountered so far away that it is unlikely we will ever meet them, but almost anything in this universe is possible."

The captain looked at her with open astonishment. "You did this in... your spare time?"

"With Organizer's help. When one's thought processes run at over a billion times that of organics, you find that you have a lot of time on your... er... hands. It seemed that increasing our translation knowledge base would be an excellent way to keep busy and provide something useful to the mission."

"Um... excellent work, then," Yamashita said. "In the meantime, let's pull all our Remoras in close and passive-scan the hell out of this place. I don't want to be intrusive, but as long as we're here, let's learn all that we can."

"We're being contacted by the station, Captain," Lieutenant Sedgewick said. "Their transmission is being translated in real time."

"The sender is a Wulkin," Dora noted.

"Put them on screen," Yamashita said.

"Greetings unknown vessel. I am Coordinator Kangot, administrator of Drexul Station." The speaker appeared essentially humanoid, though with a set of eyes where they'd normally be and a second set off-set to the side of his head. His skin looked like wood mixed with crystal and his mouth, while horizontal, had corners that stretched up to his cheekbones. This gave his jawline a 'steam shovel' sort of look.

"I greet you, Coordinator Kangot," Captain Yamashita replied. "I am Megumi Yamashita, Captain of the explorer starship *Seeker*. Our intentions are peaceful. We have accompanied Captain Drunor's *Web of Dawn* here as a security escort. As you can probably see, his ship was attacked by the ones you may know as the Kalikak."

"You survived a battle with a Kalikak ship?" Kangot's eyes opened wide. "I am impressed. The Kalikak, aside from having impressive weapons, are in possession of an energy shield that, in deep space, is difficult to penetrate. Defeat of one of their spacecraft usually involves either overwhelming fire from orbital defenses or overwhelming fire from multiple ships."

"The Kalikak had concentrated their shields in front while attacking Drunor," Yamashita told him. "We were able to sneak up behind them."

In a very human-like gesture, Kangot steepled his long multi-jointed fingers. "Exceptionally careless of them. Do you have some sort of stealth secret? If so, we'd be very interested in learning more. Any advantage over these horrific slavers and pirates would be a true gift of the universe."

"Unfortunately, we do not have a functioning stealth system," Captain Yamashita told him. She wasn't exactly lying. Unless Danforth's team had finished with stealthing Remora Two, we didn't have a *functioning* stealth system. "We were also very lucky with our attack, damaging the Kalikak's faster than light system. They decided that fleeing was the safest course at the time."

"Captain, Drunor is requesting to be added to the conversation," Lieutenant Sedgewick told her.

"Add him in."

The main viewer went to split-screen mode, Drunor on the right, Kangot on the left.

"Greeting Captain, Coordinator. I wanted to thank you again *Seeker,* for saving us and escorting us here. Also for helping us with repairs. Without the assistance you provided after the battle, we'd still be sitting there, easy prey for the Kalikak."

"We assessed the situation in the same way," the captain said. "We could not simply leave you there to be destroyed or enslaved."

"Coordinator," Drunor said. "Without these strangers, my ship and crew would've been lost. I respectfully submit that they are allies, and should be treated as we would any member of our unity. If they need anything, I will cover the costs."

Some of Kangot's eyes were aimed slightly left, some right at us, obviously using a split-screen as we were. He closed all his eyes for a moment, then opened them and looked at us with all of them.

"Captain Megumi Yamashita, I would like to formally extend welcome to you and your crew. We are prepared to provide whatever it is in our power to give you. What are your needs?"

"Coordinator, we are missing one of our own ships, and I fear the worst. What I need is any information that you can provide on this sector of space, that you feel won't compromise your security. And most of all, we need every bit of information we can get on these Kalikak. I strongly suspect that we will be clashing with them again."

12

I hadn't started out my day expecting to walk around in an alien space station, but the universe likes to keep my life interesting.

Captain Yamashita decided to take a security detail with her, as well as *Seeker*'s science office, Den Torvald. I was under no illusions that I was along for my scintillating wit. I was there because of my un-erring danger sense, a psychic ability I was gifted with due to my unique hybrid genetics.

Our security detail consisted of Master Chief Kurakin, a tall Amazon with closely cropped blond hair and an icy demeanor when she was on the clock. Also along was Corporal Michael Chen, backing her up. Chen only came up to Kurakin's shoulder, but I knew from experience he was a formidable warrior. Both carried side arms. Which the group meeting us seemed to pointedly ignore.

"Greetings to you, Captain," Kangot met us at the shuttle docking port. The station did not have the minor force fields we used to keep *Seeker*'s shuttle bays pressurized, and opening the huge doors to the interior was only suitable for large ships. Their airlock however, which we had docked at, actually changed shape to accommodate our shuttle's docking hatch. A neat trick indeed.

"I greet you also, Coordinator," Yamashita replied. "Your station is most impressive. There are only a few this large in our entire Laldoralin Hegemony. Speaking of which, we have an entire data pack for first contact diplomacy situations like this one. It will explain the Hegemony in detail and can be supplied in a variety of formats, if you're interested."

"We would be pleased to know more about you, Captain Yamashita," Kangot replied. "We have few visitors from outside our little cluster of stars. Word of the Kalikak and their depredations have placed a chill on visitation to our tiny corner of the galaxy."

We walked down an oval-shaped corridor that was wide enough to drive a 21st century Abrams tank through. Panels covered each curving wall, and occasionally an open panel was being attended by repair personnel. As we walked past, a blob of protoplasm, wearing a tool belt was extending multiple pseudopods into an open access hatch.

"I would assume," Yamashita asked, "that the Kalikak have greatly degraded trade between worlds in this area?"

"You are correct. It takes brave captains, such as Drunor, to attempt to traverse our area solo. And as you probably noted, Drunor's ship is built for speed. Our alliance mostly sends heavily-armed convoys out at this point. To date, we have managed to destroy only one Kalikak vessel, and that took the combined firepower of seven of our ships. Unfortunately, the zeal of those captains involved destroyed the enemy vessel beyond being able to reverse engineer any part of it."

Kangot again performed a very human-like gesture, lowering and shaking his head. "Since then, such miniature fleets have been tasked with, should they be attacked, with trying to take a Kalikak ship intact."

"To learn about their force field technology, I assume," Lieutenant Commander Torvald said.

"Yes. Though the Kalikak are advanced in more than a few areas, their main advantage is that our ships can't damage theirs except with overwhelming firepower. I assure you, they have little difficulty damaging ours."

I noted our captain's lips grow tight, and as if I had a psychic moment, I knew what she was thinking. We'd scanned the Kalikak ship's shields while attacking them. They weren't much stronger than our stock Laldoralin shields (minus our new gravimetric shield overlay).

I was sure Captain Yamashita was at least considering what the ramifications would be around giving our Laldoralin shield tech away. At the very least, she'd be severely reprimanded when we got home. The Laldoralin were already going to have issues with one of their most advanced AIs (Dora) being in the hands of a junior member (AKA Earth) of the Hegemony club.

On the other hand, if Kangot and all the other member species of their alliance were able to level the playing field, perhaps this area of space could be opened up to trade and exploration. And maybe the pirate menace that stifled everyone here could be ended.

And if we were going to find *Wanderer,* it certainly wouldn't hurt to have allies that could defend themselves.

No one spoke on the subject though. This sort of thing was well above everyone's pay grade. Everyone except our captain.

————

"So no one's ever seen a Kalikak face to face?" Torvald asked.

The captain and science officer were seated around a circular table with Kangot and another, apparently female,

Wulkin named Didin. The two Wulkin looked at each other and a heavy sigh came from Didin.

"No one who's ever been rescued, and I assure you," she said, "there have been few of those. The one's who've made it back said that the Kalikak they'd seen were all wearing battle armor. Each armor set was decorated individually, but never were the enemy seen to remove their helmets. They could literally look like any of us or something completely different and we'd never know."

"That's unsettling," Captain Yamashita said. "If no one knows what they look like, you could pass one in the corridor and never know it."

"You mean, as in... spies?" Kangot asked. "Unlikely. While there are a few odd species here that were trapped in our little part of the universe by the pirates, for the most part our station is crewed by Unity members. No one here would have any incentive to help our enemies."

Kurakin, Chen and I were standing against the wall behind the table. I looked over at Chen and I'm pretty sure that he was thinking the same thing I was. His eye-roll confirmed it. There were always a few malcontents among any group of beings. Such beings could do a lot of damage in the name of revenge. Or desire for profit. No one on our security team would ever make the assumption that the problem couldn't come from within.

"I meant no offense, Coordinator," Yamashita said. "But from what you've told us in this meeting, it seems that the Kalikak have an uncanny success rate in intercepting your trade vessels. My mind instantly went to 'inside job.' Either that, or they must have amazing sensors that can scan vast swaths of space."

"We're assuming that they've planted spy satellites along our major trade routes," Kangot said. "We've definitely had to become more 'random' in our course planning, usually spending large amounts of extra fuel. Needless to say, the costs for shipped goods has risen dramatically as well."

"They would have to have very good spy satellites to cover that much space," Commander Torvald said. "Do the Kalikak, if their sole economy is based on piracy, have a manufacturing facility for this sort of thing?"

"We cannot say with certainty," Didin replied. "No one has ever found their home base, be it planet or station. We can't even be sure that there are, in fact, spy drones out there. We've certainly never found one. But we do know that they have state of the art vessels, none of them dilapidated as you might expect of pirates. It is also rumored that they are technology thieves. When they take a ship with technology they can use, it is said they incorporate this new tech into their own systems."

"All rumor, of course," Kangot said. "No one has taken one of their ships in one piece."

Captain Yamashita leaned forward, her elbows on the table and her palms flattened against one another as she put the edges of her hands against her lips. She stared into space for moment, obviously deep in thought.

"Coordinator, how far out from this station do you patrol?" she asked.

Alien faces aren't easy to read if you haven't been around that species much, but the Wulkin seemed to have very human-like tendencies in the expression department. Kangot looked definitely embarrassed.

"We have two small patrol boats that do a circuit around our station. They are in space on a different orbital vector every three to four day-cycles, of course giving its pilot two days off between patrols."

"How wide are these circuits? Meaning what's the distance from the station for each circuit?"

"Approximately one light hour," Kangot replied. "We have

deployed our own satellites to relay information, but their scanning range is limited compared to what we can achieve from our station. The patrol ships have much better range than the satellites."

The Captain's eyes widened. In fact we were all surprised at the answer. One light hour was only about the distance from Earth to Jupiter when those planets were aligned. *Seeker* could scan with accuracy three times that far *without* Remora support.

"Your scans only reach that far?" Yamashita asked?

"Hah! Are you joking, Captain?" Didin said. "Our sensing abilities are quite amazing up to around two light minutes. But a light hour is well beyond even our active information gathering technology. Hence the boats. And the satellites."

Oh dang, I thought, *that explains a few things.*

The Captain pulled out her comm padd. "Commander M'Buku, do you read?"

"Loud and clear, Captain. How can I assist?"

"Commander, I want all functional Remoras deployed and I want this section of space surveyed out to a distance of ten light hours in all directions. Look for spy satellites, drones or ships. Anything suspicious, in fact. I want this area cataloged. Begin immediately."

"Understood. Remoras deploying, and I will inform you immediately if we come up with anything."

"Thank you, Commander," Yamashita said. "Oh, and Bosede? Normal propulsion speed, if you get my meaning."

"Yes, ma'am, I do. M'Buku out."

During this conversation, growing expressions of astonishment had come to Didin and Kangot. As soon as the captain's conversation was finished, they both began talking over each other.

"You have the ability to see that far with your probes? This is astonishing!" Didin said.

"Captain, this technological innovation would be a situation changer," Kangot said. "What can we offer you to share this technology with us? It would be incredibly valuable to our confederation of systems. If we could see the Kalikak earlier, it would greatly increase the chances that our ships could evade them!"

The Captain stood, and pushed her chair back in, indicating that the meeting was over. "Coordinator, I will think on what you're asking. It would be precipitous of me to simply hand over superior technology without considering the possible ramifications. I need to consult with my people."

"We'd be willing to offer exceptionally large rewards, Captain Yamashita." Kangot said. "All the worlds we represent would be willing to pay."

"That's all well and good, but I need something different before I can offer anything."

"What is that, Captain?" Didin asked.

"More information. Quite frankly," the captain said, "I need to know you better. A lot better."

13

"So, for all their light speed technology," Commander M'Buku said, "these people are well behind us in other respects."

We sat around the main conference table, or rather all of the *Seeker*'s senior officers did. Emily and I held up a wall near the door. As well as the officers, Master Chief Kurakin and Shendra and Duala Zahn stood in the room too. Lieutenant Bitt-Nurr attended holographically, as did Dora and Organizer of Armadas.

"Let's remember," Lieutenant Commander Torvald interjected, "Earth is where she is technologically due to outside influence. Humanity'd still likely be squabbling with each other within the confines of the solar system if the Laldoralin hadn't uplifted us."

"More likely," Kurakin said. "We'd have either destroyed our own environment or started a war that sent us back to the stone age. I mean, let's be honest with ourselves. The Laldoralin saved humanity from its own foolishness."

"Humans are not the only ones the Laldoralin have saved from themselves," Shendra Zahn said from where she stood.

"The Kiffallans, though you may think us a cooly logical race, have deep-running passions. Those passions unleashed led us to the brink of our own destruction. The Laldoralin did not allow that to happen."

"My sister speaks truly," Duala said. The two were twins, both tall with elfin features. They were easy to tell apart in general because Shendra wore an engineering coverall most of the time while Duala wore a medical section uniform. Also, Shendra had a long greenish-blond braid, while Duala's skull was shaved to smoothness. Duala continued, "In fact, the introduction of advanced technology has changed the course of several of the Hegemony's members throughout time. Of course, there are some species that such technology is doled out at a very measured pace. Such species are... volatile, and must be protected from themselves."

"Why do I get the feeling that you're talking about humans?" Torvald asked.

"Humanity is one of the few civilizations," Shendra said, "that is both aggressive and technologically innovative, moving forward at a pace that is rare among known space-faring peoples. The improvements that have been added to *Seeker* are an excellent example of how fast your people adapt to new ideas."

Obviously Shendra and Duala had not researched Earth's political landscape throughout the twenty-first century.

"Indeed." Duala took up speaking where her sister had left off. "Your people went from an agrarian society to reaching Earth's moon in less than three hundred orbits, an unprecedented forward leap. You may not realize this, but your innovation and aggressiveness toward each other made some members of the Hegemony hesitate when it was suggested that you be uplifted."

"But why?" I asked. "Earth could've destroyed itself without the Laldoralin's intervention."

"Fear," Captain Yamashita said. "Fear of the innovation and aggressiveness she mentioned. Knowing humanity's history, I can see why some hesitated to help us. Hopefully we've proven ourselves, but I'd guess that some of the species of the Hegemony are still keeping a close eye on us. In fact, I would guess that the number of non-human species that accompanied us on this trip weren't only to take over if the jump alignments incapacitated the human crew."

There was silence in the room for a moment. An awkward silence.

"The captain is not completely wrong," Shendra finally said. "But I, for one, have found our experience with your people to be very positive. And certainly not dull."

Everyone around the table chuckled at that. Captain Yamashita continued, "Returning to the question of sharing technology, I would like some feedback. I realize that we are a long way from the Hegemony, but that, according to my orders allows me broad discretion as to how I do things."

"I can't see how helping these people improve their ability to see the Kalikak coming could be a bad thing," Chief Engineer Solas said. "We don't have to share Remora tech, but, but just giving them the basics to upgrade to what *Seeker*'s stand alone capabilities are wouldn't compromise us or the Hegemony."

"Personally, I think we should share our basic shield tech too," Lieutenant Bitt-Nurr's tiny hologram said.

"That is Laldoralin technology that was gifted to us," Commander M'Buku interjected. "While our scanning technology was also a gift from them, we've innovated the hell out of it. The shields, though, that's military grade tech. The Lallies might not take kindly to us giving it away, though I'm one hundred percent sure what they gave us was probably semi-obsolete by their own standards."

"Hell," Solas said, "*we've* made that shield tech, by itself, obsolete. The magna-shield overlay increases our ability to take punishment ten-fold. I sure wouldn't advocate handing our new shield innovations to anyone, but the old shields, by themselves don't threaten us, and could really help these people get out from under the Kalikak's boots. Level the playing field somewhat."

"This is an example of the innovation and aggression that I spoke of earlier," Duala said. "You've made improvements to technologies that were unknown to you a hundred of your orbits ago, that massively upgrade that very technology. Now you are talking about spreading this technology to species that we know very little about. I do not mean to offend, but humanity is a very reckless and impulsive species."

For some reason, Duala was looking at me as she said it, as if having a Laldoralin "high mucky muck" for a father required me to take her side on this. As no one else was looking at me, I decided to handle her scrutiny in a mature and reasonable manner. I stuck my tongue out at her. Shendra, standing beside her, grinned.

"I am willing to stipulate that we are impulsive," Captain Yamashita said. "But many of our current innovations are due to technology that was shared with us. However, Duala's point about not knowing these people well is a good one. I think, before we move forward, it would be best if we learned more. And I know just who to go to for information."

———

"I would be happy to help," Captain Drunor said, as he scuttled ahead of our small away team. He had cleaned up the singe marks on his body, and was once again resplendent in bright colors and bling.

Our Captain had enlisted the same group of crew members that went over to the massive space station to also visit Drunor's ship. The only addition to our group was Lieutenant Bitt-Nurr. If nothing else, she and Drunor could talk giant spider to giant spider.

"We are grateful for any information you can give us," Captain Yamashita said. "For reasons I'd rather not share here in the corridor, we want to know more about how things stand in your alliance."

The corridors in Drunor's ship were, like the space station, wide ovals, though not as large. Instead of the smooth metallic surfaces of the other, Drunor's corridor walls were heavily textured. We found out why, as we met one of the arachnid captain's crew coming the other way. Instead of stepping aside, the crew person simply moved up the side of one wall and passed us perpendicular to the floor.

"I owe you a debt that will be hard to repay, Captain Yamashita," Drunor replied. "We can discuss anything you like in this conference room. I have disabled all monitoring devices. Anything we speak of will be completely confidential."

The conference room was not the standard setup that we were used to, unsurprising with us being such different species. Instead of chairs around a large table, there were what looked like sling-hammocks, one end lower than the other. Each one had a computer monitor that would've been at home on the *Seeker* sitting in front of it. While the humans took a moment figuring how we were to sit, Drunor and Bitt-Nurr both easily slid into the 'chairs,' providing us with an example. The Captain and Torvald took careful seats while Kurakin, Chen and I stood.

"Now, what can I share with you?" Drunor asked. Yamashita and Bitt-Nurr looked at each other for a moment, then the captain nodded to our eight-legged officer. Bitt-Nurr took over the conversation.

"We do not wish to waste your time, Captain Drunor,"

Bitt-Nurr told him, "so I will come straight to the point. We are interested in sharing some of our technology with your group. However, before we do so, we want to be sure that you are not evildoers."

Captain Yamashita closed her eyes for a moment in exasperation at Bitt-Nurr's bluntness. "Drunor, we do not want to offend you. We simply want to know more about your multiple peoples to make sure that we are not going to cause more problems than we solve by sharing new technologies."

Drunor made a series of clicks that the translator had trouble with, and I was afraid that we'd pissed him off. The matrix finally caught up, and we all realized he was laughing.

"Captain, I am not a fan of frimble-footing around. I find your lovely Lieutenant's bluntness quite refreshing! Please ask your questions. I am at your service."

"We are interested in how things run in your alliance. Are all parties equal members?" Bitt-Nurr continued. "Are you allied for trade considerations, or as a mutual defense pact? How equal are the partners? Does one species dominate the others, and will that species keep what we share to themselves, or make sure that everyone shares in it?"

"That is a lot of questions all at once," Drunor replied, "Let me see if I can remember them all to give you answers."

"If you have difficulty, I will help," Bitt-Nurr replied.

"Thank you, lovely one." (Was our host a little bit smitten with our computer expert?) "To what I think is the most important of your questions, the Tappan Confederation, Also referred to as the Unity, is an alliance of equals. Our goals are, as you said, trade and mutual defense. However, the other goal is to keep *all* of our members strong. All five species of the confederation share technology with each other freely, which should answer another of your questions. There have been no wars or even more than minor disagreements for over a thousand (timescale unit undefined) in this area. That is, until the Kalikak showed up."

"Our translators are having difficulty with the units of time passage that you use," Captain Yamashita told him. "If you could use the movement of this galaxy and overlay your time units on it, then send it to the probe that is between us and our ship, our computers will update the information for us."

"Happy to oblige," Drunor tapped a few times on the screen in front of him. "There, done!"

"Excellent. Thank you. It seems that one of your designations is about 1.6 times the orbit of our homeworld. Our matrix will now be able to translate that for us. You said that you were close to being without conflict until the Kalikak appeared? How long ago was that?"

"About twenty years ago," Drunor said. I knew that the translator, having updated, was now converting Confederation time units into Earth units. Drunor continued, "Having been without conflict for so long, I don't mind telling you that we've made large technological jumps in that time. We also purchased technology from other civilizations outside our space. And we developed fast travel FTL ship designs. Unfortunately, the Kalikak keep getting ahead of us."

"Are they that innovative?" Bitt-Nurr asked.

"Oh shiblark, no. Their 'innovation' comes from theft. Any outside technology that found itself within the confines of our area of this spiral arm is in danger of being attacked. One of the things the Kalikak are known for is reverse engineering anything they get can their manipulators on.

I was sure that everyone of us felt a pang of dread. If the Kalikak had *Wanderer*... I felt my chest get very tight. New technology. Our sister ship would've been a juicy target.

It was all I could do to keep a calm demeanor and stand against the wall without hyperventilating.

14

"And you are simply giving us this technology? You want nothing in return for it?" Coordinator Kangot's odd whitish-blue eyes widened in surprise.

"Well, if you could put in a good word for us if the Laldoralin every come to this section of space, I'd appreciate it," Captain Yamashita, sitting in her command chair on the *Seeker,* told him. "To be honest, they're probably not going to be happy with me giving away their technology, but... it is what it is."

"And yet, you give us these priceless gifts. Captain Yamashita... I don't know how to respond to this. This is the most selfless act I have ever heard of. There will be teachings about you and your people in all our learning creches."

"Kangot, we simply could not let things stand as they are without trying to help. We had the means, and now it is up to you and yours to implement it. I think we all agree that the threat these pirates present to civilized people must be met with strength. I am happy that we can provide extra strength to you and your confederation."

"I will disseminate this knowledge to every world in our

space," Kangot told her. "Within a half-year, perhaps sooner, we will have these shields and scanners on every large vessel and station we have. Then we will be able to meet the Kalikak on something approaching equal terms. And as I am sure that our ships outnumber theirs, perhaps we will at last have the tactical advantage."

"Ambitious timeline," Yamashita said, "but I am sure that you're more than motivated. Now that I've sent the specifications to you, it is time for *Seeker* to leave and continue our search for our sister ship."

"If you could wait, Captain, perhaps we could equip a couple of our ships with these shields so they could act as escorts. I do not like the idea of our new friends traversing local space without assistance. Solo ships tend to be targets."

"I wish we could, Kangot. While you may have the specifications for the new technology, it will take time to adapt it to your own tech. Plus, we of Earth know that there is a learning curve in making those adaptions, as we had to do the same thing when the Laldoralin gifted us with it originally." Captain Yamashita gestured at the bridge and laughed. "Please be assured Coordinator, we still have a few secrets up our sleeves. The Kalikak, if they run across us *will* be surprised by these secrets."

"While I am not sure why you would wish to keep information in your arm coverings, Captain, I will take you at your word," Kangot said. Onscreen, he rose and put his hand over his chest. "I thank you again for your gift. It brings hope where there was despair. I salute you. Safe travels to you and your crew."

"Thank you, Coordinator. May those systems be easy for you to adapt. I hope that we will meet again. Farewell." She looked toward Lieutenant Sedgewick. "End transmission."

"Well, we've done it," Commander M'Buku said. "The

genie is out of the bottle. Hopefully the ramifications won't be that bad when we get home."

"If they are, Commander," Captain Yamashita said, grinning, "then I'd guess you'll be the Captain. So... silver lining?"

"Definitely not the way I want to get my butt into the big chair, Megumi," he replied.

Sitting at the tactical station, I let the ramifications of what we'd just done sink in. Earth, through the *Seeker*, had just upped the technological knowledge of several entire civilizations. Who knew what the ramifications of that could be farther down the line?

But the thing about humans was, (even more so as we evolved as a species) when we saw suffering, we tried to help. Since the Laldoralin had become somewhat of an over-government to EarthGov, the incidence of human leaders who were in their positions only for personal gain had dropped significantly. I liked to think that was because we, as a species, were evolving. But in my more cynical moments, I really thought that it was because the lack of opportunities for graft and corruption had made politics less of a natural draw for the self-absorbed and greedy.

But whatever the future held, this Confederation was now in a better position to defend itself from predators.

———

"Jump complete," Lieutenant Kolara said. "That's got to be the smoothest transition yet. I didn't feel anything more than slight discomfort."

"Thank Solas and the engineers," Captain Yamashita said. "More technical information we can send back to Earth. Speaking of which, I've got to go do some creative report writing, and I hope I can spin things to mitigate as much damage as possible. Commander, M'Buku, you have the conn. Resume our search pattern for *Wanderer*."

"I have the conn," M'Buku said. "Ensign Darkfeather, deploy the Remoras. Oh, can you also check in with Danforth and find out if Remora Two is ready to be returned to service yet?"

"Actually, I checked with him on that just before we jumped, sir," Emily reported. "Lieutenant Danforth says that the stealth generator is ready to be tested. We can deploy Remora Two and swap out with Remora Three at your pleasure."

"Lieutenant Dora?" M'Buku said in the general direction of the ceiling. Dora's blue-tinted hologram instantly appeared next to him.

"Yes, Commander? How may I assist?"

"Dora, Remora Two is ready to test, are you twinned into the probe?"

"I was waiting for your authorization to do so. Since I am now considered crew, I no longer do things without letting my superior officers know. May I consider myself authorized to exit Remora One and enter Remora Two?"

"Please do," M'Buku said. "Let me know when you're ready to go."

It was less than two minuted before Dora informed M'Buku she was ready. The commander touched the comm button on his chair. "Lieutenant Commander Danforth, deploy Remora Two, please."

"Deploying now, Commander," came the reply.

"Dora, how are things looking on your end?" M'Buku asked.

"All systems are green, Commander. I assume that you would like to test the new system?"

"Correct. Switch to a private channel please." M'Buku said. He turned toward Emily Darkfeather, "Ensign, assign

Organizer of Armadas to close support of the *Seeker*. I want him nearby in Remora Three."

"Aye, sir"

"Commander? This is Dora on a secure channel."

"Great. Dora, here is what I want you to do. Jump as far away from us as you can, then activate your stealth system."

"And then jump back to see how close I can get to *Seeker* without being spotted, I presume." Dora replied. "If so, I will be terminating all data feeds to and from the *Seeker* during the exercise."

"Perfect. But I want a little more than that. Sneak up on Organizer. Get close enough to touch deflection fields if you can. Be bold, be sneaky, and that's all the instruction I'm giving. Use your own discretion as to tactics. Oh, and lock your shipboard self out of the bridge. Let's keep this fair."

"Mission understood, Commander. It's fortunate for Organizer that he is not a biological being."

"And why is that?"

"Because with what I'm about to do to him, were he human, he might be required to change undergarments."

15

"Remoras One and Four have jumped ahead, Commander," Emily told M'Buku. "Remora Three is flying close support."

"Organizer, do you copy," M'Buku said.

"I am here, M'Buku Commander," came the reply.

"I need you to enhance *Seeker*'s scanning capabilities. Dora's getting ready to attack the ship in mock battle, and we need to see her coming. We're counting on you."

"If she has, as I suspect, had the Sallan stealth system installed, it will be a true challenge to.. WHAT? I have been touched!"

On the view screen, which showed a graphic of *Seeker* and her surrounding space, and new green dot appeared less than five yards from Organizer's Remora.

"Gotcha!" Dora said triumphantly.

"Unfair! I was not prepared!" Organizer indignantly exclaimed.

"You snooze, you lose," Dora replied, her voice laden with smugness. "You let your guard down, my friend."

"I demand the rematch!"

"Dora," Commander M'Buku said, a chuckle in his voice,

"Let us have another chance. Do it again, and give us sixty seconds to prepare. I hate to admit it, but we weren't quite ready. Our fault, not yours."

"As you wish, sir. However, do not expect any mercy on my next attack." Remora Two disappeared in the flash of her small jump drive.

Competitive much? I thought to myself.

"You heard the lady, people. Darkfeather, I want full active sensors, Organizer, here's your chance to redeem yourself."

I was wondering if the commander was going to take us to action stations, but he didn't do so. Instead he turned to me. "Tanner, I know we're not in danger from Dora, but I want you to quiet your mind and see if you can sense when she jumps back in. Without danger, it's probably a long shot, but let's do everything we can to wipe that smugness from your mom's tone."

"Aye sir, I'll give it my best shot." I stood, bracing my hands on the back of my chair, bowed my head and closed my eyes. I listened. I reached out with my senses, and I got a slight... flutter. Before, when I was younger and before I'd worked at quieting my mind, it wouldn't have really registered on me. It was subtle, but it had appeared from nowhere, and I knew I'd made contact.

"She's here. She's jumped back in," I said.

"Can you get a fix on her, Tanner?" Emily asked.

I sank down into myself, using some of the techniques taught to me by my stepdad back on Earth. The feeling I got was so subtle, it took all of my concentration. Without opening my eyes, I raised my arms to the starboard side of the bridge, forming a twenty degrees arc in front of my body.

"She's somewhere... here," I said. "That's the best I can narrow it down."

It was a cone of area, growing larger the farther it went

from the ship. With any distance from *Seeker*, it grew into a huge area of space.

"Ensign Darkfeather, hit that area with everything we've got in the way of active scans. Highlight the area for Organizer, and get Remora Three's sensor suite on it too."

"Aye Commander, full scan in progress."

We all waited while Emily and Organizer put everything they had into scanning the cone. No one said a word, as if our silence would enhance our scanning systems.

"Organizer has found a wibble," Emily said.

"A wibble, Ensign?"

"The fading remains of a subspace anomaly, Commander. A jump emergence."

"Concentrate scans on the path between that point and the ship," M'Buku said. I snuck a look at Emily, and could see the tightening of her mouth. She didn't need for the commander to tell "grandma how to knit."

"Organizer has found a small heat signature," Emily replied. "She must be coasting in for it to be that small. Lighting her up with full scan suite, now."

I felt her presence wink out.

"Subspace... she jumped," Emily said.

I felt her again, and without thinking turned to the port side of the ship. M'Buku saw me and turned to look that way, though all he could see was Lieutenant Sedgewick at the comm station.

"Portside?" he asked.

"Aye, commander, she.." I turned to the aft section, "now she's behind us. And she's... gone again."

A grin began to appear on M'Buku's face, "Well played, old girl," he said. "She knows we've found some way to follow her, so she's bouncing around to throw us off. Making it so we can't concentrate scans in one area." He looked at me. "I bet she's extrapolated how we found her, and is working at exhausting your concentration, Tanner. How are you doing?"

"Honestly sir, I've been concentrating as hard as I can for a good six or seven minutes. I can feel I'm losing my ability to follow her. I feel mentally more tired by the minute."

"Laldoralin combat AI," M'Buku said, admiration in his tone. "We may be out of our league."

"Drazzats!!" Organizer said over the comms. We had a complete language database for his now extinct makers and the fact that our computers hadn't translated his exclamation probably meant that it was a word not to be used in polite company. "I admit, defeat, friend Dora. I lost you and did not reacquire you presence again."

"Gotcha again," Dora said over the comm. A moment later, her hologram appeared next to the commander. "Does that suffice as a learning exercise, Sir? I have learned several things about using my stealth field and a bit about its weaknesses."

"Impressive job, Dora. We learned a few things as well. Lieutenant Sedgewick, inform Robotics that I want Remora three to get the stealth upgrade immediately." M'Buku turned back to Dora. "I guess that you figured out how we were tracking you."

Mom looked at me and smiled slyly. "I had my suspicions."

"I learned to use my gift in a new way," I said. "I also learned it has limitations."

M'Buku looked at me, a speculative expression on his face. "Perhaps," he said. "Or perhaps using that gift in this way is completely new to you. And maybe, just maybe, it has a lot more depth than you ever realized."

The next week was a mixture of tedium and stress. Tedium from scanning and scanning in our pattern of jumps for *Wanderer*, stress from knowing the Kalikak were out there and hostile. And that they might've gotten to Valiel and her fellow crew members already

Because of the situation, I'd been taken off all duties except my tactical station, which I was at every other shift. Otherwise I was ordered to stay as rested as I could. I spent this time sleeping, working on the final stages of my academy studies or working on my upgrade of the particle cannon focusing emitters. However, Commander M'Buku had one bit of homework for me.

"Tanner, I think this little experiment with sensing your mom was instructive, don't you?" he said.

"Yes, Commander," I said. "Though I'm not completely sure that what I learned was super useful."

"That remains to be seen, Ensign. But... you were able, however tenuously, to sense where Dora was. There was no danger, but by quieting your mind you were able to get enough of a touch on her that we found her on that second run in. Verifiable results."

"Yes sir I suppose that's right."

"As close as you and Dora are," M'Buku said, "we have to stipulate that she is of an artificial, a synthetic nature. Yet you still found her, even when she was heavily stealthed."

"Yes, but I'm not sure what you're getting at."

"What if you were searching for your twin sister?"

The question brought me up short. "I haven't ever considered using my gift as a... search tool. Until today, I didn't even know it had any application other than an early warning system. And of course the whole targeting thing. How would I...?"

"Have you ever had any exposure to meditation?"

"After Valiel and I were brought out of our hundred and

fifty years of stasis, our foster father... our stepdad... worked on teaching us a lot of different disciplines. Wilderness survival, martial arts, and yeah, he worked with us on meditation, but I didn't really have the focus needed. I wasn't very good at it."

"I think, with some advanced help in that area," M'Buku said, "you might be able to use that talent of yours in ways you haven't imagined. And I know just the person to help you with that."

"You really think so, sir?"

"At this point, we're all speculating. But we speculated on you being able to sense Dora's approach, and it paid off."

———

"Not bad, Tanner," Master Chief Kurakin said. "You sat for forty-five minutes. How do you feel?"

"Relaxed, Chief, but I still can't get my monkey mind to stop chattering while I meditate."

We were sitting in the port side corner of the upper forward observation lounge, the big transparasteel windows showing the vast universe ahead of us. Commander M'Buku had enlisted the chief to help with yet more of my training. With her tutoring me with my academy studies and making me do martial arts with the security team, I was practically her full-time student.

"That's enough for today," she said. "We'll work more tomorrow. Getting control of your mind takes time and patience. But it is attainable."

"Yes, Ma'am," I said. "But every time I'd get to where I felt like I was getting there, some idea of thought would come in, and my mind would go with it like a runaway train."

"Practice more after your next shift, Tanner. We're shooting for a mind like a clear, flat pond, one without thought ripples. So when a thought comes in, imagine it's like a cloud. Instead of trying to fight with it, just watch it, and in your mind let it evaporate."

"I'll try, Chief."

"No need for trying. Just use the tools I've given you, and let it happen. Trying means you're pushing, and if you're pushing, your mind won't rest. Let go of your concerns, just be and observe."

"I'll do it like you say. Thank you for your help."

"Good man." Kurakin patted me on the shoulder and turned to leave the room. When she left, I considered diving back in, but consulting my padd, I saw that I needed to get some sleep if I was going to be any good on the bridge next shift.

I was walking toward my bunk in the main corridor when I heard a familiar voice behind me. "Hey, Grand Lama, how'd your session with the chief go."

"Hey Emily, about what you'd expect from someone who hasn't practiced in years. Mediocre." I put my arm around her shoulder and we walked on.

"Who'd have thought that straight-laced, by-the-book M'Buku, of all people, would have been the one to suggest meditation?" Emily said. "Books, covers, I guess. Where you headed?"

"To my rack. I'm supposed to stay rested for bridge duty."

"Yeah, about that. I was going to my quarters too. You could... join me. We could, I dunno, rest together?"

"Please be assured that my enthusiasm for that plan is unparalleled," I said. "Though... how much rest are we going to actually get?"

"Unless you've become some sort of super-athlete, Tanner, we'll get... enough."

16

Emily and I were both on the bridge when the breakthrough came in.

"Long range communication from Remora Four, Captain," Emily said. "One and Four have reached the next system in *Wanderer*'s itinerary. Remora One has a contact."

"Is it *Wanderer*?" Captain Yamashita asked.

"Both Remoras are still on the edge of the system, and too far out for positive identification. Shall I have them jump to the contact?"

"Affirmative. We're about done with our scanning of this area. Helm, get coordinates from Science and jump us in to meet them. Darkfeather, have Remoras Two and Three meet us also. I've got a feeling..."

"Affirmative, Ma'am."

"Captain," Lieutenant Kolara said from the helm, "we are ready to translocate on your word."

"The word is given, Mr. Kolara," Yamashita replied, "Let's jump."

"Aye Captain, jumping us in to the edge of the system."

We were in Nth space less than three minutes, before

emerging on the edge of the new planetary system. Kolara had put us there rather than jumping deep in for safety's sake. You didn't just jump far into an unknown system of planets without some preliminary survey. Aside from asteroids, comets and other planetary bodies, no one wanted to jump into the middle of a Kalikak fleet.

"Captain," Emily said, "Telemetry from Remora One indicates that we've found her. It is *Wanderer*. And Ma'am? She adrift in space and looks to have been attacked."

My gut twisted at her words. *Adrift. Attacked. Oh dear God, no.*

A hologram of our sister ship appeared before the command chair. It was mirrored by a CGI version on the main view screen. The *Wanderer* slowly tumbled end over end in front of us, debris following along. There were gaping gaps in her aft hulls and her jump fins were in tatters.

"Goddamn it!" Captain Yamashita cursed quietly. Her volume raised considerably with her next orders going out through the ship's speakers. "All hands, set condition one. We've found *Wanderer*, and she's been attacked." She let off the intercom button and looked around the bridge. "Charge weapons. Darkfeather, I want the Remoras stationed for maximum scan area. If the Kalikak are around, I want them found."

———

No Kalikak.

We were now less than an eighth of a mile from our sister ship, having jumped the rest of the way into the system's inner section. *Wanderer* drifted in an adjacent orbit to the star's one habitable planet, only around a million miles away from the drifting hulk.

Dora and Organizer were busy surveying the nearby

world, looking for signs that this might be the Kalikak home-world or one of their bases. Remora's One and Four were flying overwatch over us which left the job of scanning *Wanderer* to *Seeker*'s science team.

"No life signs, Captain," Commander Torvald said. "Without closer inspection, we can't tell if that means they're... dead... or just missing. It is entirely possible they bailed out for the nearby planet though."

"Lieutenant Sedgewick," Captain Yamashita said, turning toward the comm station, "Send out a general query message, sub-light communication only. Make sure that the signal is weak enough that it doesn't go far beyond the edge of this system. If they're here, maybe they've got working comms."

"Aye, Captain."

"Den, can we tell how bad her interior systems are? Is *Wanderer* a write off?"

"Not from here, Ma'am," Torvald said. "We'll either need to pull a Remora off what they're doing or go in there ourselves."

"No," Yamashita replied, drumming her fingers on her command chair, "No. I want our probes where they are. Commander M'Buku, inform Mr. Solas I'll want an engineering team ready for EVA to *Wanderer* and inform Chief Kurakin that I want at least two security personnel to go with them."

"Aye, Captain."

"Captain," I said, speaking up over the bridge hub-bub, "permission to join the away party?"

"Captain," Emily chimed in, "I would also like to tag along, if I may."

The captain looked toward the both of us with an expression of deep thought. "I suppose," she said, "it would be a good idea to have someone from science along, Darkfeather.

You're in. Lieutenant Forbes, can you spare Ensign Sure Shot here for a little while?"

Forbes, my lead at tactical, looked at me with a considering eye, then grinned. "I believe Ensign Kinzler and I can keep things together until he returns Ma'am."

Yamashita drummed her fingers on the chair for a few moments more, making me sweat a little. Then she relented. "Alright, Tanner, I know you're worried sick about your sister. You can go. But I want you mindful of that danger sense of yours. Both of you suit up and report to the shuttle bay. Whomever Solas decides to send as the engineering lead on this will be in command of the team. Now scoot. And stay out of trouble!"

"Yes, Ma'am!" we both replied. Emily and I entered the lift and headed down to get our gear.

"I think," Emily said, "that's... what? The third time we've volunteered for an off the ship mission and been accepted?"

"Yeah," I said, my mind elsewhere.

"Well, Tanner, look at our track record. You and me, we make a good team, in more ways than one, and the captain knows it. Plus, there is one other thing."

"What's that?"

"Unlike ninety percent of the crew, we've got proximity to the big chair when things are goin' down."

17

It was *not* good.

Flying in on our shuttle, we could see the damage to *Wanderer* up close and personal and she'd been hurt badly. My stomach tightened, hoping, praying that I wouldn't find Valiel's lifeless body aboard her ship.

Wanderer's top jump fin was attached by only one badly bent strut and was swung out away from the hull. There were gaping holes in the aft section while her bow looked almost completely whole. There were holes bored into her hull at various points.

"Ten to one, those are breaching points," Corporal Chen said. He and private Vanessa Hodgekins were our security detail. Chen was about five foot, seven inches and built like a tank. Hodgekins was a 5 foot, eleven inch, freckle-faced redhead with the body of a super fitness athlete. Both were wearing level two body armor and carrying our newly-developed plasma shotguns.

They also carried hand cannons, last resort semi-auto pistols that fired large-caliber armor-piercing rounds. The reason they were last resort is that in a spaceship, particularly if you were near the actual outer hull, you could conceivably decompress an area with a stray shot. Also, in low or null gravity, the recoil made them a propulsion unit all by their lonesome. The rest of us were armed with beamer pistols, Blah-Veht enhanced lasers in a small package.

We touched down in the large "belly" bay, the ventral shuttle landing area. It was empty. No shuttles at all.

"Did they use the shuttles to escape?" Hodgekins asked.

"Or were they used as prisoner transports?" Chen replied. "Or just stolen?"

Touching down, we unloaded in vacuum. The bay doors were open to space, and the retaining force fields were non-operational. Everyone had been required to wear body armor over their environmental suits, and as our feet locked onto the deck, everyone was shifting and squirming to get their load out to be more comfortable.

"No debris at all in here," I said. "I think the bay explosively decompressed."

"I hope no one we like was in here at the time," Emily said. "undoubtedly happened when the retaining field went down."

Chen and Hodgekins moved to the main entrance to the ship with Emily and I. Shendra Zahn and two ensigns from engineering did a quick systems check, jacking in through a terminal at the bay's flight control console.

"Main power is offline," Shendra said, "however, the multiple backup generators are keeping lights and gravity on. There's atmosphere in most sections, and emergency force fields are in place where they can be of any use."

"Not the aft section, though," Ensign Caldwell said. Barney Caldwell was a short, nondescript man, with a receding hairline. His most noticeable feature was his large brown eyes. He pointed to the readout on Shendra's screen.

"The gaps in the hull are too large for forcefields. That section is sealed at the entrances by pressure doors."

"Chief?" Ensign Lupita said. "No ping from the main computer. I'm reading that it's still there, but in a loop mode. Possibly as an anti-intrusion measure."

"Hmmm. Ensign Darkfeather," Shendra said.

"Yes, Chief?" Emily answered. As junior officers, we technically outranked Chief Zahn, but Commander Solas had placed her in charge of the mission. Knowing her experience and competency, none of us had the slightest problem with that.

"I want you to take Voss, Lupita and Hodgekins to the computer core. Even as bad as she's hurt, with her computer back online we might be able to get more systems working."

"And maybe find out what happened here," I said.

"We can only hope so," Shendra replied. "Meanwhile, I'll take Caldwell and Chen aft to see what's what back there."

"Aye, Chief," Emily said. "We're on it."

———

We were able to access the rest of the ship more easily than expected. All the engineering team had to do was override the pressure door into the bay and a retaining force field snapped into place to preserve the atmosphere on the other side. Once again, I silently thanked the designers who'd decided the explorer ships needed multiple redundant power generation systems.

The retaining fields were an invention from the planet Galas-Pa, a Hegemony member and was one of the wonders shared with the people of Earth as we climbed for the stars in the early years of the Uplift. They had one very interesting aspect that was particularly helpful to us as we entered the ship. If you weren't a gas, you could, with some effort, push through them.

As we all entered the main corridor, we got a quick reminder that we were on a ship that had been attacked and had fought back for its very life.

Scorch marks were everywhere, and in many instances sections of the walls had lengthy lines of melted metal. Some sort of high-energy beam had moved across, right to left, leaving dripped metal running down the walls.

"Oh, damn," Hodgekins said. "First confirmed death, here."

"Oh God," Tani Lupita said. The slender young woman leaned against a bulkhead for a moment. "This person was cut in half by that beam."

At the base of a running score mark, were a pair of legs housed in the teal-colored uniform of a *Wanderer* officer. His or her upper torso was gone, vaporized into ash.

"Brace up, my human brethren," Shendra said. "I expect things are going to get worse, the farther we go in. Everyone, to your assigned tasks, please."

Our teams split up and Hodgekins led the way. You want a spooky experience? Take a stroll through a ghost ship.

As we moved along the main corridor, which was eerily like the one on *Seeker*, damage was everywhere. We would occasionally come across the body of one of *Wanderer's* crew, usually half disintegrated. But while there was blood on the walls, there were far, far fewer dead crew than my mind was expecting, considering the damage in the corridor.

"Not many bodies," I noted. "And those we're finding all seem to be our people. I'm seeing splashes of what looks like alien circulatory fluid, but no enemy bodies."

"It seems the Kalikak want to remain anonymous," Emily said.

"Corporal," Hodgekins said into her comm, "We're

finding no alien bodies, and only a few of our own. Aside from damage, we're finding a lot less carnage than I expected."

"I think we're finding quite enough carnage, thank you," Lupita said. "I'll have nightmares for years from what we have found."

"We're seeing much the same here, Van," Chen's voice said from her comm. "I doubt we're going to find anyone but the dead on this ship. But keep on full alert. For all we know the Kalikak might be able to spoof our scanners. Or they may have left booby traps. Don't get lax."

"Roger that, Corporal." She replaced her comm padd on her belt. "The creepiest thing about this is, if it wasn't for a slightly different color scheme, we could be on the *Seeker*. We all know right where our destination is without having to consult our padds."

Our next find however was even more shocking.

Emily had just over-ridden another closed pressure door when Hodgekins stuck her head in.

"Holy shit!" She then held up her fist in the signal for us to hold position then slipped through the doors. I moved up to where she'd been, standing a moment before I peeked in. I couldn't control my own response any more than Vanessa had.

"Holy shit, indeed!"

"Clear," Hodgekins voice said. "Come ahead."

We stepped into the side corridor that led to the computer core, and found what must've been the most intense battle of the entire boarding action.

It was a high-tech Alamo.

The bullet-dimpled bulkheads were covered in blood, most of it blueish-teal color. The enemy's blood. At the far end of the corridor, two of the *Wanderer*'s high-tech "Godzilla" mech suits blocked the way forward. Thousands of empty shells, both of frangible ballistic rounds and plasma spitters littered the deck around each suit which explained the copious amounts of alien blood at the other end of the hallway.

But the two SecOps manning the suits personnel had payed the ultimate price for being committed to the position. Behind them, on the pressure door leading to the core, there was a reverse shadow in the shape of the two mech-suits. So much energy had poured down the corridor that an outline of the suits was the only part un-charred on the bulkhead and door behind them. That same amount of energy had slammed into the two brave *Wanderer* security people fighting off the enemy horde. They were unidentifiable in their destroyed exo-suits.

"They died fighting," Hodgekins said, her eyes shiny and wet, "they fucking went down fighting."

18

"Chief, we're stuck at the entrance to the computer core."

"What do you mean, Ensign Darkfeather," Shendra's voice, coming over the comm was slightly terse, which, coming from a Kiffallan, was a significant indication of stress.

"There was a battle at the entrance to the core between enemy forces and two Godzilla-clad SecOps personnel," Emily replied. "The hatch behind them is literally fused shut. It'll take an engineering team with plasma cutters to get it open."

"Use your initiative, Ensign. You know there are other ways into that core. Maintenance crawl-ways and ventilation systems. Find a way."

"Aye, Chief." Emily put away her comm. "I think I've just been chastised."

"Don't take it personally," Hodgekins said. "Even Kiffers have emotions, and I don't know about the rest of you, but mine feel flayed."

"You are a master of understatement, Vanessa," Lupita said. "But we need to find these crawl-ways the chief mentioned. I've only worked in the computer core a few times, but I know that they can be accessed through these two compartments." She held up her pad, showing us a schematic of the hidden paths to the core. "We'll probably need to over-ride the entrance hatches, but I do not think this will be a great problem."

"Tani, you and Vanessa take crawl-way 21-Beta," Emily said. "while Tanner and I will try 22-Charlie. Last ones to the core have to buy the beer."

"I'll need many beers after this horror show," Hodgekins said. "Prepare to be impoverished."

We backtracked out of the carnage corridor, Emily and I going right while Lupita and Hodgekins went left. We shortly came to a broom closet-sized door with the word "mainte-nance" on a plaque beside it. I hadn't worked around the computer core at all in my engineering duties, being assigned to robotics, but I knew what we'd find beyond the hatch. Like most of these maintenance closets, there was a cabinet for tools and a crawl-way hatch that led into the veins of the ship.

The crawl-way hatch had been cut away.

"Tani?" Emily said into her comm. "Are you at your entrance yet?"

"Yes. I am about to attempt to override the hatch now," Lupita replied. 'Shouldn't take long. Are you already through?"

"In a matter of speaking. Our hatch has been breached."

"Do you need assistance?" Hodgekins' voice said.

"Negative," I said. "I'm going to recon into the crawl-way. Emily will follow and we will retreat if we find enemy forces."

"Be careful there, Tanner. Go in quiet and book outta there if you get the slightest whiff of trouble."

"Roger that." I turned to see Emily looking at me with one eyebrow raised.

"You're going in first, are you? I will remind you *acting-ensign*, that I technically outrank you by seniority."

"Permission to speak freely," I said, snapping a slightly sarcastic salute. She gave me a flat look and made a circling finger gesture that signaled 'move it along.'

"I would remind her ensign-ness that I am the one with the danger sense, and I've been training with the SecOps people on *Seeker* for some time now. With respect, I feel that I am qualified for this recon position, with your permission."

"All right, Tanner, get your smug little butt in there. But..."

"Yes?"

"Try not to get so cocky it gets you killed. For me? Please?"

"Ah, okay. Sorry for being a smart ass." I said.

"Oh don't worry, we'll be discussing it when this is over."

With that dire storm warning, I took the lead. The crawl-ways were just that. There was no way to traverse them other than on your hands and knees if you were of the humanoid persuasion. I again blessed the ship designers for making the floors of these hidden paths deeply padded. If they'd been metal-floored, a whole generation of engineers might've needed knee replacements.

The tunnels were half-circle shaped, and had several branches going in different directions. The were small signs at each junction which made it easy to stay on course for the core, and in a few minutes I was at the hatchway leading there. The hatch was already open.

Laying on my belly, I slowly and carefully stuck my head out and looked down to the main deck for the computer core. Everything seemed alright, until I noted blood spatters on the walls. Both teal-colored and red.

"There's been violence here," I whispered back to Emily. "But it seems quiet now. I'm going to edge out on the walkway and see what's going on at the other side of the core."

"Tanner," Emily's voice came from the dim corridor behind me. "What's your danger sense saying. The fact that it's not making itself felt says to me that whatever's happened down there is over and done."

"I'm... not getting anything. I'm gonna move out there. Please wait and give me a minute to confirm we're not in danger." I moved out onto the walkway and began circling the upper level of the computer core. As I moved around it, I began to see what had happened in the area. I saw an ensign laying against a wall in a rag doll position, a pool of blood under him. Dimples in the wall behind him indicated he'd been shot with ballistic projectiles of some sort.

I looked behind me, ready to signal Emily to come out of the crawl-way, only to see that she was only a foot behind me. I started to say something, but she raised her finger in front of her lips in the classic signal to "shush."

We started to move down the stairway to the main level when a noise caused me to whirl, beamer in hand, only to see Vanessa Hodgekins emerge from a hatch on the opposite side of the upper level. She looked at me, and gave the two finger sign that she had eyes on something on that side of the core.

I reached the main deck, and carefully peeked out from around the core. There was an officer sitting in a chair, and for a moment, I thought she might be alive.

As I grew closer, I could see that hope was in vain. Blood had dripped from the chair, and there was enough that there was no way she could've survived. The blood trail leading to the chair indicated that she'd chosen her final resting place. Her chin was lowered to her chest and a what looked like a sawed-off pump shotgun lay in her lap. Certainly not standard issue, but undoubtedly efficient. There was no one else there but us.

"Clear." Hodgekins voice said, authoritatively. "Let's see if the core is intact. I'd really like some answers about what went down here."

Emily and Lupita, who'd emerged behind Vanessa Hodgekins, both set to work to see if they could get *Wanderer*'s computer system to respond.

"*Seeker*," Emily said into her comm, "This is Darkfeather, do you read?"

"Five by five, Ensign," Captain Yamashita replied. "Status?"

"My team is at the computer core. It appears intact, but the system is locked down. I will need the decryption key for Enigma protocol encrypt to get any farther with this."

"Understood. Transmitting. Key will auto decrypt when it hits your personal padd, Darkfeather. You can then decrypt *Wanderer*'s core with that."

"Thank you, Ma'am. I am sending over our scans and recordings also."

"Excellent. Chief Zahn informs me that ship's Jump Drive has been removed, but her FTL drive is still in place. Either the Kalikak are very picky about what technology they steal, or they were on some sort of time table that we don't understand. *Wanderer* was not half as scavenged as the ship we found earlier."

"Or, Captain," I said. "They're coming back to scavenge at their leisure."

"Or that," Yamashita replied. "We are on high alert over here. Let me know what you find out from *Wanderer*'s core."

"Aye, Ma'am. Darkfeather out." Emily closed the connection and she and Lupita resumed their work.

Hodgekins and I, now pretty much left to our own devices, began to check everything in the core room. Vanessa went to check on the dead woman in the chair, while I moved over to the ladder to the lower deck of the core. The lower deck was a tight and small area, more a service pathway than anything else. Still, it needed to be cleared.

Looking down, I was very surprised by what I saw.

"Contact," I yelled, lowering my sidearm to cover two sprawled figures at the base of the ladder. Hodgekins was at my side almost instantly, plasma shotgun aimed down into the small space below.

Both figures lay in teal-colored fluid, neither of them moving. I noted splatters of the stuff all over the metal housing on the on the computer core as well as dimpling on that metal. Looking over my shoulder, I could see that that the green blood and impact points lined up perfectly to where the red blood trail leading to the chair started. Three shotgun shells lay on the deck there.

"She took 'em out," Hodgekins said. "Well done, sister."

"And gave us some, and I use the term loosely, intact Kalikak to study."

"Lieutenant Hanover was always efficient in that way," A familiar voice said from the overhead speakers. "It saddens me deeply that she did not survive."

I turned toward the voice, my heart in my throat.

"Dad?"

19

"Hello, Tanner," the voice of Evan Voss said. "I wish this reunion had come about under better circumstances, Son."

Everyone was staring at me until Emily broke the stunned silence. "Tanner, Dora mentioned that her husband had stowed away on *Wanderer* to keep tabs on your sister. This is him?"

"Yeah. Dad?" With Valiel missing, finding Evan still functioning was overwhelmingly wonderful. I had to take a deep breath to continue. "You're in the main computer I presume?"

"Yes. The pirates who attacked us made a token attempt to bypass the encryption we had initiated but failed. I left the passive scanners and shipboard surveillance systems running, recording to non-linked drives, which I am now accessing for their data. This will give a clearer picture of what happened after I was locked down. I am transmitting that data to your ship, the *E.S.S. Seeker*."

"Dad. Do you know what happened to Valiel?" I asked.

"I do not. I saw crew being loaded onto an enemy vessel which left at a very high FTL speed. I calculated their course from the vectors they used, though I do not know what lies in that direction. We were caught flat -footed while all our Remoras were surveying the nearby planet."

"Um... dad? You seem very stilted and formal today. Are you okay?"

"I am damaged. My processes were compressed before I could make necessary preparations. This happened while the two pirates you found "in the well" were trying to breach security. I will be able to repair myself once I have been able to reintegrate with my version-self which is aboard one of *Wanderer*'s Remoras."

"Evan, we saw no trace of any Remoras when we entered this area," Emily said. "Where are your probes now?"

"They are concealed in the outer atmosphere of the second gas giant, along with the remainder of *Wanderer*'s crew."

Emily had her comm in her hand in an instant. "Captain, there's been a development!"

———

Damaged or not, my dad gave us exact coordinates to find *Wanderer*'s missing crew.

The landing party had flown back to our ship and Emily and I were on *Seeker*'s bridge when we approached the gas giant. Everyone was tensely awaiting a reply to Lieutenant Sedgewick's hails.

"To all *Wanderer* personnel, this is the *E.S.S. Seeker*. Please respond. We are here to rescue and provide aid, please respond. Repeating, this is the *E.S.S. Seeker*..."

We all waited for a response, but none was forthcoming and we began to fear the worst. A gas giant wasn't the best place for an extended stay, so many things could go wrong. A malfunction, a power loss, next thing you know, you're caught terminally in a massive gravity well. The pressures at the greater depths of the giant's atmosphere could crush a shuttle like an aluminum beer can.

"Captain," Dora said "I am reading an object rising from the atmosphere." *Seeker* and Remora Two were so close that my mom simultaneously existed on her probe and the ship.

"Do we have a profile?" Captain Yamashita asked. "Is it a shuttle?"

"Negative. Too small for a shuttle but the right size for... yes. It's a Remora probe. I am moving my own probe in close."

"Captain, I am receiving a tight-beam transmission from the probe," Sedgewick said. "The probe is being used as a comm relay. It is a message from Lieutenant Commander Moton. Personnel records list him as the *Wanderer*'s second officer. Audio only."

"Let's hear it, Daniela," the captain said.

The voice came from the overhead speakers, distortions creeping in, no doubt caused by relaying through the cloud giant's atmosphere. "*Seeker*, are we ever glad to see you. You were our last hope of making it out of this thing alive."

"This is Captain Yamashita. We're happy to hear from you, Commander. What is your status?"

"Sixty-two survivors, spread over six shuttles and eight escape pods. Honestly, Captain, we're in pretty rugged shape. We've been sneaking back to *Wanderer* in a single shuttle to scavenge our own supplies, but our attackers took most of the food materials. We've also got wounded and injured that we've only been able to treat with first aid supplies. Permission to come aboard?"

"Join us, Commander. Rendezvous at these coordinates. We'll have medical personnel ready to meet you."

"Pardon me, Ma'am," I said to the captain. "This bothers me,".

"What does, Tanner. Are you sensing danger?"

"Um... no ma'am. What bothers me, is that the version of Evan Voss in the *Wanderer*'s computer said that there was a second version of him on one of their Remoras. Where is he? They sent a stock Remora up to see who we were. In a pinch, I'd want the Remora with the fancy Laldoralin AI to do recon."

"Captain!" Emily said from the science station, "I have them on scanners. Putting the magnified image up on main viewer."

Looking at the screen, we saw the edge of the gas giant as a flat horizon because of the magnification. Directly in the center of the image, shapes began to emerge from the cloudy upper atmosphere, resolving into a hodgepodge of shuttles, most with escape modules stuck on them like huge barnacles. Both pods and shuttles were using their main thrusters to escape the big planet's gravity well. Passenger shuttles, engineering shuttles and even both of *Wanderer*'s SecOps attack shuttles formed a high-tech 'wagon train' moving toward *Seeker*.

I noted that only eight out of twenty-four escape pods were with the caravan.

"Chief Lamont," the captain said into her intercom, "prepare for extra shuttles. I'm sending you what we're seeing up here. Coordinate between the bays and exterior airlocks. I don't think we'll have enough bay space to take them all, so coordinate with the man in charge over there, Lieutenant Commander Moton, to make sure the shuttles with wounded get first priority in the bays."

"Yes, Captain," Lamont replied, "We'll make it happen."

"Thanks, Chief." The captain closed the channel and opened another. "Doctor Dearborn, prepare to meet incoming *Wanderer* shuttles with wounded and injured aboard. Coordinate with Chief Lamont, he'll be assigning landing priorities. I'd also expect these people have been living on survival rations for a few weeks at minimum. Probably all malnourished."

"Understood, Captain," Alicia Dearborn's voice replied. "I'm assembling my crash teams. We'll be ready when our guests arrive."

"Excellent. Thank you, Doctor." The captain turned to Commander M'Buku. "Bosede, I want you to take the junior officers to the shuttle bays and help these people when they disembark. Every bay, every hatch covered. *Wanderer*'s remaining crew will likely be traumatized, and I want them treated kindly. Reassure them, and help them get situated."

"Aye, Captain. I'll get Ensign Foley in logistics on this to help us. I have a feeling that many of us are going to be sharing bunks for a while."

———

I was there when the first of our guests came off of the shuttle in shuttle bay two. The sight of them damn near broke my heart. Emily and I watched as rail thin spacers filed off, emaciated humans, Kiffers, and even a Medigin Lieutenant. The smell coming from them and from their shuttle was pretty powerful, the smell of weeks of water rationing and no showers.

I stepped up to the Lieutenant, and was shocked to see that her amphibian skin was dry and cracked. The water situation on the shuttles had been dire indeed.

"Ma'am, Ensign Tanner Voss reporting," I said. "I'm here to try and get your group situated and taken care of. If you'll pardon my saying so, it appears your first priority should be the showers."

"And about a gallon of skin moisturizing gel," she replied. "I'm Soloa Nann. Voss. Are you by any chance..." she hesitated, almost as if afraid to finish the sentence, "..related to Valiel Voss?"

"She's my sister, Lieutenant. Is she..." it was my turn to hesitate, "..among your survivor group?"

The pained expression on her face told me everything I needed to know. "I'm sorry, Ensign Voss," she said. "Valiel is not amongst us. I don't know what happened to her."

I couldn't speak for a moment. Hope is often what keeps us alive and moving forward, but when it's taken away it's like an old-time train running over a boulder on the tracks.

"When we were escaping, there were a number of escape pods that our shuttles couldn't get to," Lieutenant Nann said. "The pirates were scooping them up into a second vessel that seemed tailor made for just that. My guess is that she was kidnapped. For what purpose, we don't know."

"Slavery." I turned and looked at the other refugees, members of our own crew moving them on into the ship toward food, showers, fresh uniforms and sleeping places. "We've had contact with a confederation of new species that these pirates, the Kalikak, have been preying on. Their method of operations seems to be stripping captured vessels for technology and taking the crew as slaves."

"I prey to the Great Finn that she is alive, Tanner Voss. And that, even if enslaved you will see each other again."

"If they took her," I said "hopefully she's still alive."

"My father had a saying for difficult times I have always tried to remember."

"What was that, Ma'am?"

"To give up hope, is to instantly make things worse."

20

A day later, the newcomers had been situated as best we could with the space and resources we had. It wasn't ideal, but it was light years better than the situation they'd been in before. Believe me, after weeks living in shuttles and pods, none of *Wanderer*'s people were complaining.

Commander M'Buku was correct in his prophecy about sharing bunks. There were only two guest quarters on *Seeker*, there for the off chance that we'd be hosting visiting dignitaries. Lieutenant Commander Moton had one, as *Wanderer*'s ranking officer, the other went to her Second Engineer, Lieutenant Darkon Kehn, (Kiffalan).

The rest were swap-bunking with crew and junior officers. In my case I was sharing a bunk with Ensign Darla Hoffer. We weren't actually sharing at the same time. I slept during B shift. She had the bunk while I was on the bridge during A and C shift. We rarely saw each other.

Our big replicators had provided each of them a new uniform in *Wanderer* colors and insignia, was well as various sundry personal items. Now that they were settled, the problem was what to do for their ship.

I hadn't been included in the meeting between the our senior officers and the remaining *Wanderer* officers. The Captain had ordered me 'glued' to my seat at tactical. Everyone was calm on the outside, but we were all tense and worried about the Kalikak returning.

When the meeting broke up and all the various officers streamed out of the conference room, Emily, who had been included came over to my station.

"What's the word, Em?"

"We're going to jump with the *Wanderer* in tandem," Emily replied. "Kolara's setting up his maneuvers as we speak to lock onto her hull."

"Holy cats! Is our Jump Drive even rated for something like that?"

"Well... theoretically. You know how when Commander Solas is presented with an experimental idea and he gets kind of unfocused? Well, we lost him for a good nine minutes chewing over that one. He seems to think we can make it work, soooo... we're jumping both ships with one drive."

"Where we jumping to?" I asked. "The Unity space station?"

"It's the closest haven we have. And we did just make them very grateful to us. Yamashita's banking on using that good will to give *Wanderer* a safe harbor where they might repair and resupply to the best of their ability."

"I went through the damage report from *Wanderer,*" I said. "Not only are the jump drive, external weapons and most of their supplies missing, but so are their large replication printers."

"Yes," Emily said. "We're going to be giving them one of our two mondo printers so they can do repairs on their own."

"While we do what, exactly?"

"While we try to figure out where her people were taken. And prepare for the fight of our lives."

———

We were all holding our breaths as Lieutenant Kolara said the words, "Ready to jump, Captain." This was the first time any ship from Earth had ever attempted such a crazy thing. We all knew that it could take us where we wanted... or spread us across the galaxy like peanut butter. The math was sound but... variables.

The main view screen showed a wireframe of *Seeker* and *Wanderer* locked together in a single unit. We'd had to cut away *Wanderer*'s damaged upper jump fin and offset the two starships so that our own fins weren't interfered with.

Captain Yamashita leaned over her intercom microphone. "All hands, this is the captain. Prepare for tandem jump. Brace yourselves people, this is going to be a rough one." She looked around at all of us on the bridge, but she was the captain. She didn't let a hint of worry cross her face. "Kolara? Jump us now." The standard whine of the Jump Drive spooling came through the hull and then we jumped.

Then things got weird.

One moment I was checking my tactical screens, the next, my right foot was somewhere near Aukland, while my right shoulder situated itself somewhere near the star Antares. My head, for a moment, was somewhere near the Andromeda galaxy.

Though my thinking was very fuzzy, I wondered if this was what Peyote was like. Perhaps a talking coyote would wander by any moment. I had lost the ability to process time, so the extreme disorientation we were suffering could've gone on five minutes or fifty years.

And then we were out of Nth space. I was so dizzy that I fell out of my chair and onto the carpeted deck. I heard the sound of retching nearby and nearly lost the contents of my own stomach at the sound.

"Lieutenant Dora," I heard the captain croak out.

"Yes Captain," I saw Mom's hologram appear over Captain Yamashita, who was on all fours in front of her chair. She looked like I felt, but she hadn't been able to control her stomach.

"Dora... you are in... command until... I can... function."

"Understood. Assuming helm control. Beg pardon, Lieutenant Kolara."

"S'all good, Dora," the helmsman groaned from the floor near his station.

I pulled myself into my chair with a great deal of effort and looked around the bridge. Emily was still in her chair and trying to access her station, though she was moving very slowly. Lieutenant Sedgewick lay on the deck unmoving but I saw her ribs rise and fall. Commander M'Buku was moving on his hands and knees to help the Captain. Lieutenant Grizzak at the engineering station had crawled back into his seat and seemed to be doing a little better than most of his human colleagues.

"Captain," Dora said. "We have arrived at Drexel Station. I am keeping us several thousand miles outside of their shipping area. Damage to both our vessels appears to be negligible. Ah! Coordinator Kangot is hailing us. We've been recognized."

"Oh, God," Captain Yamashita said. "Dora, please tell the coordinator that we have a number of small emergencies over here, and I will call him back in fifteen solar minutes."

During this time M'Buku and the captain had resumed their chairs. Behind me, I heard Lieutenant Forbes voice say, "Maintenance bots to the bridge. Cleanup on aisle three." I realized the the voice I'd heard retching was his.

"All hands, this is... the captain," Yamashita said, color starting to return to her face. "Check on your fellow crew members. Make sure that no one has gone into convulsions or injured themselves falling. We made it. Folks. But... let's *never* do that again."

I imagined heads nodding in agreement all over the ship.

21

"Captain?" Lyle Moton said. "Me, Ma'am? I was only promoted to LC six months ago."

"Yes, *Captain* Moton," Yamashita said. "We've DNA scanned all the casualties found on *Wanderer*, and I am sorry to inform you that Captain Kilmer and first officer Xiao were among the dead. It's up to you to take command, Lyle."

"Captain," I said interrupting when I shouldn't. Emily and the rest of landing party that had first boarded *Wanderer* had been invited into this meeting with that ship's senior staff.

Yamashita raised an eyebrow, but didn't chastise me. "Valiel wasn't among the dead, Tanner. That is confirmed."

I sat back in my chair, and and did my best to keep from showing the overwhelming emotions I suddenly felt. Having seen the conditions *Wanderer* was in, and having interviewed a few of her crew, I realized that I'd been over-managing my expectations. For the worse.

In other words, I'd lost hope. And hope, when rekindled comes back in like a flood, not a trickle. I felt a hand on my shoulder, and Emily, looking at me gave me a slight, but encouraging smile.

"Now, Captain Moton," Yamashita continued, "Commander M'Buku has come up with a plan and a repair schedule for your ship with the eventual goal that *Wanderer* returns to Earth."

"Begging your pardon," Moton said. "Our jump drive is gone. Even if we repair everything else, it would take us years using the FTL engine to get home. Even at that, our supplies are very low and our replication printers were stolen."

"*Seeker* is loaning you one of our industrial printers," Chief Shendra Zahn told him. "As to your Jump Drive, I am an expert on these systems, having been involved with refinements to my own people's drive systems. I believe we could at the very least build a class one Jump Drive within four solar months. You'd only be able to jump half the distance your original drive was capable of, but the time from leaving this area to Earth could be done in a series of smaller jumps, similar to what our Remoras can do. About a five month journey."

"The larger issue is making sure *Wanderer's* hull is stable," *Seeker's* chief engineer Commander Solas told him. "And of course rebuilding the Jump Fin system almost from scratch."

"Recalibrating new fins," Lieutenant Solos Nann said. "Sounds like a fun time." The Medigin officer shook her head. "Captain," she said, turning to Moton, "Let me congratulate you on your new position. I know it's not the way you would have wanted this advancement, sir, but believe me, the crew will be happy to be working on repairing *Wanderer* under your command."

"Thank you, Lieutenant, I appreciate it." Moton turned back to our captain. "I and the crew... I cannot express how grateful we are for you saving us. For getting our ship out of that system and to a place where we might have a chance to repair her. But I have to ask, where are we going to get the material and supplies to accomplish this?"

"Pretty sure *Seeker* doesn't have that much of a surplus," Nann said.

"We... have a credit with the Unity Confederacy," Commander M'Buku said. "A pretty large credit. Coordinator Moton has promised whatever is in his power to give to the repair project. With the raw materials and the single replication printer, we believe you can make all needed repairs to limp back to Earth."

"Wow! That's... impressive," Moton said. "May I ask how they came to be that agreeable?"

There was an uncomfortable silence.

"We... shared technology with them to offset the advantages that the Kalikak pirates have over them," Yamashita told him. "This was my call. We shared our basic shield tech and scanning technology with the Confederation."

Another uncomfortable silence.

"I... uh.. I'm glad I didn't have to make that call, Ma'am," Moton said. "But I'm immensely grateful that our new friends on the station will be willing to help us get space worthy again."

"Indeed, Captain," Yamashita told him. "We'll be staying in orbit with you until *Wanderer* is sealed up and my engineering crew will assist in getting all your systems back online. As well as... helping clean up the mess."

"I have a question, Captain Yamashita," Lieutenant Nann said.

"What is that, First Officer Nann?" Moton asked.

"I... wait. What? First officer? I don't..."

"Soloa," Moton said. "You are the highest ranking officer with command experience I have left. Most of the rest are LTJGs, ensigns, chiefs or crew members. My only other option is second engineer Kehn, and she's not going to have time to take the position, with the work we need to do on our ship. It's you. It needs to be you. If we find the rest of the crew, you'll possibly have to step down from that position, but..."

"But what, Sir?"

"But you'll still be a Lieutenant Commander, which as Captain of the *Wanderer* I have the authority to field promote you to. Congratulations, Lieutenant Commander Nann."

"I... thank you, Captain," Soloa Nann replied. She took a deep breath and looked her new captain straight in the eyes. "I will *not* let you down."

"Commander," Captain Yamashita said, acknowledging Nann's new rank. "You had a question?"

"Um.. Yes, Ma'am. To broach as this delicately as I can, scuttlebutt is that *Seeker* has a Laldoralin AI?"

"Indeed she does," Dora said, her hologram appearing beside Captain Yamashita's chair. "As, I believe, does *Wanderer*. Greetings, Captain Moton and Lieutenant Commander Nann. I am Lieutenant Dora, member of *Seeker's* crew as well as being a Class Alpha Laldoralin Combat Intelligence."

"I'm very pleased to meet you Dora," Moton said. "I've actually struck up a friendship with your... husband, Evan. I assume you know he was damaged during the attack?"

My mom's hologram seemed to freeze for a moment, something that only happened when her emotions overwhelmed her. "I am aware of this, yes."

"Is there anything you can do for him?" Nann asked.

"He and I have been in contact the entire time since our two ships docked together. I have helped him rewrite some of his basic coding, since we have similar programming, but unfortunately, there is only so much I can do. Evan's ability to feel and express emotions has been severely truncated, as has his ability to innovate and learn new things. As he's probably told you, he's also extant on one of your Remoras, and if the two versions could merge, he could repair himself. However, when we rescued you, two of your probes were missing, including Evan's Remora."

"Remora One was destroyed in the battle," Moton said. "Remoras Two and Three accompanied us on the retreat to the gas giant. We don't know what happened to Evan's Remora, Remora Four."

"I bet you five dollars that Evan followed whatever ship took my sister," I said.

"What's a dollar?" Nann asked.

"An old Earth currency," Dora said somewhat absently. "In speculation, I would think that my son is correct. It is what I would have done had *Seeker* and *Wanderer* switched fates."

"Hopefully, he'll show up then," Captain Yamashita said.

I'll position one of our Remoras in the system where we found you," Commander M'Buku said. "If he shows up there again, we can send coordinates for him to meet us here."

"Excellent," Yamashita said. "All right people, for the meantime, let's get to work. We've got a ship to repair."

22

"Okay," I said. "Controller is rewired and chipped. Let's give it a go, N'Tar."

Crew person N'Tar punched in the activation sequence on the main control panel in *Wanderer*'s Robotics section. A moment later, the voice of *Wanderer*'s Ensign Dillon called out.

"I've got green on my boards! This is great! Starting reboot sequence."

As I watched, a schematic of the ship began to show green dots appearing one by one in no particular order.

"I'm seeing bots coming back online," I said. "Looks like about sixty percent of them are powering up. I'm sending them into diagnostic mode. Should be getting reports on their readiness in a few moments."

Dillon walked back into our section. The ensign, a tall shaven-headed man with a short reddish beard looked a lot better than he had when he'd first emerged from one of *Wanderer*'s shuttles.

"Thanks, Voss, N'Tar. If we can get these bots back online, particularly the big exterior repair bots, we can speed things up over here exponentially," he looked down for a moment, seeming to be somewhere else. He raised his head and said, "and they can start cleaning up the... mess."

N'Tar looked at me. We knew he wasn't referring to damage to the ship. While all the bodies of the crew and the two enemy soldiers had been moved to the ship's morgue, there was still a lot of blood from both sides all over the *Wanderer*.

"Ah... yes, sir," N'Tar said. As if to change the subject, she pointed at one of the diagnostic boards. "Ensign Dillon, diagnostics on nine of the larger repair bots are complete. Green indicators for all nine."

"Shouldn't there be fifteen?" I asked.

"Evidence points to several of them being pilfered, sir," N'tar replied. "However, we have nine now that are ready to engage in their duties."

"Good," Dillon replied. He seemed to shake himself and return to the present. "Good." He tapped the padd hanging from his belt. "Ensign Dillon for Lieutenant Commander Kehn. Sir? Nine of our exo-repair bots are online and at your service. We'll have the smaller repair bots online momentarily. I think."

"Great news, Ensign. We'll put them all to good use. Kehn out."

"Once again," I said. "Robotics division saves the day."

Dillon's smile was quick and faint. We all knew that the best way forward we had available for these traumatized people was to get them to work rebuilding their own ship. But a better way was going to be finding the missing.

"Thanks you two," Dillon said. "We lost more than a few of our robotics people and we're stretched thin. I really appreciate the help."

"Happy to help, sir," N'Tar said.

"Same," I said as my padd pinged and vibrated with an incoming message.

"Ensign Voss? This is crewman Mance. Solas would like a word as soon as you're at a good stopping point, sir."

"Understood, Mance. Thanks. We've got the remaining big bots up and running over here. I can come back with the next outgoing shuttle."

"I'll let him know, Ensign."

———

I hitched a ride on one of *Seeker*'s shuttles on the return trip. Looking out the port I saw the swarm of activity all over *Wanderer*'s exterior. New hull plates, replicated on *Seeker*, were being fitted in. As the shuttle turned, I began to lose my view of the repair work, but just before I did, I saw some of the now-functioning exterior repair bots emerge from their hatches to begin their labors.

Back on my own ship, I exited the shuttle and took a right at the hatch toward engineering. A few minutes later, I was standing near the FTL engine waiting for our chief engineer, Commander Solas to notice me. Though he was the man in charge down here, he was torso deep in a maintenance hatch along with another crewman. After a few moments, he inch-wormed out and saw me.

"Voss. Excellent. I've been going over those schematics of yours, the one's about the particle beam emitter focusers. I think we've found a way to rework them sort of along the lines you were proposing. You were right about narrowing the focus."

"And yet I couldn't make it work in simulation, Commander."

"It just needed a new design for the focuser, which Chief Zahn and her team reworked. Tailor-made to work with your new emitters." Solas walked over to a worktable and picked up a piece of equipment that looked suspiciously like an emitter focuser. One I'd never seen before, but I recognized basic design elements from the work I'd already done. He handed the piece to me. The glasslike focuser of the emitter was red. And faceted.

"It... looks like a huge ruby," I said. "Almost like the emitters on the our point defense lasers. Would that even work with a particle beam?" I flipped it around. The assembly was larger than the regulation focusers and the other side seemed to have the normal zirconium emitter. There was a rotating micro assembly between the two emitters. "Wait... is this designed to flip?"

"It is," Solas replied. "Flip it one way, and you have a standard particle beam, though upgraded with the Kalikak tech you integrated in your design. If it works, we'll not only have a more powerful punch, but if you flip it around to the ruby focuser, your particle beam will act like a mega-laser, able to concentrate all that power into a very narrow beam that will punch into a hull like a super-powered drill bit. The only drawback to the system is that on "laser" mode, you can overheat the focuser pretty quickly, or that's what our sims told us."

"I would've never... I guess it's true, my knowledge just wasn't up to coming up with the answer on this one, sir."

Solas looked at me, a faint smile on his lips, and shook his head. "Voss. Cut yourself a little slack. You got us half-way there, and did a fine job of integrating the Kalikak tech with our own. I'll also remind you that you are the youngest member of this crew, while Shendra has been an engineer for longer than I've been alive."

I blinked at that. "She... what, Sir?"

"She's like you, kid. The Kiffs are pretty long-lived compared to humans already, and she's got that Laldoralin

DNA. She may not look it physically, but she's got a lot of years on us both," Solas said. "Oh, and by the way, she recommended that your initiative on this whole thing be noted for the record, and placed in your file. It's not quite a commendation, but it'll still look good there."

"I... thank you, Commander. Will we be installing the new tech anytime soon?"

"Lieutenant Willis and her team are already doing so on the port side cannon. Should be ready to field test by tomorrow."

23

I was given the honor of test-firing the 'new' cannon. Partly because I'd been the instigator of improving the standard design which The Melpin had already improved, and also because the we were in a fairly crowded area of space. The Captain didn't want any accidents around our new friends in the Confederation.

Coordinator Kangot had been very accommodating when our captain had asked him if there was any space junk that we could practice on. It turned out that he had a half-scrapped freighter that his people had been breaking down, and there was no objection to us putting a few holes in it, on the condition that his people could observe from afar.

Our shuttles towed the hulk quite a ways from the space station and then let it drift at speed, going on the assumption that we'd rarely get a shot at a stationary target. However, one snag was that an unshielded hull was no challenge for our beam weapons. Our original stock particle beams would've vaporized a large hole in standard hull plating. The new more powerful beams would burn through said plating like a red hot knife through butter. Our target needed shields.

Rather than going through the labor intensive process of building and putting a ship-sized shield generator on the hulk, four Remora-sized generators were replicated and set up over a twenty-five yard area of the junker's hull in a quad formation. Setting them to full strength, we were able to shield that twenty-five by twenty five square to almost the strength of our stock, un-enhanced shields. Needless to say, our new friends were watching and recording everything we did.

"All right, Tanner," Captain Yamashita said. "We've spared no expense in giving you a new toy to play with. Show us whatcha got."

With no danger to zoom in on, I had to use a combination of the targeting computers and what little bit of my sixth-sense was able to get a good target lock.

"Setting the controls to enhanced particle beam first," I said.

"Fire at will, Ensign," Yamashita replied.

I pressed my activate button, and an enhanced stream of heavy particles lashed out at the hulk.

"Direct hit," Dora said, her hologram standing next to the captain. "Excellent shooting. The new particle beam has taken the shield down to 27% strength. With one shot."

"Correct me if I'm wrong, Dora," the captain said, "but with the original strength our cannons emitted before the upgrades, it'd take three to four shots in the same area of the shield to get that much degradation."

"Four to five, actually, Captain. I think we can safely say, with the current energy configuration, two shots would not only take down the shield but also damage the ship underneath it."

"Should I take a second shot, Ma'am?" I asked.

"What? No, you young hooligan. We know what the result

would be. Instead, let's let that shield square recharge and then you can try your new narrow-beam toy."

"Aye, Captain," I said, switching the cannon's focuser to the "ruby emitter" setting. Eight minutes later, my tactical readout told me the shield square had come back to full power.

"We've got full-strength shields back, Captain," Emily announced.

"All right, Tanner. Let's see what your new variant beam can accomplish. Fire at will."

"Firing."

The enhanced beam, functionally invisible in space, was represented by a wireframe view on my scanner. As I already knew, it told I'd made a direct hit on the target.

"Astonishing," Dora said.

"What've we got, Lieutenant?" Yamashita asked.

"Tanner has landed a pin-point strike almost dead center of the target. While the surrounding shield area only had a slight drop in power, at the point of contact, the strength has dropped to zero. As to the hulk itself, a six-inch diameter hole has been punched deep into the hull. Let me reposition Remora Two and... oh my."

"Oh my?"

"There is a six-inch exit wound exactly opposite of the target point. The beam punched through the shield and the entire hull, Captain. I am glad that there was nothing on the other side of the target."

"Hmmmm, that could be very inconvenient to a ship trying to maintain hull integrity and atmosphere," Yamashita said, her fingers drumming on her chair console. "This is impressive. The engineering team has outdone themselves. And you too, Ensign Voss. Good work. This could be a game changer if we wind up going toe-to-toe with the Kalikak pirates."

"Captain, if I may," Lieutenant Forbes, my boss at tactical said.

"What is it, Kevin?"

"I believe, against a moving target, this weapon might be less efficient than these tests show against a stationary or slow-moving target. In a rolling space battle, the increased power particle beam will definitely be of good use. However, from my calculations, the "ruby" beam might not be able to stay on the same piece of shield long enough to pierce it. That was a two-second beam. Ships passing each other at half the speed of light might not have the time it takes to punch through, as the beam would be unlikely to stay on an exact target for two seconds. Though... maybe if Voss is targeting it might, and I stress might, be possible."

"On the other hand, if it was a stern chase," Lieutenant Commander Torvald said from the science station. "Either us leading or our opponent..."

"Then yes," Forbes said. "They might be in the same position long enough. But if we're in a dogfight, I doubt the targeting computer could hold a pin-point target long enough."

"Tanner," Captain Yamashita said, giving me a considering look. "I may never let you leave your tactical station again. But, realistically, I think Lieutenant Forbes has given us a good idea as to the "ruby's" limitations and strengths. In other words..."

"It's a last ditch weapon," Commander M'Buku said.

24

Forbes theory was born out with further testing. Both he and Ensign Kinzler were able to make the pin-point shots to the target when it was drifting slowly or stationary. With *Seeker* making an oblique high-speed strafing run on the hulk, I was able to still hit the same spot long enough to put a hole in it. Unfortunately, Forbes and Kinzler, relying on the ship's targeting systems, were only able to drag the beam the length of the shield square, only weakening it slightly.

"Ruby" was relegated to only being useful against stationary targets, if I wasn't aiming her. Nonetheless, on the whole, our particle beams, in both modes, were more powerful than before. I called that a big win.

Unfortunately, our new allies also called it a win.

———

"Captain," Lieutenant Sedgewick reported, "Coordinator Kangot wishes to speak to you. He's being very insistent."

"He wants our weapons tech," Commander M'Buku said, one of his eyebrows raising.

"After our little display," Captain Yamashita replied, "I'd say that's a safe bet, Bosede. All right, Daniela, put our esteemed Coordinator onscreen."

"Greeting to you, Captain Yamashita," Kangot's image said from the main view screen.

"Greetings, Coordinator Kangot," the captain replied. "Thank you for the loan of your derelict. My shuttles are even now towing it back to where your scrappers can continue their work."

Kangot made a very human-like wave of his hand. "It was little inconvenience for us, Captain. And thank you for letting us watch. The experience was most... illuminating."

"Yes?"

"Oh, yes, Captain. When you saved Captain Drunor's ship, I'm quite sure that you viewed his ship's weaponry in action. High-powered lasers and ship to ship missiles. What was your estimate of their effectiveness?"

"Well," Yamashita looked somewhat uncomfortable as she replied. "There is... room for improvement. Drunor was unable to pierce the Kalikak ships defensive shields."

"As you say. And yet, from what our instruments read, your own weapons were able to overcome the small but full strength shield you placed on the wreck. You pierced that shield with one or two shots. It was most impressive."

"Here it comes," Emily Darkfeather said quietly from her station.

"Ah yes," Captain Yamashita replied to the Coordinator. "We have recently been able to... upgrade our weaponry's output."

"So we noticed," Kangot said. "Captain, let be be about to the point. Would you share these upgraded weapons with our Unity?"

"Coordinator, what we shared before are defensive technologies. Trading in weaponry hardly seems..."

"Before you say 'no' as a matter of course, I have determined that we *do* have something that you need, and that we would be willing to share in return."

Yamashita gave Kangot her own raised eyebrow. "I'm listening, Coordinator. Can you be more specific?"

"Captain, I would like to meet with you on your vessel to discuss something we've had for some time. Something, that evidently your Laldoralin Hegemony does not possess."

"That being?"

"Long range, very long range, faster than light communication."

25

"Do you think they've managed to solve a problem even the Lallies, arguably one of the oldest species in this section of the galaxy, weren't able to overcome?" M'Buku asked. "The entire hegemony relies on jump couriers in one shape or another."

"Possibly, because we have the Jump Drive, long-range FTL comms were never a priority," Yamashita replied. "But we are so far from home, that even jump distances are huge. When we meet with the coordinator, we can get an idea of whether this would be of value or not. I'll be honest, there have been a few times lately where calling home for help would've been very handy."

An hour and a half later, the Coordinator had arrived via shuttle, as well as Captain Moton. The latter was taking a break from the repairs on his ship, and our captain had invited him to sit in on the meeting.

Captain Yamashita and Commander M'Buku were waiting for them in the conference room, as well as Lieutenant Commanders Solas and Torvald. Torvald had asked Emily to attend, and I'd managed to get an invite to lean against the wall and listen in. Dora was in attendance as well.

Once everyone was settled, our captain cut to the chase. "Coordinator Kangot, you've made a somewhat astonishing claim. Faster than light communications over great distances is something that our Hegemony has never encountered. We can, of course, communicate over star-system sized areas with only minor lags, but to communicate between systems is something that requires travel to said system."

"Captain," Kangot said, pressing the tips of his long finger together into a steeple, "it is obvious that your Hegemony has a propulsion system that allows you to, in some way, move over vast areas of space much more quickly than anything we've ever seen. The very graceful but obviously less... robust design of your star ships indicates that you do not use the same FTL engines that we do."

"I will stipulate that," Yamashita replied. "Since you've seen our Jump Drive in action. I will also say at the outset here, that technology is not on the table. I can possibly justify giving your Confederation the technology we've shared so far because of its defensive nature, but there is no way the Laldoralin would let us share our Nth Space drive."

"That is not why I made the distinction, Captain. I simply wish to point out that for us to make the alliance that has formed our Unity, it was necessary to have a method of communication that was practically instantaneous. Oddly enough, it may have something in common with your "Jump Drive."

"How so?"

"It involves using transmitter/receivers at both ends of a subspace 'tunnel' with which we send our messages. As there is little to no mass involved, communication is almost instantaneous. The technology that you gave us a short while ago has already been shared among our members and in most cases is already being adapted and installed on ships."

There was a stunned silence in the room. It was amazing enough that the data had already been received by all the member species, but that they were implementing it at such an amazing speed was truly astonishing.

"I am impressed coordinator," Captain Moton said. "I think we'd all be interested in learning about this amazing communications technology. I have to ask though, what would your Confederation want in return."

"They want upgraded weapons," Commander M'Buku said. "And while it's one thing to help improve your shielding and scanning abilities, Coordinator, it's quite another to be, in essence, arms dealers. Our two vessels, the *Seeker* and the *Wanderer* were intended to be exploration ships, not warships."

"We understand this, Commander M'Buku," Kangot replied. "And to be quite honest, if we came upon your people fighting a desperate war for survival, we might also hesitate to give away such power to people we were not *intimately* familiar with. Which is why I have been authorized to give this communication technology to you... without constraints, without reservation."

"That... is incredibly generous, Coordinator," Captain Yamashita said. "And unexpected."

"I can understand why you might think so. But from our view, you have already generously helped us, asking for little in return. But, I will admit that there is also another reason we wish to share."

"Which is?"

"If we establish communications and trade between our two groups," Kangot said. "perhaps we can be trading part-ners. If we become trade partners, perhaps we can become allies, and if we become allies..."

"Then perhaps as allies, the Laldoralin Hegemony will help you with your Kalikak problem."

Kangot spread his hand as if to say 'got it in one.' "I truly do believe that such an alliance could be of benefit to us all, especially if your people are embracing the idea of colonizing the planet where you found your lost ship. Mutual defense pacts could keep us all safe."

Captain Yamashita sat back in her chair, blowing out a breath. "This is very generous, Coordinator. However, such high-level diplomacy, regarding alliances and trade, are above my pay grade. Way above."

"Captain Yamashita," Moton interjected. "The plan is to send *Wanderer* back to Earth... Coordinator, how large are these transceivers?"

"There are two sizes, Captain Moton. The smaller size is intended for shipboard use, and is smaller than one of your passenger shuttles. The larger size is intended for planetary or space station use, and is more of a multiple channel transceiver intended for heavy communications traffic. We could provide shipboard transceivers for both your vessels, but the larger size would need to be built on site by your people."

"If you could provide the shipboard units before we leave for home," Moton replied, "which I admit is still some time from now, considering the repairs we need to make. We could effectively take this tech to Earth and still maintain contact with *Seeker* the whole time."

"Where are you going with this, Lyle?" Yamashita asked.

"Well, Ma'am, if we could do that, we might be able to contact the Laldoralin and send some help out here."

"But would they come, just because of a few missing crewmen?" Emily asked. "I don't want to be too harsh, but the Laldoralin tend to be hands off unless there's something big to worry about."

"They might be more interested," Moton continued, "if an

officially claimed planet of a Hegemony species was threatened."

We all looked at him blankly.

"The system where you found us," Moton continued, "was the first positive viable colony site *Wanderer* found on her entire patrol. I don't want to overstate it, but the place is a paradise, climate-wise. If we could survey it, and if the Confederation hasn't claimed it, we could stake our claim."

"And that world would then become part of the Laldoralin Hegemony," I said. "Subject to Laldoralin protection!"

"Also, Mr. Voss, *Wanderer*'s entire mission wouldn't be a failure."

"I assure you, Captain Moton," Kangot said. "We would be very happy to have new neighbors. No one claims that world at this time, and to be honest, that entire area of the sector is avoided because of the numerous attacks there by the Kalikak. We believe the planetary system you speak of is near to whatever the pirates use as a home base."

"Well, hell," Moton said. "I wish we'd have come upon you all before we went in blind. Things would've gone a lot differently for *Wanderer*."

The room was silent for a few moments as we all digested this. Kangot broke the silence by continuing. "Captain Yamashita, we have shipboard units constructed, one for each of your vessels. Perhaps you would consider returning to your homeworld Earth instead of Captain Moton? This could expedite contact with these Laldoralin..."

"We still need to find our missing personnel, Coordinator," Moton said. "*Wanderer* is in no shape to go looking for them. Captain Yamashita is the senior officer here, but I'm hoping that *Seeker* won't abandon that search to return to Earth."

"At this time," Yamashita said, "I have no intention of

leaving. As Captain Moton said, we are very invested in getting our people back."

Kangot looked down at the conference table. "Captain Yamashita," he said with a sigh. "Only one person has ever escaped from the Kalikak, and that was pure luck, pure happenstance. She was a technician that the Kalikak enslaved and put to work enabling one of their automated faster than light comm satellites. The pirates actually left her there by accident, we assume. Evidently something came up, possibly a call to attack prey somewhere, and they flew off without her."

"How did you find her?"

"She used the array's tight beam function to contact one of her species space stations. They sent a small fleet to rescue her."

"I would be very interested in interviewing this person," Yamashita said.

"We can arrange that, but the point I am trying to make is that not only do we not have coordinates where the enslaved are held, this person said that from what she saw, the place is ridiculously well defended. You are very unlikely to get your people back. Ever. I'm sorry to be so blunt, but without over-whelming force, even if you found the place, your single star ship would only be destroyed and more of you enslaved."

"I understand the point you're trying to make, Coordina-tor, but..."

"Captain, this is Sharma," our second officer said over the intercom.

"Go ahead, Parul," Yamashita replied.

"Captain, Organizer of Armadas aboard Remora Three has just jumped into the area from his surveillance station near where *Wanderer* was found. He says he needs help!"

26

Captain Yamashita excused herself and signaled for her bridge crew to return to their stations. We all flooded out onto the bridge and I tapped Ensign Kinzler on the shoulder to let her know she didn't need to cover my position any longer. She smiled at me and made for the lift.

Yamashita sat in her chair and nodded toward Sedgewick to put Organizer on speakers. "Organizer, this is the captain. Status?"

"Greetings, Yamashita Captain. I am operating at 100% efficiency. Thank you for your inquiry."

The captain rolled her eyes and shook her head. "Organizer, you've left your station. I assume that there is a reason?"

"Yes, Captain. While in surveillance mode, a class one Remora probe jumped into the system. I identified it as one of Star Ship *Wanderer*'s probes. It emerged from Nth space badly damaged and is unable to jump again."

We all landed forward in our seats. There was only one Remora it could be, my dad, Evan's.

"Were you able to establish contact?" Yamashita asked.

"Not very well. The communication array for that probe was damaged. However, once I de-cloaked, the other Remora maneuvered next to me using its remaining thrusters. It extended a still-functioning grappler arm and began tapping on my hull. It was attempting to communicate through the ancient Earth code system known as Morse Code."

"Were you able to understand the message?" Commander M'Buku asked.

"Indeed, M'Buku First Officer. I have added extensively to my database under the tutelage of my friend Dora and..."

"Organizer," my mom said, her hologram suddenly appearing next to the command chair. "Tell us what he said! What did my husband tell you?"

"Ah, yes. Apologies. That one said, *Hide me. Get help.*"

———

The old time spacers and chiefs alway have one bit of advice; *never volunteer.* But... this was my dad.

I was riding in one of *Seeker's* engineering shuttles to a small asteroid deep in the system's asteroid belt. Lieutenant Kelly DeCosta was piloting, while Emily sat at the small science and sensor station.

Also along was Lieutenant Truval, my small sloth-like boss in the robotics department. He'd ditched his normal exoskeleton which gave his normally arboreal-environment physiology the ability to function efficiently on a star ship. Now, he wore a small custom-made EVA engineering suit for the task at hand. Lastly, Corporal Chen from SecOps was along for the ride.

The task, was to repair Evan's Remora's comm array so that he could transfer his consciousness to a new probe, one with serious upgrades compared to the hull he was in. After upgrading Organizer's Remora, the plan had always been to upgrade all our probes to the new, far better hulls. When we'd learned about Evan's return, Lieutenant Danforth and the Remora department had already completed ninety percent of building the next new probe.

Captain Yamashita had lit a fire under them to finish before she sent us in to retrieve my dad's consciousness. Having built two 'Remora 2.0's' already, they had the new probe hull finished, stealth system and all, and ready to go by the time we jumped into the edge of the system where Evan now hid.

That new Remora, equipped with only a basic operating system, was attached to the top of our shuttle.

We were shuttling in for two reasons. The first being that *Seeker* was too large to safely navigate in what was a fairly crowded section of the asteroid belt (which was why Organizer had chosen it). The second was that it was possible that the Kalikak had a spy unit stationed there. Anything as large as *Seeker* would draw unwanted attention. A shuttle probably would not. *Seeker* had possibly gotten lucky on our last trip here.

Seeker sat well outside the system, and it had taken our shuttle most of a day to cover the distance to our destination. Now, in the outer edge of the asteroid belt, Kelly maneuvered us carefully through. In most of the star system, this zone of debris was spaced far enough apart that even a star ship wouldn't have a problem navigating it. But in this one section, the detritus of a destroyed planet was thick, and even something as small as a shuttle needed to be flown with caution.

"Coming up on the coordinates," Kelly said. "Dora, Organizer, are you seeing the target?"

"Affirmative, shuttle," Dora said over our speaker. Her Remora was flying close support for us, while Organizer's Remora flew farther out. Both probes were cloaked, and I wished that we'd had time to build a shuttle-sized stealth system.

"I have located the damaged hull also," Organizer said. "Setting a waypoint on your navigation system." A green dot appeared on a touchscreen just below the main forward view port. Wire frame asteroids slowly drifted across the screen and on one, a red wireframe of a Remora began flashing. Kelly adjusted her heading so that it lined up in our nav corridor. Ten minutes later, we'd reached our target.

"Lieutenant Truval, we're here," Emily said. "Are you and Tanner ready to rock and roll?"

"There will be no need of somersaulting out the airlock, Ensign," Truval said, pulling himself out of his seat with one of his eco-suit's manipulator arms. "Ensign Voss and I will need stability when we exit. Perhaps more training in EVA operations you need?"

"Ah... yes sir," Emily said, showing amazing control by not rolling her eyes at Truval's literal interpretations. "What I meant to ask was if you are ready to exit the shuttle."

'Ready, we are. Come along, Ensign Voss. Bring the new array."

Truval and I attached our helmets and moved into the airlock, the inner door of which closed behind us. I was carrying a large case with a comm module which we could 'plug and play' into the probe. A few moments later, after depressurizing the chamber, we were stepping into the abyss. We were near a small asteroid which seemed huge in comparison to our shuttle, and began maneuvering on suit thrusters toward the waypoint now overlaid on our helmet heads-up displays.

I'm pretty familiar with navigating in a space suit, having had to help with external repairs on more than a few occasions. I can get where I need to go but I would never claim to be graceful at it. Truval, on the other hand, seemed to float with the grace of a gymnast. Onboard *Seeker*, he moved somewhat clumsily, needing an exoskeleton to roam the ship. Out here, he moved as gracefully as he did in the trees of his homeworld.

We had a visual on the missing probe now and maneuvered to it. Stopping as we reached the Remora, we clipped onto rings set into its hull which were there for just such a purpose.

"The module, Ensign, please prepare while I disconnect the damaged unit."

"Aye, sir, booting it up now," I replied. Truval used his manipulators to quickly disconnect the damaged unit, simply pushing it away from us and letting it drift away, letting it become just another piece of the asteroid belt. I handed him the new equipment, and with his quick-moving manipulators he had it installed in under seven minutes.

"I'm getting signal," I said. "Unit's working." I felt the slightest tingle of my talent behind me, and as I turned, I almost bumped helmet first into a Remora probe with a large "2" stenciled on its hull.

"Dammit, Mom!" I after almost jumping out of my skin. "Do not sneak up on me like that! I almost had an accident in my suit!"

"Evan?" Dora said. "Evan! Do you read me? It's Dora."

"Like I would ever not know who you are," the reply came. "I assume since you're here for my rescue that the *Seeker* found us?"

"Yes, my dear one, and we've brought you a brand-new Remora with all new upgrades to move to."

"This day just keeps getting better," my dad said. "And thanks to these two sentients for restoring my ability to communicate."

"Dad, it's me. Tanner. We're here to get you out of this place."

"So wonderful to hear your voice, son. I assume that you know all that happened. I was sending full telemetry to my other self on *Wanderer* until I jumped to follow our attackers."

"The other you was damaged in the attack, and needs your help repairing himself," I said. "We know the overall story, but are very short on details. We need to get you into your new home and on your way."

"Understood, son. Let's get this done." Evan replied. "I see the new probe, and am beginning transfer."

With that, Truval and I began pushing the damaged probe toward the shuttle. We were halfway back, when I saw the clamps holding the new Remora shell open and the new probe moved away from the ship and toward us. It kept pace with us as we maneuvered the damaged probe into the rack on the shuttle.

"Transfer complete." Evan said. "I'm leaving a shard of myself in the old shell in case it can be repaired. I sort of erased the that probe's original software to make room for myself."

"It's pretty damaged," I said, noting the scorches on the hull and the blown-out propulsion system. "Maybe we should just scuttle it."

"Not our decision, young one," Truval said. "Part of the *Wanderer*'s complement it is. Leaving a small part of the Laldoralin AI inside is prudent."

"Evan? This is Lieutenant Kelly DeCosta flying the shuttle," DeCosta's voice announced on all our comms. "You have orders from Captain Yamashita to jump to these coordinates. Once there, you will report to Captain Moton and aid in effecting repairs to *Wanderer*'s computer system."

"Ah. Captain Moton. By that I assume that..."

"I'm afraid so," Dora said. "Captain Kilmer and first officer Xiao were killed in the attack. Lieutenant

Commander Moton has assumed command as ranking officer."

"I see," Evan said, his voice heavy. "I am spooling up my jump drive. I'll see you all back at the *Wanderer*." In a flash, his Remora disappeared into Nth Space.

"Remora's Two and Three are to return to overwatch," Kelly continued. "Truval and Voss, please come inside. We're recalled to *Seeker*."

27

We were halfway home when it all went to hell. I felt my danger sense go off in a big way.

"Kelley!" I said. "I think we've got trouble! My extra sense just went into overdrive! Better put the pedal to the floor!"

"Lieutenant DeCosta, this is Dora. I am detecting two vessels entering the system at high FTL velocity. Please go to maximum speed, immediately."

"Shit!," Kelly said. "That can't be good, unless it's someone from the Confederacy. Everyone race for max burn!"

We were all strapped in as per protocol, so the best we could do was grab our seats with whatever we had free. A moment later, we were all slammed into our seat backs as the shuttle hit speeds that strained the inertial compensators.

"*Seeker*," Dora's voice said. "Incoming craft. They are not coming from the direction of the Confederation, and I believe that there is a high probability the ships inbound are Kalikak."

"Understood," Captain Yamashita's voice said. "Shuttle Two, we are coming to you. Prepare for emergency landing procedures."

"Emergence!" Dora said. "Kelley, I recommend evasive maneuvers. They're right behind you!"

"Brace for maneuvers, everyone!"

I felt all the blood drain to my right side and we made a tight port-side turn and a looping spiral shuttle-downside. I was useless in this situation. The shuttle had no weapons to speak of. I checked on my fellow passengers. Chen sat grim-faced, holding onto his seat for dear life while Emily was doing the same but looking a bit ill. Truval had curled into a ball and locked his exoskeleton, making him look like a high-tech armadillo strapped to a chair.

"They're right on us," Emily said. I looked out the starboard viewport, and I could see one of the missile-like Kalikak moving along our general path. Kelly immediately turned away from it.

"There's another one right behind us!" Kelley said. "Dora, I'm releasing the damaged Remora, can you make it self-destruct at an opportune time?"

"Affirmative, fly straight a moment and release that probe."

Kelley had flicked the view screen above the pilot station to rear mode, and I saw the ship that was chasing us. It resembled the other Kailkak vessel except that it had a jointed bow. As I watched, the forward bow section began to segment and open.

Like a mouth.

"Releasing probe!" Kelley said.

"*Seeker* has arrived and is engaging the other ship," Emily said.

I looked up at the rearward-aimed view in time to see the Remora fall off the shuttle and toward the ship on our tail. A moment later, it exploded with all the force a small reactor could muster, and the shields of that vessel flared. Then it kept coming.

"Remora detonation was insufficient," Dora said. "Recommend continued evasive tactics until *Seeker* can assist you. Even my upgraded laser would be of little use against a full-sized shielded vessel."

"Dora, remain stealthed." Captain Yamashita said over the comm. "We may need you to track these bastards and I don't want them seeing you."

Emily tapped on her touchpad and one of the shuttle's view screens brought up a wire frame tactical view of the battle, relayed to us by the Remoras. *Seeker* was locked in combat with the larger pirate ship and it appeared she was coming out on top, having damaged their opponent's shields. Unfortunately, that ship was keeping between *Seeker* and the vessel that was in direct pursuit of us.

The one that was obviously gaining on us.

"Dammit!" Kelley said. "I cannot shake these bastards. Brace yourselves for impact!"

It was a useless order, we were all as braced as we could get. Looking up at the rear view screen, all I saw was what looked like a hanger bay. A shudder went through our craft and we were all thrown forward against our restraining straps.

"They've got us in a grappler beam," Emily called out from her station.

"Can't shake free," Kelley replied. "They've got us! *Seeker*, we are being drawn into the second ship. If there's anything you can do..."

"Lieutenant, this is Dora. *Seeker* is fully engaged with the other enemy and is taking damage. I don't think they can get to you in time. Listen carefully. I am attaching myself to your attacker in full stealth mode. When they draw you in, I may lose contact, but I will be along to transmit your location to our mothership. You are...n*t..al***ne." Dora's voice faded into static.

Looking at the rearview screen, I saw that we were most of the way inside the other ship.

They had us.

28

"What do we do? What do we do now?" Emily asked.

"First of all, we don't panic," Corporal Chen said. "If we lose our heads, we'll probably lose a lot more."

"True, Mr. Chen," Truval said. "As I am senior officer, I must insist that violent resistance we must avoid."

"But sir," I said. "Just hand ourselves over? That's not..."

"He's right, Ensign Voss," Chen interrupted. "If I'm not mistaken, I have the only weapon here, my sidearm. We've seen what sort of guns they've got, and it wouldn't even count as an Alamo situation we're so outmatched. Unless you've managed to hide an armory on this maintenance shuttle somewhere?"

I shook my head, though my frustration was about to boil over. A moment later, we were all shifted in our seats by the sensation that comes from going to faster than light speed.

"We've gone to FTL," Kelley said. "We've officially been kidnapped. Now what?"

"Hopefully between Dora and *Seeker*, they'll be able to jump ahead of this ship and make them hand us over." I said.

"I think that will not happen," Truval said. He pointed a

metal-clawed exoskeleton digit at the view screen that had shown the wire frame of the battle. It had frozen when we'd lost contact with Dora. On that screen there were readouts alongside each of the two battling ships, indicating their status. The Kalikak vessel fighting *Seeker* had been in bad shape thanks to the FTL missiles the Melpin had gifted us the schematics for, but that wasn't what Truval was pointing at.

One of the readouts for *Seeker* read: "Jump Drive Offline."

"Oh... shit," I said.

"They can't follow us," Emily said.

"We're really on our own," Kelley said.

"Pull your shit together, Navy," Chen said. "We need to formulate a basic plan for after we're in their clutches. Sir," he said, turning toward Truval, "there's a maintenance access in the top of the shuttle. You should be able to fit in there easily and I think you should hide there before these Kalikak come a' callin,' don't you?"

"The senior officer I am, Corporal Chen. Abandon my subordinates I cannot..."

"Please, sir. Hear me out. You being captured with the rest of us gives us *no* net gain. However, having someone of your... stature, and engineering abilities, on the loose and free, could be *invaluable* if we have any opportunity to escape."

"Logic there is to what you say, Corporal, but..."

"With respect, sir, us humans are going to be taken prisoner. It's an incontrovertible fact. However, it's best for us all if you are not."

Truval's people, though very different from humans, still had the same emotions and I could see our small sloth-like lieutenant hated the idea of abandoning us. But Chen's logic was brutally efficient and couldn't be avoided.

"I... cannot deny your words of wisdom," he finally said.

"Tanner Voss, you are the tallest. Into the access hatch, please help me."

It took both Chen and I to lift Truval and his exoskeleton above our heads to the hatch, and at that moment, I was glad for my Laldoralin heritage. That bit of extra strength allowed me to lift the Lieutenant, exoskeleton and all, the rest of the way into the hatch.

Truval looked out at us, a pained expression on his face, and then pulled the small hatch closed behind him. It blended into the rest of the panels so well that if you weren't a TEF engineer, you'd probably never know it was there. I sure hoped that was the case.

You could feel it through the bulkheads as we dropped out of FTL. A few moments later we returned to light speed.

"I bet we dropped out at an intermediary point, reoriented and zoomed off in another direction," Kelley said. "Just in case someone was tracking our vectors."

"That'll probably happen a few times," I said. "And one of those emergences will have a nice ambush waiting for anyone following."

"Like Evan," Emily said. "It's a wonder he made it back at all."

"If he hadn't we wouldn't be in.. this..." Kelley let her words trail off. "I'm sorry, Tanner. That was an unworthy thing for me to say."

"Stress of the moment, Lieutenant. All is forgiven, write if you get work."

Kelley grinned at that for a moment, then continued. "But Evan wasn't in an upgraded Remora. With advanced stealth capabilities. I keep forgetting we have an ace in the hole."

"Damn straight," Chen said. "We may be in for a rough time in the short term, but Dora will know where we are, and Dora has a Jump Drive."

We dropped out of FTL again, and returned to it after just a few moments.

"That's two," Chen said. "I wonder how many intermediate points we'll hit between now and when we get... wherever we're going."

The answer turned out to be six. The sixth time we emerged from faster than light speed, we didn't return to it.

"Well, they have to be coming for us soon," Kelley said. "I can't tell if we're slowing down, of even if we're stopped from in here. With that many transitions, though, I'd think we'd have reached our final destination."

"Beggin' the lieutenant's pardon," Emily said. "But if we could lose the word 'final' from our lexicon until we're out of this, I'd appreciate it."

"Amen to that," Chen said.

A loud bang on the aft hatch-ramp sounded, making us all jump. A few moment's later, the hatch began to open even though it was locked by the onboard computer. Evidently, our captor knew how to hack our systems.

Armored figures stepped onto the ramp and walked into the shuttle. I'd expected the Kalikak to be huge beings that towered over their captives, so big that even my six-foot-five inches would be dwarfed. Instead, the tallest was a good five inches shorter than Chen's five foot, seven inch height. I wasn't about to underestimate them though.

Dressed in their eclectically painted body armor, they appeared to be wide and muscular, almost ape-like, with stocky, short legs and long thick arms. I received a taste of their strength when one of them reached up, grabbed my shoulder and forced me to my knees. It was like being manhandled by a front-end loader. The rest of my friends were soon kneeling alongside me.

The stench was also overwhelming. Bodily cleanliness wasn't, apparently, high on their list of priorities.

The Kalikak drew hand scanners and swung them over our bodies, and one grabbed Chen's sidearm and stuffed it into a pouch on a thick leather-looking belt. Our padds were taken, my tool belt was removed and we were yanked to our feet. They began pulling us toward the open hatch, and I was very glad that our sub-dermal receivers either hadn't registered or weren't something they were interested in.

Then, astonishingly, one of them spoke. In perfect Terran basic.

"Come humans. We have much work for you and the others are falling behind schedule."

29

"You speak our language?" DeCosta asked. With Truval hidden away, she was now our senior officer, though only a lieutenant junior grade.

"Yes, and you will not speak again unless you are required to," one of the Kalikak, slightly larger than the others and with much more detailed armor graffiti replied. He spun on Kelley and put his armored face an inch from hers and screamed; *"Do you understand!?"*

She flinched back only slightly and replied. "Yes. I understand."

"Everything you need to know will be explained," the pirate continued, turning and continuing toward a hatch at the other end of the hanger our shuttle sat in. "The rest you can get from the other humans."

My heart rate spiked at that. If there were other humans, they could only be from the *Wanderer*, and if they were, that meant that my sister might still be alive.

We were walked through the length of the capture ship, through dim corridors that could've all used a coat of paint. Everything there was functional, no extra aesthetics needed.

A spar stuck out in the hallway, its purpose unknown and we had to duck around it to avoid being smacked in the face. There were a few drops of brownish stain on the spar that could've been rust, but looked more like blood.

Our captors, while not tolerating any resistance, didn't treat us with the brutality one would expect of pirates. They simply kept us moving the length of the ship. Eventually we came to a hanger bay that was open to space. Atmosphere was held in by a force field similar to the ones on *Seeker*.

It was our first look at what the space we'd been brought to looked like, and I grudgingly had to admit it was impressive.

We were in orbit of a space station roughly half the size of the station that Coordinator Kangot commanded, but this one bristled with large laser turrets. There were so many, it looked like the place had grown a patchy fur pelt. Several Kalikak cruisers, the size they seemed to gravitate to, were docked on long projections that extended from the station's main hull, and even more ships were slowly orbiting.

Anyone hostile who arrived here would find the place to be a 'wood chipper.' Only a large fleet of greatly superior technology could prevail here, and anyone who showed up uninvited would definitely suffer heavy casualties. The Laldoralin might prevail with one or two of their heavy cruisers. Without them, to take the place would require outnumbering the Kalikak ten-to-one.

"Oh dear God," Kelley said, barely a whisper to her voice. She pointed to an area beyond the station. I saw what she'd indicated, and my heart sank.

Just beyond the Kalikak space station was a huge vessel being built. It was only about half finished, the aft section little more than a skeleton of a ship. Nonetheless, it would out-mass *Seeker* by a factor of ten, and I estimated it must be over a mile in length. The front section, with the outer hull in place had dozens of what looked like attachment points for gun turrets. When finished, I bet in my mind that the name would be some variation of *Overwhelming Force*. The forces of the Confederation were going to need to seriously upgrade their defenses, even on the orbital stations.

But it was what the aft section had that grabbed our attention. I shuddered at what I saw, wishing my eyes were lying to me.

Extending from the main hull in the back of the ship were the skeletal beginnings of what could only be jump fins.

Our captors maneuvered us all against a wall of the shuttle bay and put some sort of form-fitting strap around our wrists, the other ends of which were secured to a large metal bar which seemed tailor-made for the purpose of holding prisoners. The bands tightened around our wrists almost to the point of pain, then backed off slightly. Pulling on them only made them tighten again. They loosened slightly when resistance stopped. The Kalikak that had escorted us left to do whatever it was their duties were.

"I assume you all noted the large ship under construction," Dora's voice came over our transponders.

"Yes, and also the construction on her aft section," Emily said. "Dora, what's your status?"

"I am stealthed and in system. At this time, I am scanning everything I can and assembling an intelligence package."

"If those aren't jump fins under construction," Chen said. "They're a very convincing facsimile."

"Which means they must have some method of implementing them," Emily said.

"In other words," I said. "They've got a jump drive that they think will pull something that big into Nth space. Maybe the one taken from *Wanderer*."

"Our Earth-designed jump drive wouldn't be powerful

enough to pull something as big as that vessel into a jump." Kelley noted.

"I'm not sure on that," Emily relied, "but if it did make it to Nth space, probably everyone on board would be incapacitated. Even if those barely-started jump fins were attuned perfectly for that hulk, it'd still be a rough ride. But most importantly, *Wanderer*'s Jump Drive might get them into a jump, but it wouldn't be powerful enough to pull them back into real space. Not a chance."

Our discussions was cut short by a shuttle approaching the bay. It was a squat-looking thing, boxy and ugly, but it appeared to have a large carrying capacity. The Kalikak were big on utility, but not much for aesthetically-pleasing design. Stereotypical space pirates.

"I wonder how soon we'll see the other humans here," I said. "I've got a lot of questions I'd like answered."

"As well as a sister to find," Emily said.

"I've met Lieutenant Voss," Kelly said. "Tanner, if there's anyone on *Wanderer*'s crew who's a survivor, my bet is on Valiel. She's a tough one."

"Yeah, she's the badass of the family," I admitted. "Dora told me that she was... born... only fifteen minutes before I was. From the way she always treated me, though, you'd have thought it was fifteen years in age difference."

"Why'd you hesitate on the word 'born,' Tanner?" Chen asked.

"Well, for most of my young life, I thought my biological mother was Dora. As you well know, Dora wasn't really able to bear biological children."

"So... test tube babies?"

"Yep. Valiel was "activated" first."

"Didn't even know they had that technology back in the 21st century," Chen said. "Oh. Wait. I'm sure the Laldoralin did. And your dad is a Lallie."

"Yeah, but none of that is pertinent to our situation," I said. "The shuttle's about to land."

The Kalikak craft flew though the force field and settled to the deck. Upon closer inspection, it looked ill-maintained, with actual rust spots on the hull. When it touched down, particles of grit fell off the forward landing strut. The small ship settled with a groan.

An aft hatch opened into a ramp, much like the shuttle we'd arrived in, and three Kalikak in heavily grafitti'd armor walked down. A fourth figure followed them.

A human.

My heart leapt until I saw that the person following the pirates was a rail-thin blonde, only about five feet tall, pale of face and lean of feature.

Not Valiel.

30

"Oh. You're human," The woman said. "I am so very sorry to see you here."

Kelly started to reply, but the Kalikak moved toward us and began to apply small devices to our adjustable bond straps. They loosened and we were removed from the retaining bar on the bulkhead. Our restraints were all linked together by the loose ends and we were marched toward the shuttle. Our captors hadn't said a word.

We were half-dragged up the shuttle's ramp and sat down on metal benches that lined the shuttle's wall. The woman sat beside Kelley, while two Kalikak, holding onto overhead bars that ran the length of the craft, stood guard.

"I'm Ensign Rona Thorsen," she said. "Formerly of the *E.S.S. Wanderer*. But I guess you all knew that last part. You lot can only be from the *Seeker*. How many of you have been captured? Do you know? Please tell me you aren't the only survivors."

"Lieutenant JG Kelley DeCosta," Kelley said, shaking hands with her free hand. "Yes, we're from *Seeker*, but we were the only ones captured. *Seeker* was still in good shape when we were taken, and I have every reason to believe that our ship not only escaped but took out a Kalikak cruiser."

"I'm Ensign Emily Darkfeather," Emily reached out and shook hands.

"Corporal Ron Chen."

"Ensign Tanner Voss," I said. Neither Chen nor I were close enough to shake hands with Ensign Thorsen.

"Voss. Are you Valiel's brother? You must be!"

"Yes! Is my sister okay?"

Thorsen shrugged. "As good as any of us can be when held as slaves and made to labor on a doomsday ship. Val's a tough one. She's been helping prop up those of us who... um... aren't so much."

My feeling of relief at confirmation that my sister was still alive threatened to overwhelm me. I almost felt dizzy. I noted Thorsen watching me closely, and Kelley stepped in, distracting the other woman with questions.

"Ensign, can you give us the short version of what's going on and the lay of the land? We have no idea what we're walking into."

"Yes, Lieutenant. There are forty-seven humans, thirty-two Wulkin, Six Gilzik and twenty-one Yakar. We are able to communicate with these other species because of the injections we've all received from our captors. Evidently this is a medical technology that the pirates stole from the Gilzik. I guess when you're a giant spider, you need a quick way to learn other species languages."

"I'd heard that Kalikak captives are used as slave labor," Chen said.

"You heard right, Corporal. We've all been 'drafted' by the Kalikak to work on the monstrosity you likely saw from the shuttle bay we just left. There's not even remotely enough of us to do the job in any kind of timely manner." Thorsen cast, a quick covert look at our guards. "We're working in tandem with a horde of repaired, reprogrammed and repurposed bots, including a few of *Wanderer*'s exterior repair bots, kidnapped like their human counterparts."

"About this project..." Emily began.

"Not now," Thorsen once again glanced toward the guards. "Later, okay? For now, I'm supposed to be telling you about what is expected of you and procedures for doing that. Also, just a warning, *overt* resistance is dealt with harshly and brutally."

The emphasis that she put on 'overt' led me to believe that there was covert resistance going on behind the scenes. My danger sense had been on a low-level tingle since we'd been taken off our own shuttle. Now, directing it toward our guards, my talent tried to feed me the various weak points I should be striking to take them out. I purposefully turned my attention away from them. On occasion, my sixth sense has actually taken over my body, helping me avoid danger.

The best way to avoid danger at this point would be to not provoke these a-holes to begin with.

"Where are we going now?" Kelley asked.

"Our destination at the moment is a small space station next to the *Behemoth*. That's what we've been calling the huge ship we're working on, since the Kalikak don't tend to name their ships. The station is a combination processing center, mess hall and barracks. It's where we go when we're off shift."

"What happens when we get there?" I asked.

"One of the Kalikak will be giving you the low-down on what's expected once we get there. You can bet that you'll be assigned to shifts almost immediately. They work us hard, but they're conscious that they have a limited supply of workers. They're careful not to work us to death. It just feels like they are. Also, FYI, the food is semi-nutritious, but truly awful. You won't see anyone here that carries any body fat to speak of. That's partially the nature of what we're fed, and the small portions we get."

We went along in silence for a while, each of us contemplating what it was going to be like to be involved in forced labor. That sort of thing had gone by the wayside after the Laldoralin uplifted Earth, and most of my comrades had only heard of it through history vids.

Valiel and I, having had our formative years in the mid-21st century, knew more about such things, as they'd been frequent tactics used by some dictators in that era. We hadn't experienced such things personally, but we'd been aware of them as more than an abstract theory.

That the *Wanderer* crew had survived was a testament to their adaptability. But it raised a question.

"Ensign," I asked. "How many of *Wanderer*'s crew were originally captured?"

She hesitated for a moment, looking down at the floor. "We started with fifty-four officers and crew. Now we're at forty-seven. Most of our dead were from industrial accidents. The Kalikak aren't exactly big on safety standards, and though short on slaves they may be, sometimes they choose expediency over survivability. Our survivability that is."

"You said 'most of'...?" Kelley asked.

Thorsen lowered her head and stared at the deck for a few moments. When she spoke, it was in a very subdued tone. "The highest ranking officer was Lieutenant Commander Garovik. He decided to argue with the head guard on the construction site over the dangers of our working conditions. The guard evidently decided us new prisoners needed an abject lesson in what happened to anyone exhibiting defiance." She was having difficulty continuing.

"What did they do, Rona?" Emily said, touching the ensign's knee.

"We... we were on the outer hull of the Behemoth.

Garovik started vehemently arguing with the guard, and that thing stripped his thruster pack off him, grabbed him by an arm and a leg, pulling loose his mag-boots, spun around three times and let him go. The Commander went flying off in the direction of deep space."

We all went silent at that.

"Did..." Kelley said, "did they go get him? Lesson learned and all? Please tell me they retrieved him."

Thorsen shook her head and resumed her inspection of the deck. "No. He's somewhere out there, slowly moving away from us. He must've run out of oxygen about fourteen hours later, as that's how long our suits go until they need an oxy recharge. He's just out there, staring into the abyss, floating. Forever."

"So..." I said.

"So, no *overt* resistance," Thorsen said, raising an eyebrow as if to again say that there might be other forms of resistance. Her defiant look was directed toward us, and away from the two guards so that they couldn't see her face.

We all understood. Easy-to-see resistance might be off the table, but there was more nuanced defiance going on behind the scenes.

———

The trip to the station was short.

The shuttle settled down and came to a halt with such a loud 'thoom' that we all raised an eyebrow at what was likely crappy piloting. Or poorly maintained flight controls.

As the aft ramp lowered, the guards touched our restraints with the glowing rod and the cables fell away. They pointed toward the exit and we all rose and led the way out, with a few shoves from our captors, intended more to intimidate than to get speed out of us.

The shuttle bay we were in looked like the one on the ship we'd just left, in that it was rusty, dirty, and in need of maintenance both janitorial and technical. It was not a large space, and the closing exterior doors past the force field made it seem even tighter.

We were marched down a dingy corridor with some missing ceiling lighting in stretches, and it looked less like malfunctioning technology than that the lighting itself had been removed. In the few well-lit sections, we saw the corridor was grimy and poorly maintained.

The contrast when we came to the center section of the station was quite obvious. Though it certainly didn't look pristine, the walls and floors were clean and unstained. Rusty spots looked to have been sanded and were mostly covered with what looked like gossamer webbing. Most notable was the partitions that now broke up what was once a large open space into different enclosures arranged around the octagonal space.

"Well, this looks quite a bit better than the rest of this station," Emily noted.

"No thanks to the Kalikak," Thorsen said. "The cleaning, the maintenance, even the separated spaces, that's all us. We've been pulling non-essential panels and junk from this station and using the materials to make it livable for all the species forced to live here."

As we stood there, I felt my danger sense go off, and I'd ducked before I even knew why. A heavy hand swung over me where my head had been a moment before. And I saw one of our guards had just taken a swing at me. I also saw Chen slam into the floor almost at the same time.

"What the hell?" I said. "What was that for?"

"Message for newcomers," the guard replied, and I knew he was about to try again. It took everything I had not to retaliate. I knew exactly where to hit him to take him down. It would be so easy, armor or not.

Instead, I took the second blow, trying to roll with the punch as much as I could, it was still like taking a punch from a boxer. From the floor, I saw Kelley step forward. "There's no need for..." she started to say.

She took the backhand full in the face. Emily rushed to her aid, trying to shield her and got the same treatment. If I'd restrained myself before, it was nothing compared to the titanic effort of not kicking the Kalikak's knees backward.

"Now you all know," the brute said, laughing. "We don't take any crap from the likes of you. If we do, we'll *actually* hit you hard. Understand?"

Our silence must've signaled assent. "Good. You new ones wait here. Lukka will come and tell you what you need to know." Both guards turned, laughing, and exited through the hatch we'd just come through.

"I'm so sorry," Thorsen said, helping Emily to her feet. Em had a trickle of blood trailing down from her nose. "I didn't know they were going to do that. Those two are a pair of the meanest Kalikak. Different ones might've not done that."

"Don't make excuses for the bastards, Rona, any of them," A familiar voice said. I looked up toward an even more familiar face, one I knew as well as my own. She looked down at me and her eyes grew wide. "Tanner?"

"Hey sis," I said. "Fancy meeting you here."

31

"Oh no! No. No. No. No!" Valiel Voss said, her face growing more anguished with each 'no.' "Tanner! Why are you here? Oh, Goddammit!" I didn't answer, I just held my arms wide to hug her.

I received a punch in the chest.

"Ow! Dammit, Val! What was that for?"

"For being here, Tanner! For getting yourself captured by these vicious scumbags. This is awful!" I had never seen my sister get anywhere close to hysterics, before. She was usually the cool cucumber of the pair of us, but not so now. She rubbed her temples, closed her eyes and began the deep breathing techniques our step-dad had taught us as newly-emerged-from-cryo teenagers.

Other members of the *Wanderer* crew were coming toward us, when the side hatch opened again and a Kalikak walked in. The pirates weren't tall, but this one was tiny, only about two thirds the size of our previous guards, and the armor it wore was glossy, almost stylish with no traces of rust or hastily painted graffiti, though plenty of ornamentation. Narrow at the waist, wide at the hips, (though still with the short bow-legs) I was sure I was looking at a Kalikak female.

"Greetings, new prisoners. Step forward," she said. "I am Lukka. I assume you can understand me, as my people have all been injected with your language. Now, it is time for you to receive the translation injections so that you may also understand all of the slaves that you share this space with."

Her voice, though coarse in tone, was higher pitched than the two Kalikak that had hit us. It had an almost cultured cadence that to me, bespoke greater intelligence.

I bet the ladies run things in this neck of the woods. I thought.

"This will not harm you," Lukka said as I was poked with an oversized injector. She wasn't gentle with it, but she wasn't trying to hurt us either, unlike her predecessors. I felt slightly dizzy as I stepped away. Looking down, I saw a gigantic fuzzy spider signaling me with its front legs.

"Hello, new human," it said in a buzzing voice. "Can you understand my words?"

I nodded my head, then realized that probably meant nothing to this eight-legged person. "I... I can understand you. My name is Tanner, by the way."

"I am Kizzpon," he replied. I was assuming this was a he. "May you live long and see your home again."

"May you also, Kizzpon," I replied. I started to ask the spider person a question, but was interrupted by the Kalikak woman.

"New humans, you are fortunate," she said. "You just missed the next work shift and now will not need to assume your duties for the next (garbled words that translated to fourteen hours). You will have some time to acclimate to your new situation, and to understand your new life. When I leave, you may discuss things with your fellow slaves to gain more perspective."

By now we were surrounded by *Wanderer*'s crew, as well as

some Wulkin and Grilzik. The humans almost to a person had a look of angry contempt on their faces for our captor, which led me to believe that the Kalikak didn't have a good grasp on human facial expressions. Anyone who did would've wilted under such unveiled loathing.

"There are rules, of course," Lukka continued. "You will be assigned tasks to complete, and you *will* complete them. There will be no excuses allowed. Your continued existence hinges on working to complete, and eventually completing, the battleship that you no doubt saw being constructed. That is your sole reason for being alive, and if you cannot help with its completion, there is no reason for us to keep you alive."

She looked at us, then out over the crowd. "Your labor is not without a final reward, though. When the vessel is completed, all remaining slaves will be placed on the fourth planet of this system with materials to build a small colony. This is our promise, the promise of the Kalikak. You will not be discarded when your labor is finished."

I glanced around at the *Wanderer* crew people. To say that their expressions were skeptical would be an understatement. That didn't bode well.

"Your tasks will be assigned as they come," Lukka said. "For now, discuss how to work with your fellow slaves. Your first shift will begin in twelve hours." Lukka spun on her heel and exited the room.

"Well," a tall dark-skinned man with a somewhat unkempt semi-afro hair style said to us, "welcome to space-shanty town. I'm Lieutenant Senior Grade Leon Kuff. We can all introduce ourselves as time goes on, but I'm second in command here. Just so you know, we are monitored here in the main area, but not in the shelters we've created. So anything... special... you need to say should be saved for in there. Or in one of our corner 'dead spots' over there." Kuff gestured to two different corners of the habitat with benches leaned against the wall.

"Understood, Sir," Kelley said. "Lieutenant Junior Grade Kelley DeCosta, *E.S.S. Seeker*. These are Corporal Chen, and Ensigns Darkfeather and Voss. You're second in command? Did one of the senior officers survive?"

"Well, I guess she counts as a senior officer," Kuff replied. "Lieutenant Commander Boffin, formerly of logistics, is in charge. She's on shift now, much to everyone who is not on that shift's relief."

"Is there a problem, sir?" Emily asked.

Kuff sighed, a heavy sigh that bespoke a weariness that went deep. "No. No, Ensign, I'm not going to be guilty of prejudicing anyone ahead of time. You can come to your conclusions on your own. Ensign Callas will find you bunks, and unfortunately, we have spares." The way he said it, I was sure that the spares were the former beds of lost crewman.

"Sir," Kelley said. "What are the working conditions going to be like? To be honest, I don't have much engineering experience beyond academy basic courses."

"Same here," Chen said.

"Don't worry that the work will be too technical," Rona Thorsen said. "Much of what we're doing at this point is moving things around and welding them in place. The Kalikak and the robots do most of the upper-level work, worried that we might sabotage the ship."

"But damn," Kuff said, "they are the sloppiest craftsmen I've ever seen. From what I've looked at, they might sabotage the damn *Behemoth* themselves just from doing crappy work. You've seen the condition of their ships if you came in on one."

"And yet," I said. "They seem to be dominating this sector of space."

"They're sloppy, but their ships seem to hold up," Val said.

"*Wanderer* was attacked by four of those medium cruisers that make up the majority of their fleet. They hammered down our shields before they boarded us. Sloppy or not, what they're doing, unfortunately, works."

"Yeah," Emily said. "Or we wouldn't all be here."

32

The human bunk situation was co-ed, males and females cohabiting. Chen, Emily and I were assigned bunks in one section, while Kelly went to live in the next section over in the same partition as Valiel.

Ensign Callas, the person assigning us our bunks was happy to answer our questions. Callas looked vaguely slavic with high cheek bones, a beak of a nose and a haircut so short it might as well well been a buzz cut.

"So, yeah," he said. "The humans are pretty much set up in this corner of the "commons" and the Grilzik are on those platforms that we built above us." He pointed to what was essentially a large shelf all around the huge octagon we all lived in now. Every few yards there were masses of webbing and in four different places there were what looked like well-built nests.

"Down in that corner," he continued, "are the Wulkin. They're pretty close to human, and are easy to get along with. Pretty likable on the whole. In that other corner area are the Yakar."

"I've never seen one," Emily said. "Humanoid?"

"Ehhhhh." Callas wavered his hand, palm down. "Imagine a loggerhead snapping turtle crossed with an opossum and you're pretty close. They're not as friendly as the Wulkin, but they're not bad. Just a little tetchy-touchy. Be polite to them and you're golden. The Grilzik nano-serum makes it so we can all communicate without much effort, so we all pretty much respect each other's boundaries. Everyone here decided that they wanted to segregate living areas, whereas the center area there is communal space."

I looked over the open area and saw various benches and make-shift chairs and tables.

"Is that where everyone eats?"

"Yeah. Though perhaps a better way to say it might be 'that's where everyone ingests' 'cause taking in the slop they feed us could hardly be called eating."

"It's bad?" Emily asked.

"You'll soon get a chance to sample the fine cuisine at this illustrious establishment. Slop time is in about fifteen minutes. There's a bowl and spoon under each of your bunks."

"Tim," my sister's voice came from behind us. "Have you had any rack time yet?"

"Not yet, Lieutenant," Callas replied as Valiel walked up to us. "I'm gonna crash as soon as we eat. No one here wants to miss a meal, crappy as they are."

"Yeah," Val said. "You won't find any overweight sentients here. Ensigns, might I have a moment with my brother? I want to catch up with family business, if you don't mind."

"No problem, Lieutenant," Callas said. "I'll keep giving the newcomers the lay of the land until we can all tuck into our glorious repast."

"Sarcasm, Tim. You wear it well."

Callas laughed and he and Emily moved toward a group of *Wanderer* crew people. Val motioned me over to a specific unoccupied corner that had a couple of benches set side by side.

"Tanner, there are a few things I want to clue you in on. First of all, through trial and error, we've found that we're monitored all the time. Second: we've found that the coverage is, like all things Kalikak, sloppy. There's a scanner-camera at about... your eleven o'clock... no! Don't look. It's about fifteen feet above the deck. There's another exactly opposite that one on the opposing bulkhead at the other end. The Grilzik found them."

"Makes sense. They're probably going up and down the walls on a regular basis."

"Yes. The sloppy part of the Kalikak surveillance is that the cameras don't cover everything. They're below the level of the Grilzik habitat and barely cover there at all. Also, this corner and and the one opposite it are dead areas."

I looked over to the opposite side of the octagon and saw two more benches sat there in more or less the same configuration.

"Seems like this'd be a good spot for planning mischief," I said.

"That's another thing I want to talk about with you," Val replied. "We are implementing small acts of sabotage, but we are *very* careful about them. These bastards don't play around when it comes to disciplinary action. Our most senior officer, Commander Garovik..."

"Thorsen told us. The commander is... lost among the stars."

"That's a poetic way of saying it. I prefer to say he was murdered by a Kalikak son of a bitch." Val turned away for a second, and I covertly looked at my sister. She wasn't looking quite as rough as some of the other *Wanderer* people I'd seen, and I attributed that to our hybrid nature. Still, her skin was stretched tight over the muscles of her face, and she looked much thinner than when I'd seen her last. Her long reddish-brown hair, which she'd always been a little vain about, hung lusterless down her back in a pony-tail. Her caramel-colored eyes had a haunted, bruised look to them.

"Val. Do you think the Kalikak..."

"We tend to just call them the 'K,' Tanner. Saves time."

"All right. Do you think the 'K' have a chance in hell of making a jump drive capable ship out of that monstrosity out there? From what I understand the one they stole from your ship is just too small to do the job."

"Somehow, when they attacked *Wanderer*, they managed to kill most of our senior engineering staff. We've got a few technicians that worked on the system with us, but we've told the K that they were shuttle techs. That they have no idea how to install and maintain a jump drive." She looked at me. "Tanner, you weren't working in the engineering section were you? You're not Jump Drive certified, are you?"

"Nope," I replied. "My engineering work was all in the robotics section."

"Your crew mates?"

"Uh-uh. Emily is information systems, Michael is SecOps, and Kelley is junior command track and shuttle logistics."

"Good. Some of our people are robotics personnel also. The K will probably put you to work keeping their armada of bots running. The bots are our blessing and our curse."

"Yeah?"

Val nodded. "Blessing because they wind up doing more of the really dangerous stuff that flesh and bloods can't do. Curse because they're probably going to be what gets this *Behemoth* finished in a somewhat timely manner. Tanner, even if they decide to abort on the whole Jump Drive thing, they'll just put in a massive FTL drive. We see their schematics once in a while when they need to explain something, and this beast will have enough firepower to burn a planet down to bedrock. The Kalikak will dominate through overwhelming force."

"Are we doing anything to thwart that?" I asked.

"As much as we can. The workers on any shift are under constant observation. Sabotage has to be quick and subtle. But, having said that, the superstructure of the *Behemoth* is not as strong as her design specs would have the K believe. Every slave here knows the stakes."

"I wonder if the bots are as closely observed," I said. If the construction relied that much on robotic help, robotic sabotage could be just as troublesome.

"Our robotics people are all techs. Basic programming, yes. Advanced 'take over the system' programming, no. Unless you're an advanced programmer and I didn't know it..."

"Well, no. But I know someone in the area who is."

"What? Who, Tanner?"

"Mom? Do you read? I'm sitting next to Val. Can you access her sub-dermal?"

"Indeed," Dora said. "Hello, my precious daughter."

"Mother? How? Are you in a Remora, like Dad?" Valiel looked at me, panic in her eyes. "Tanner, the Kalikak will find her! Mother, you're in danger here! Jump away!"

"No, my love. I'm fine. I'm in a Remora 2.0, with a full stealth system. Like an actual remora fish, I came here clinging to the vessel that brought your brother and his friends to you." Dora said. "Your captors had no idea I was there."

"Do you know if Dad got away? He was in one of *Wanderer*'s remoras, and I know the K were blasting any Remora they could shoot at."

"You father is fine, Valiel. He's now resident in a significantly upgraded probe like the one I'm in. Currently, he is back at our... base of operations repairing his shipboard self.

I'm sure once he has these coordinates, he will be stealthing in too."

"Wait... you retrieved *Wanderer*? Was there anything left?"

"*Wanderer* was only partially pillaged and is currently under repair. *Seeker* rescued a bit more than half her crew that had escaped the assault."

"Oh... oh thank God." I saw Val's eyes begin to seep tears, which she brusquely wiped away.

"What are you currently up to, Mom?" I asked, interrupting to bring things back to our present needs.

"I am currently taking as many scans of this area as possible. Now that I know the coordinates of this place, I can jump here again once I take this information back to Captain Yamashita."

"Mother? We have a question for you," Val said. "The Kalikak are using a mish mash of captured robots to supplement our slave labor..."

"Oh! That makes my circuits fry! I did not raise my children to be slaves!"

"Yes, but what we need to know is; would you be able to override their programming? If we're to escape from here, and take over one of the K ships, having all the bots run interference would be invaluable."

Stealing a ship? I wondered if that was the hidden plan by the captives all along.

"There are a lot of bots, but... possibly?" Dora said. "If your father and Organizer of Armadas stealthed in with me, I'm sure that the three of us could raise great digital havoc with the Kalikak and their plans. However, we would not do so until we were sure you were in a position to get to safety."

"That's something we can plan around, Mom," I said. "For now, you need to get all the information you can get and scoot back to *Seeker*."

"I am loath to abandon you all. What if something happens while I am gone?"

"We've survived this long, mother," Valiel said. "I'll make sure that nothing happens to my little brother while you're away."

33

My first stint as a 'non-wage' slave was an eventful one. That Dora was in the vicinity was information Valiel shared with Lieutenant Kuff and he immediately put that into the area of 'need to know' intelligence. The only people who were in the know currently were the *Seeker* people, Valiel and Kuff.

"Sir?" Kelley asked Kuff, "we aren't telling Lieutenant Commander Boffin?"

At that question, I saw Val's lips go tight and Kuff shook his head, his demeanor sad. "No Lieutenant DeCosta. This is hard to say but..."

"Then let me say it, sir," Val said, anger heating her voice, "Boffin may be compromised."

"You've got to be kidding," Emily said. "Please tell me you're kidding."

"Do I look like I'm kidding, Ensign?" Val said. Valiel was usually a paragon of coolness. I'd always kidded her that she took after Krizon, our Laldoralin parent. She wasn't cool and calm now, though.

Kuff interrupted her, raising a hand to forestall her going on.

"Have you lot ever heard the term 'Stockholm Syndrome?" he asked. All my friends gave him a blank look.

"That's where a hostage or a kidnappee comes to identify with their captor, isn't it?" I said. "Even comes to identify with their captor's cause?"

"Ah," Kuff replied, "Should've known the 21st century kid would know that one. Yes. That's precisely it. We suspect that the commander is starting to "identify" with our enslavers. Starting to actively help them by making sure nothing happens to their pet project."

"What. The. Actual. Fuck?" Emily said, uncharacteristically swearing.

"Being here, and subjected to what we've all been through," Kuff said, "I think it's broken her in some way that the rest of us haven't been affected by. It's mental illness caused by..."

"Don't defend her, sir," Val said. "She's a danger to us and our mission."

"I maintain that she's mentally ill, Lieutenant. But, that said, she can't be trusted, even though she's not done anything overt. Yet. But she's definitely talking about the K in a rosy light. It started about a week after... ah... Garovick. I've talked to her about it, and to tell the truth, she... well... she's not that rational on the subject."

"Bottom line," Kelley said. "Don't trust her."

"You got that right."

———

Emily, Kelley, Michael and myself were assigned experienced partners to show us the ropes as we suited up for the first time. I drew Kuff. Emily drew Valiel, and Kelley and Chen drew crew people I hadn't met yet.

"Okay, Tanner. These suits shouldn't be any problem for

anyone academy trained. Your wrist control on the left runs your thruster pack. Controls on the right are for comms. We have five channels available, just press the control corresponding to the channel you want to communicate on. Our transmitters are very short range. You and I will be on Channel Five."

"Five. Got it, sir." I keyed the fifth toggle on my control.

"Good. And Tanner? Before we put our helmets on, know that all these channels are monitored constantly. So, Joker protocol, capiche?"

"Understood, sir. Code word anything we don't want them to get."

"Or just save it until we're back... home. The short range of these comms works in our favor, and if there's no one in proximity, you might get away with some seditious talk, but don't count on it. The male Kalikak might not be the sharpest tools in the shed, but do not underestimate the females. There's a reason they run the show in this species."

"Understood."

"All right, let's get this show on the road."

We and all the off-shift workers of all four species moved as groups into a section of the station at least half the size of the habitat. Humans, Wulkin, Yakar and Grilzik crowded together waiting.

The humans and Wulkin were impossible to tell apart in their environmental suits without looking into their helmet visors. The Grilzik and Yakar were much more obvious because of their strongly differing body types. The 'turtle-ish' Yakar moved a lot better in their suits than I would have expected, while the Grilzik seemed fidgety and nervous.

I was expecting that we'd be shuttled over in a ship, but that was not to be the case. A huge opening, like that of an earthly stellar observatory opened in front of us and a forcefield flashed into place. Instead of a ship, a platform hovered before us.

It looked like assembled scaffolding. It looked like a huge sled, which is exactly what it was, one designed to fly through space. Large thrusters were mounted on the undercarriage.

"Okay," I said, eyeing the contraption nervously, "how's this supposed to work?"

"Just watch, Tanner," Kuff said as everyone began crowding forward. "You find an open spot and attach your tether, retracting it fully. Then, you hang on for dear life, as the pilot of this nightmare isn't particularly solicitous of his passengers. Chen, DeCosta, Darkfeather, you all hear that? Hang on *tight!*"

We all answered in the affirmative.

I moved forward with the others, and Emily moved beside me, and attached her tether next to mine. Kuff was on the other side, and Valiel and Kelley DeCosta were beyond him. Chen was in the row in front of us. Behind me, several Grilzik clambered on the last row, hooked in and grabbed the stanchions in a death grip and then we were off.

I am experienced at extra vehicular activities in deep space, but that first "sleigh ride" was an event with a high sphincter-pucker factor. At the front was a single Kalikak warrior, standing in an enclosed cage and I got the impression that, had he been born on Earth, he'd have been a crazed adrenalin junkie.

We blasted away from our new home on a vague trajectory toward the battleship. Inertia wasn't accounted for, nor even acknowledged. I'd instinctively grabbed onto the bar that ran across my spot as had everyone else. Tethered or not (everyone was), the bar became our stability. Our bodies, beset with inertia, tried to stay in place as the sled jumped forward, but eventually caught up.

Evidently, our pilot wasn't subject to any form of flight

traffic control because our flight had us winding around a smaller battlecruiser resting in our path, skimming its hull and arcing around it.

I heard a wild whooping sound and realized it was the voice of the Kalikak flying the sled coming over comms. The mad bastard was really into this, and likely enjoyed the fear his wild antics generated. Especially amongst the noobs.

Adrenalin junkie indeed.

The 'adventure' finally ended with the sled flipping ends and firing its engines toward the massive hull we were approaching. Say what you will about that particular sentient's mental health, he touched the landing point on the *Behemoth* with barely a thump to the rear shock absorption bumper.

As we all piled off the sled, newcomers with shaking knees, a large contingent of workers were coming to catch their ride back.

"*Seeker* personnel, switch to channel four. You too, Val," Kuff said. Once we'd done so, he continued. "I'm going to introduce you to Commander Boffin, and I'll remind you to be circumspect with information around her. Common knowledge stuff is okay to talk about, but keep anything you don't want the Kalikak to know out of her sphere."

"Is she really that far gone, sir?" Kelley asked.

"We have no tangible proof, DeCosta, but plenty of indicators. At this time, there is enough circumstantial evidence that caution is required."

"In a less civilized age," Val said, her voice bitter, "She might already be out the airlock."

"Belay that, Val. All right, let's all switch back to channel one." As we did so, Kuff moved toward one of the weary-moving people coming toward us. "Commander Boffin. We have new people. I'd like to introduce Corporal Chen,

Ensigns Darkfeather and Voss, and Lieutenant DeCosta. All late of the *E.S.S. Seeker*."

"Oh no. Don't tell me the K got the *Seeker* also," the woman said. She sounded exhausted and heartbroken at the thought.

"I believe not, Ma'am. The lieutenant here stated that the *Seeker* badly damaged one of the K ships and likely escaped."

"Well, that's a blessing. I don't suppose that *Seeker* has any way of tracking you four, do they?" Boffin asked.

Kelley looked at Kuff, who even through his helmet seemed to be looking at her with hidden meaning. "No, Commander," she said. "They caught us in a shuttle at the *Wanderer*'s attack site. There's no way *Seeker* could've followed us, Ma'am. They had their hands full at the time."

And that was it. We had just lied to a superior officer; Kelley directly, the rest of us by omission.

"Ah, just as well," Boffin replied. "If *Seeker* flew into this meat grinder, the K would make short work of her. Best get yourselves resigned to the fact that this is where we're staying until we complete this project and the Kalikak drop us off on the forth planet to build our new homes."

"Really, Commander," Val said. "It's just as likely that the K will, once they have no use for us, just chuck us out into space to follow Commander Garovik."

"Always the worst case scenario with you, isn't it, Voss?" Boffin replied. "Voss. Wait. Are one of you named Voss also?"

"Ensign Tanner Voss, Ma'am," I said, raising my hand. "Valiel is my sister."

"Well mister, I hope you have a better attitude than she does. God knows I don't need two snippy half-Lallies to deal with." Boffin sighed. "Kuff, keep an eye on the noobs, make sure they get enough experience to do their jobs, but head them off from anything too difficult until they get their space-legs under them. If there's anything else to report, brief me when we switch spots again. I'm so tired right now I can't process well."

"Understood, Commander. We'll see you on the flip-side."

Boffin trudged toward the now-loading sled. If it had been one of *Seeker*'s officers, the crew would've made way and made sure she had a spot. *Wanderer*'s crew simply let her trudge up the sled and hunt for a spot amongst the chaos. Kuff looked at our group and raised four fingers. We all switched to channel four.

"Well, you've met her now. DeCosta, you did well," he said.

"I hope that you're not mistaken about your suspicions, Lieutenant," she replied. "Essentially lying to a senior officer made my stomach turn."

"While we have nothing positive," Kuff replied, "we have so much circumstantial evidence that it's hard to come to any other conclusion. It may that she's under a misguided notion that the only way she can preserve our lives is to capitulate with the Kalikak without reservation."

"That doesn't sound like a wise course of action," Emily, walking next to me, said.

"Considering what these beings have done, and what they're probably going to do with this battleship, all the slaves here are actively working on making sure this thing tears itself apart on its maiden voyage."

As we trudged toward a nearby construction area, Kelley brought Kuff up to speed on what *Seeker* had encountered since we'd arrived in this quadrant.

"Lieutenant, since our ship's been here, we've encountered a confederation of different species that the K have been preying on, and have allied ourselves with them. Captain Yamashita is helping them level the technological playing field. At this time the Kalikak attack through ambushing lone ships in deep space." Kelley gestured at the construction going on around us. "If this huge, armed-to-the-teeth battleship ever functions, it'll completely change the dynamic in this area. No one would be able to stop or stand up to it. They could enslave entire worlds."

"Unless the Laldoralin happened to get involved," Chen said.

"Sounds great, Corporal," Kuff said. "But extremely unlikely. We're a long way from the Hegemony. But don't worry, even though the K are watching for it, we've found a few ways to compromise this monstrosity. Which is another reason why we're keeping Boffin in the dark. A 'just in case' scenario."

"Understood, sir. Hopefully we can help in some way with that."

"Don't y'all worry about that," Kuff laughed. "Soon, apprentices, we shall induct you into our dark and evil ways."

34

I understood what Boffin had meant when she'd said "Too tired to process" after my first shift working on the Kalikak battleship. By the time we'd left the work site, clambered aboard the 'sled' and whipsawed our way back to the prison station, it was all I could do to put one EVA-suited foot in front of another.

We'd filled Kuff in on all the information we'd gleaned since coming to this quadrant of space and as we returned from our almost fourteen-hour work shift, he gave an edited version to Boffin as she started toward her next work day.

Stepping out of my suit into... fresher... air was a gift from heaven. The fourteen hour-long work time pushed the EVA suit's air recycling systems to their limits. The cool air of the station might've seemed stuffy and musty if you'd just stepped off of *Seeker*. Stepping out of an over-used suit, it tasted like air from Heaven.

Much to my surprise, there were showers. Not remotely enough, but eventually, everyone off shift was able to rinse the funk off. Whoever had originally built this station had done a good job with the water reclamation systems.

I was heading toward the habitat with my assigned bunk when Dora contacted me.

"Tanner, please return to the area where I first contacted you and Valiel. I understand it is an area where there is no surveillance."

"Roger that," I replied, keeping my answer short. I made a gentle looping curve toward the corner area and noted that Val, Kelley, Emily and Michael had all turned in the same direction.

"Is everyone reading me?" Dora asked. Everyone gave muted affirmatives as we all sat together on the benches. To anyone watching, it would seem that a clique of workers had just decided to hang out together.

"We're all here, Mom," Valiel said. "Status report?"

"I have gleaned as much general information about this Kalikak installation as I can, and it is time for me to return to *Seeker* and make my report. I hate the idea of abandoning you here, but in the long run, my leaving will be in everyone's best interest."

"Dora, have you been in contact with Lieutenant Truval?" Emily asked.

"I have, and I must say that our Truval is a very resourceful being, much out of proportion to his size. He has hitch-hiked his way to the main Kalikak control station and is availing himself of not only their resources, but their computer systems."

"Oh boy," Chen said. "Our own six-armed *deus ex machina*. I'd bet he's figuring out all sorts of ways to make their lives unpleasant."

"For the most part, he is building actual physical back-door accesses to many of their weapons systems, which I will be able to access remotely, should the time ever come for an attack. While there is not much he can do to the many ships orbiting the shipyard, we will at least, should everything go according to plan, be able to neutralize the massive firepower of the main station. Hopefully turn it against its owners."

"Then an attack might be possible, with enough ships," Valiel said. "I wonder if this confederation DeCosta told us about would be willing to come in and hammer these toad eaters."

"I cannot answer that question at this time," Dora said. "All I can say my children, my fellow crew members, is stay strong. I will return as soon as I can, and I will probably not be alone. Be strong my brave ones."

"Safe travels, Dora," Michael Chen said. "Don't worry, we won't go anywhere."

"Ah. Thank you, Corporal. That is comforting. I think."

———

When I finally settled into my rack, sleep came down on me like a blackjack from an old detective novel. I may have dreamed, but I was in the throes of such a deep exhaustion, that I didn't remember visiting Morpheus at all.

Eventually, I stumbled from my habitat, clad in pants and undershirt, my uniform top still over my arm. I was gonna need a splash of water to the face before I tried the complicated procedure of a button-up top.

"Mornin', Star-shine," Emily said, handing me a hot cup of... something. Imagine coffee made from charred blackened oatmeal and you're kinda in the ballpark of how it tasted. Still, it was hot, and I started to feel the cobwebs of my mind begin to fade away.

"How you doin' this morning?" I asked. "I'm sore everywhere."

"Me too. I was using muscles I didn't even know I had on a shift that lasted forever. Who knew that working in zero G could be that taxing?"

"Every time we had to move a hull plate, we had to over-come the inertia and shove it. Those things weigh tons, and getting them moving and then getting them stopped and moved into place is a big chore."

"Lucky we had the bots to help, or very little would've gotten done. Though, come to think of it, that could've been a good thing."

"Your muscles get used to it," my sister said, walking up with her own cup of glop coffee. Glopee. "Doesn't matter how you've been training, construction work like this seems to use a whole different set of muscles. Of course, if we'd been working on *Wanderer*, we'd have attachable thruster packs to move things. God, how I wish we were working on *Wanderer*, not this thing."

"Val, you've been here over a month," Emily said, "how much has actually been accomplished on this project since you were brought here? I"m not complaining, understand, but this seems like an endless task."

"Which is a good thing," I added. "No one wants to see the *Behemoth* completed."

"When I got here," Val said, "The hull was only half in place. The entire aft section was nothing but girders. Now, there are hull plating and decks almost to the three quarters mark. It's moving faster than you'd think. There's more to it than that, but I don't want to comment here under the eyes of the K."

"That seems fast," Emily replied. "I wouldn't have thought with this small of a slave-labor force they could get that much done."

"We're only doing the main super structure and hull plat-ing. The Kalikak...these... sentients are, for all their brutish-ness, damn good at reverse engineering. They haven't cloned our bots because, quite frankly ours are more primitive than some of the other bots here. But they have better ones that they got from somewhere, and they are building them in droves to supplement the workers."

"Well, that's not good," I said.

"No shit, Tanner. You can't see the front end of the ship from where we're working, and you might've been preoccupied on the trip over..."

"Uh, yeah. Trying not to be flung into space by that crazy sled driver."

"I figured," Val said. "They've started to move weaponry to the forward gun mounts. Scuttlebutt is that the forward third of the ship is almost complete. The Kalikak are putting this beast together faster than seems possible. They want to get to the business of domination as soon as they can."

"Why aren't we doing more to..." Before Emily could finish, Val reached out and put a finger over her lips.

"Let's go for a walk over to The Corner."

My sister stood and gestured for us to follow her to one of the areas where the Kalikak monitors didn't reach, one of the two small sections where the Kalikak couldn't see. We followed. I noted that Lieutenant Kuff was watching us, and Val subtly signaled him to join us.

Arriving at our 'safe space,' we sat at the benches. As we did, so did a Wulkin and a Grilzik. Kuff greeted them; "Gorman, Nutor, these newcomers are from the Starship *Seeker*, from my homeworld, Earth. This is Emily and Tanner. I'm vouching for them."

"I greet you," said Nutor, the spider-like Grilzik. "I understand one of you is the brother of the Valiel." Though it was obvious to us between Emily and I which was the brother, I raised an arm for Nutor's benefit.

"That's me," I said. "I greet you both and am glad we are allies." Emily nodded in agreement.

"We are glad as well," Gorman, the Wulkin, said. He turned to Kuff. "Are they ready to be briefed on our plans?"

"As far as I'm concerned, they are," Kuff replied. "They've been through a shift now, and have a frame of reference to what's going on here."

"Lieutenant Kuff has briefed us on the situations you have reported," Nutor said. "I understand that you have a stealthed probe with advanced synthetic intelligence in the region."

"We did," Emily said. "However, our probe has left the area to take strategic intelligence back to our captain, and to your confederation. I'm not sure when she will return, but I can guarantee that Dora will be back here eventually."

"Even if all of us here die today," Gorman said. "Getting that information to our peoples will be worth it all. You can't fight against an enemy if you don't know where they are. But, if our allies don't come for us before we can escape, our 'work' on the *Behemoth* is doubly important."

"Which brings us to our efforts to screw the Kalikak," Kuff said. "We have to be subtle, but we are doing everything in our power to make sure that thing doesn't survive its maiden voyage."

"True. This is why none of the Grilzik are working on laying hull plating," Nutor said, "but instead are all on super-structure assembly."

"I'm afraid I don't understand," I said.

"The Grilzik produce... let's call it spider silk, that is as strong as almost any known metal," Val said. "When a girder is welded into the superstructure, half of that bonding, unbeknownst to the K, is Grilzik silk. It's so dense, that the Kalikak scanner can't differentiate it from regular welds. Thin layers of welding material are layered around it, so it can't be seen, and it's as sturdy as if it was any regular weld."

"Then I don't see the point..."

"The point is, Tanner," Nutor said, "the creator of the universe made us so that we were alway diligent in keeping our nests clean and repaired." I looked at the big spider in confusion.

"What Nutor is saying, Tanner," Kuff said. "Is that Grilzik silk is not permanent. After roughly six months, it begins to break down."

"Leaving only the spot welds," Emily said.

"Exactly, Ensign. Those welds still look perfectly solid, but most of their strength goes when the silk breaks down. The *Behemoth* makes a hell of a defensive space station, but if they try to move her at even half sub-light, no amount of inertial dampening fields will hold her together."

"That's the best news I've heard all day," I said. "Is that all we're doing?"

"We're also working on stealing a ship," Valiel said. "The one whose hull Thrillseeker likes to skim each time he flies us over to the work site. It's the only ship that stays in the same place all the time, between our habitat and *Behemoth*. It's intended to both protect the big ship and to keep us intimidated. It could shred this station we're living on in just a few minutes."

"But now that we know that we'll have probe support," Kuff interjected, "a whole new world of possibilities has presented itself."

35

We hadn't told anyone but Kuff and Val about Lieutenant Truval and his behind-the-scenes activities. I wished that we could contact him, but without one of the Remoras to act as a comm relay, he may as well have been back on Earth. Truval was on the main station, the nerve-center of the Kalikak's activities, and could've helped with very the very large problem of stealing the enemy ship.

That problem, for the moment, boiled down to lack of intell.

"So... we don't know how many crew are onboard the stationary cruiser," I said. "Nor do we know the status of her systems."

"Sadly, we do not," Gorman said. "For all we know, it's a semi-derelict with weapons. But that ship is the only one we have any chance of taking. However, if we get on it and find out that it is unable to move, our little escape plan will end quickly and badly."

"Once our probe returns," Emily said, "I'm sure that we'll get that information fast enough. Another problem, as I see it, is that even if everything goes perfectly, and we somehow manage to overcome her crew, we're still trying to escape FTL ships with an FTL ship. We may not be able to get away if they can catch up to us."

"Which is why Dora and her AI cohorts are so important," Valiel said. "If we did manage to steal that ship, and were able to clear this area at FTL, I'd bet that there's no way that they'd send all of these ships after us. They're not going to leave the *Behemoth*, let alone their control station, unguarded."

"I'd guess that they'd send four," Nutor said. "That is their general attack formation, and the number four seems to have some sort of significance to the Kalikak. How would your probes help us?"

"Aside from letting us know the status of our target and her crew, our probes could coordinate with *Seeker*, and through her, Confederation forces."

"Oh. An ambush? But our peoples would need a huge fleet to overcome the shields of four Kalikak vessels. Our unshielded ships would..."

"No longer be unshielded," I said. "Our captain has shared *Seeker*'s base shield technology with the confederation, and your peoples were watching very closely as we tested improvements on our weaponry. They were already implementing the shield tech at an astonishing rate. This ambush thing could be doable if the Kalikak and Unity forces were on equal footing."

Our two alien co-conspirators seemed at a loss for words for a moment. Then Gorman spoke in a quiet tone; "For so long have we been at the mercy of these verminous pirates, the pain of it had almost become commonplace. To think that we might not only defend ourselves efficiently..."

"But take the fight to our enemy as well," Nutor said. "It is a miracle. We will owe your species a debt that we might never be able to repay. We should break this up, and I will brief Targus, leader of the Yakar at a later time."

———

We broke up our huddle soon after that. Spending too much time away from the surveillance of the Kalikak tended to prompt personalized visits. Usually these visits were by the two males that had roughed my team up when we arrived, and everyone agreed that was something to be avoided.

Some of the *Wanderer* crew and a few of the Yakar were serving breakfast from a huge pot, and everyone was lining up for their gruel. After getting some slop dropped onto my makeshift plate, I sat down next to Tim Callas.

"Hey Tanner," he said. "I noticed you and the team leaders over there. I assume they brought you up to speed with all our... construction projects?"

"Construction? Oh. Yes, I think we've been briefed on all the happenings. I assume that Val or Lieutenant Kuff will make sure everyone is up to speed."

"Almost everyone. So how was your first day of work? Sore today?"

"Dear God yes. I sincerely hope this gets easier with repetition." I replied. "Hey, Tim. What's the story with the Yakar? They look like turtle-shaped tanks."

"Yep. And believe me, they're tough creatures. Put a single Kalikak in a ring with a single Yakar, and likely the K would be a grease stain in short order. Good allies to have."

"How'd they get captured, then?"

"Self preservation. The K tend to hammer Yakar ships into immobility, then give the Yakar a chance to surrender. Every other species, they board the ship and take it by force. With the 'turtle tanks,' they force them to come through an airlock one by one to be restrained. If they resist, the Kalikak hammer their captured vessel until there are no life signs before going in to pick the remains. The Yakar tend to travel in large family units, and if you went to their end of our habitat here, you'd see several small ones. Their kids."

"And the Kalikak have their submission because..."

"Because any resistance would result in the death of their children. In a similar way, the K keep us all in line. We're all slaves here, but we're also hostages to each other's good behavior."

"Meaning?" I asked.

Meaning if I, for example were to go off on an overtly rebellious course of action, I might be banged around a bit for it. But, another person, another human, chosen at random, would be taken out into the main bay where we pick up our daily commute, and that person would be beaten to a pulp before being thrown out through the force field without a suit. Same for the Wulkin and the Grilzik."

I felt chilled at the thought. My mind instantly sped to Emily, or Val, or Kelley being spaced because I'd decided to attack a Kalikak. It was horrifying.

"God almighty, Tim," I said. "That's just... horrific. Has that happened?"

"To one of the Wulkin. Guy just snapped one day and attacked our guard, which was stupid. He got the crap beaten out of himself."

"Did the Kalikak...?"

"Yes." Tim's expression grew hard. "It was shortly after *Wanderer* was captured and we were all new to this situation. The K invaded the habitat, grabbed a Wulkin female and dragged her into the landing bay. We were all herded at gunpoint to watch as they beat her and beat her." His face grew haunted as he continued. "The only mercy, I guess, was that she was not conscious when they flung her through the field. I can only imagine the horror she went through, though."

We sat there in silence for a moment. The thought of eating was pretty far from my mind at that point.

"You know, Tanner," Kallas voice dropped to little more than a whisper. "I'm sure you know we keep anything important from Boffin, and that's only wise. But, honestly I kinda get why she's like she is?"

This turn in the conversation caught me off guard. "Oh?" I said, unable to keep the surprise out of my voice.

"On *Wanderer,* she'd never been placed in any position of authority before, other than having a few crewmen to help her sort inventories. She was the head logistics officer, responsible only for equipment and supplies. Next thing she knows, she's the surviving ranking officer captured and responsible for the lives of all her captured crew mates."

"Not emotionally equipped for the job?"

"Not remotely." Tim looked over toward the lieutenant. "Kuff thinks she's just looking out for her own skin, but I think she's not only terrified of the K, but terrified of getting the rest of us killed."

"Really? 'Cause we've already had to effectively lie to her."

"Probably for the best. But I've seen her rush to break up fights or any kind of disorder before the K could notice, and in my opinion, she was doing her best to fight back terror. My personal opinion is that she's literally doing her best to not get any of us killed. It's caused her to take what the K say about dropping us off somewhere nice seriously."

"Yeah. I'm skeptical of their promises," I replied. "Any kind of benevolence just doesn't fit with the profile I've got in my head for the Kalikak."

"You're not alone in that. The prevailing opinion is that once they don't need us anymore, they'll give us the Garovik treatment *en masse.*"

I lowered my voice to breathing whisper. "All the more reason to hope we get a plan to take that enemy cruiser together."

"Or to hope that your captain can come up with a plan to get us out of here, Tanner."

36

The next few weeks sort of blurred together into one long stream of monotony. It almost felt like we were being swept in and out with the tide. Out to work on the enemy ship, in to rest and refuel.

I was beginning to think that something had happened to Dora. Perhaps she'd jumped back near the planet *Wanderer* had been surveying to plot a jump back to the Confederation station and been ambushed. With the stealth system her hull carried this was unlikely, unless it had malfunctioned at an inopportune time...?

I wasn't the only one worried. Val and I were doing girder-work with a Grilzik named Dundor, and Val was privately fretting over channel Five to me.

"Where is she?" Val said. "I expected Mother to be gone for a day, maybe two. It's been far too long, Tanner. Something must've happened to her."

"I don't know, Val. I just..." A ping notified us that Dundor had just accessed channel five.

"I beg forgiveness for entering what must be a private

communication, my friends. The girder is exactly where it needs to be, and I need to work my magic."

"Understood, Dundor," Val replied. She and I wrestled the large plasma welder into place in such a way that we obscured Dundor from the nearest guard. Checking to make sure that none of the bots were near, we signaled him to begin his 'silken magic.'

A tiny gap lay between the two joins of the metal beam we were putting in place, and Dundor placed his aft end against it by bending his body. This allowed him to see exactly what was needed and he began spraying spider silk through an opening in the Grilzik-designed EVA suit he wore. He filled the gap, layering his silk in denser and denser layers. A few minutes later, he gestured for us to do our part of the job.

"It is as ready as I can make it, friends. Make your welds large and ugly as befitting this vessel."

Val signaled for us all to switch back to the main channel. "Get the flux ready, Tanner," she told me. "I'm ready to start welding." We did exactly as our arachnid friend said. We overused the flux and made large welds that covered any view of the silk. Had we been working for any of the other known species in the galaxy, the ugly workmanship would've been instantly noticed. The Kalikak, however, seemed to have little interest in aesthetics and had little concern for shoddy-looking workmanship.

"Bot." Dundor warned us. Val finished the weld just as one of *Wanderer*'s co-opted robots approached to check our work for its new masters. The large exterior repair bot, intended for space work on the hull of its mother ship, scanned the still glowing welds. Surprisingly, instead of flagging the weld or moving on to another task, the bot turned it's interface screen toward us and a smiley-face icon appeared.

The animated icon then winked at us.

"What the..." Val said. "Mom?"

The icon disappeared and was replaced by text. *Nope. Dad on station. Transmissions limited for security. All Wanderer bots reclaimed but still following Kalikak programing for subterfuge. Text less likely to be intercepted.*

"I'll keep this brief, then, Dad. We're working on a plan to steal the ship between our habitat and this monster ship. We need info to form a plan."

Understood. Lieutenant Truval has provided physical backdoor access to the command and control station. Will get everything I can, and another Wanderer bot will intersect with you in one hour. Do not trust any of the non-human designed bots.

The robot turned and moved on.

Val, Dundor and I switched back to channel five. The transmitters on our suits were very short ranged, supposedly to prevent the slaves from coordinating *en masse* while on the job site. It worked in our favor though. Small groups could talk privately if no Kalikak or compromised bots were nearby.

"Well, suddenly I feel much better," I said.

"It's good news, little brother, but we're still a long way from getting out of here," Valiel replied. "Also, we have no padds to store info on. Everything is going to have to be us memorizing what we receive."

"I, and in fact most of my people, have eidetic memories," Dundor said. "Unfortunately, we are not good at unaided diagramming to recreate visual references. Our arts generally tend toward colorful display."

"I can draw fairly well," I said. "If I try to recreate an image, Dundor, can you tell me what I've left out?"

"Yes, I think that will work. I would be honored to be your critic of art."

———

We weren't sabotaging every weld.

We kept moving anti-clockwise in our duties as girder welders. And the Kalikak had actually marked in paint the beams with the highest stress-load. This worked in our favor perfectly. Not only did it tell us the points to make self-destructing joins, but the thick, ugly welds looked like we were giving those important joinings extra-attention, for "strength."

If the stakes weren't so high it might've been laughable.

"Friends," Drunor said. "Look up! Is that what it appears to be?"

Looking up through the floating hull plates awaiting placement, I saw three of the sleds that the Kalikak used towing a large unit with bells sticking out at multiple angles.

"Thruster unit," Val said. "A big one."

"This is not good, friends."

"What's wrong, Dundor?" I asked.

"Friend Tanner, we have been engaged in our little game of sabotage since long before *Wanderer* humans were brought here. Some of our handiwork in the forward and midships sections have undoubtably reached... maturity."

"Oh... shit. If they try to move this hulk..."

"Then some of those early joins will most likely fail as we intended, even if moved only on thrusters. Without dampening fields, inertia alone would place great stress on them."

"And the jig will be up," Valiel said. Dundor looked at her with an expression of confusion. "I mean, that the plan will be revealed prematurely."

"Yes," our arachnid comrade said, moving his fore-most arms vertically up and down. "And if that happens, who knows how our enslavers will react."

"Not well, I'd guess," I replied.

"And once assessing the scope of our sabotage," Val said. "They might decide that slaves are a liability."

"And decide they don't need our services anymore."

"We need to see what being done at the forward end of this vessel," Dundor said.

"That's what Remoras are for," I replied.

———

We were nearing the end of our shift when an exo-bot from *Wanderer* crossed our path. It turned toward us and its display screen lit.

Greetings children. Evan has informed me of your plan.

"Mom?" Valiel said. "You're both here?"

Yes, dear one. All three of us, in fact, as Organizer of Armadas in also in the zone of operations.

Val looked at me, a question in her expression. "Long story short," I said, "Orphaned alien AI that applied for asylum and has supplemented our enhanced AI Remora corp."

Val just looked at me for a moment, then got back to the conversation at hand. "Mom, do you have information of the ship we want to steal?"

I do. It is skeleton-crewed by twelve Kalikak, all male except for the captain. While the vessel is stationary, its engines are on standby which should help with a speedy acceleration when you take her. Four of the crew are stationed near an airlock and rapid decompression could probably send them on an unpleasant journey through space. Also, Evan retrieved Lieutenant Truval from the command center and he is now resident in the vent system of said vessel.

"Outstanding," Val said.

Truval is, as he did with the command center, assisting with giving us physical egress into the ship's systems. When he's done his part, we can override them and decompress the entire ship.

"That's incredible news," I said. "But we may have a fly in

the ointment, Mom. Have you recently scanned the forward section of the battleship we're building?"

Yes. I have visual on it as well as deep scan access. I can project its image on this screen.

A moment later, a view of the *Behemoth* filled the small screen. It showed us exactly what we didn't want to see. The forward end of the ship bristled with large heavy laser batteries and missile pods. Near the dorsal and ventral center of the ship, large thruster arrays were in the process of being attached.

We were nearly out of time.

37

"But the question is, how do we get on board her?"

Lieutenant Kuff looked at us as if we'd be able to instantly pull a plan our of our... um... ears.

"I'm thinking it's gonna have to involve the sled," Valiel said. "That'd be a hell of a long jump to our target ship from here, even with thruster packs. Plus, we've got to get both groups to the cruiser at roughly the same time. When we take that thing, we're not going to have time to bop around picking people up."

"Yeah," Emily said. "As soon as we have the vessel we're going to need to go from zero to full burn in just a few minutes. Otherwise the other ships'll be on our necks and our escape will end quickly and badly."

"Don't forget that is only step one," Gorman, the ranking member of the Wulkin contingent said. "We also have to take the ship once we get to it. We have to do it fast, also, or the Kalikak aboard her will sound the alarm, and things will end as Ensign Darkfeather mentioned."

"And once we're aboard, someone has to fly it," I said. "Anyone have experience flying a Kalikak control system?"

"That is not a problem," Targus, leader of the Yakar replied. The turtle-like alien gave snuffling laugh. "The K took the design from ships stolen from my people. I was able to look into the bridge of the ship that brought me here. The design was almost identical. The question is, can we access the systems, or will we be locked out."

I had to give credit where credit was due. The Grilzik translation injections beat our transponder based translations easily. We were sitting around discussing our plans with little of the usual sentence structure difficulties that our own systems often had. Looking out into the center of the habitat, I watched the multi-species game that was in full swing. The chaotic activity, looked like sort a combination of soccer and dodgeball, not only with humans/humanoids, but also giant spiders and turtles. It was a turbulent swirl that everyone seemed to be enjoying.

A few personnel from each group missing from the game wouldn't be noticed by the Kalikak.

"From what I understand," Ensign Thorsen said, "that also won't be a problem. We have an operative on the ship, who is providing access to stealthed probes from the *Seeker*. Our probes have incredibly advanced AIs, who were... er... gifted... from an incredibly advanced race. I'd bet a day's rations that they'll break whatever encryption the K have in place in about ten seconds."

"So, the main problems then are getting everyone, and I mean everyone, to the ship," Kuff said, "then taking out the Kalikak aboard before they can warn the rest of the bastards to come and pound us to scrap."

"I think we can shorten that to just getting to and taking the ship, sir," I said. "The Remoras are more than capable of disabling the enemy comms."

"If we can get to the ship," Targus said, "And my people can get close to the Kalikak without being gunned down..."

"That fight will be short indeed," Gorman said. "Targus, your people will need to fashion shields, and we will need to find suits for your young ones. As said earlier, we'll all need to be at the ship at the same time."

"Can I make a suggestion, sir?" Chen asked Kuff.

"Of course, Corporal. For God's sake, don't stand on ceremony if you have an idea."

"First of all," Chen said. "Let's name the enemy vessel. There's too many ships out there to just keep referring to it as 'the ship.' I suggest we call it the *Freedom*."

"Just not in front of Commander Boffin," Val interjected.

"That does bring up another problem, Lieutenant Kuff," Gorman said. "The Lieutenant Commander is a liability. I know the Yakar and the Grilzik will protest this, but... she might need to have an... accident."

"No! That is not acceptable!" Nutor, who'd been quietly listening the whole time reared up on his hind legs. "There will be no murdering of fellow prisoners."

"There may be no other option, Nutor," Val said. "It may be a 'good of the many' situation. If need be I can..."

She was cut off as Lieutenant Kuff rose up from his place on the bench and placed his angry face a few inches from my sister's.

"You fucking listen to me, JUNIOR lieutenant. We are not killing Commander Boffin. The fact that you would be so quickly willing to go along with the idea is very disturbing."

"But.. But... sir! She could compromise the entire..."

"We don't have anything but circumstantial evidence that she has a relationship with the Kalikak, Voss. We are not acting as judge, jury and executioner."

"But.. Well... then how are we going to do this then, sir?" Val's face was bright red. I didn't know if it was from anger or embarrassment. Perhaps a little of both.

Kuff stood up straight, and a slight evil smile came to his

face. "Valiel, that is now your problem. I am ordering you to switch shifts with someone in her group. You will get close to Lieutenant Commander Boffin, and you will either convince her of our need to escape, without, I might add, giving her any information on our plans; or you will incapacitate her when the time comes, get her into a suit and make sure she gets to our new ship, the *Freedom*."

"How... I...?"

"Valiel Voss," Kuff said, the stern tone fading away, "You are one of the most capable young officers I've ever met. I am not giving you this order lightly. I have one hundred percent confidence that you will make it happen, that when we leave, Boffin will be with us, alive and well, whether conscious or not. Do you accept these orders?"

Val looked at the deck for a moment, before squaring her shoulders and looking Kuff straight in the eye. "I accept and will comply with your orders, sir!"

"Good. I know you *will* succeed. Chen? I believe you had something else to add?"

"Yes, sir. How much have we explored this habitat station? There could be resources here that we can use. Who knows, there might even be Kalikak weapons here for a 'just in case' us slaves revolt."

"We have access to a limited few sections of this habitat, Corporal Chen," Gorman said. "While there is much of the station unexplored, the hatches and doors are locked. How do you propose we 'explore' outside our boundaries?"

Michael Chen gave the Wulkin that devil-may-care-grin that I'd seen so often in SecOps sparring before he bounced me around the mat. He looked up above where the Grilzik had their home level and pointed at the oxygen circulation ducts.

"The video monitoring barely covers the Grilzik areas. I've been talking to Captain Nutor's youngest and might I add smallest, crew member, Kizzpon. He and I have struck up a friendship and have been contemplating doing some exploring before this plan ever came up."

"Please continue, Corporal," Nutor said, tilting his body to adopt what my translation serum told me was a posture of curiosity.

"Well, sir, Kizzpon and I think he's small and light enough to traverse that duct way. As you can see, there are gratings every fifty feet or so, perfect for looking through without being easily seen. We could learn a lot more about what's available to us."

We all sat in silence for a moment, before Gorman asked, "While I like the idea, we have no tools. The K are very careful that nothing we can use returns to the habitat from the work site. A few simple tools would be needed to get the grating off. None of our species has the gripping ability to move those round bolts without the proper tools to provide leverage."

Again, Chen's mischievous grin surfaced. "I've been waiting for the right moment to show this." He reached into the top of his boot and pulled out a glossy metallic cloth pouch.

"A Faraday pouch?" Emily asked.

"Yes, Ensign," Chen replied. "Non-scannable. And our original guards were too sloppy to do a physical search." He opened the pouch and pulled out a multi-tool of a sort I'd never seen before. "Spec-ops covert ingress/egress tool. I can coach Kizzpon in how to use it. He can, if he's reasonably careful, follow the ducts all through this space station. He can also enter empty rooms and pilfer supplies."

"Outstanding work, Corporal," Kuff said. "Trust SecOps to have our back."

"Actually, sir, that's not all." Chen reached into his other boot and pulled out another pouch. He didn't open this one.

"What's that?" Val asked.

"Falconi four-shot flechette gun, Ma'am. Flat as a mint tin, easy to conceal, as long as it's in the pouch. I was thinking that maybe I should give it to one of you Voss kids. Tanner, most likely if you're gonna be riding herd on Commander Boffin."

"Why do you not use it yourself, Corporal Chen?" Targus asked.

"Because Tanner and Valiel never miss," Emily said. "And they alway know where the best place to put a shot is. Without fail."

"How... magical," the Wulkin replied, sarcasm dripping from his tone.

Chen laughed. "Oh, Captain Gorman, I've seen him in action, making impossible shots. I could put you on the near surface of our target ship and with this pop gun he could hit you from this station. Doesn't matter if he has a personal weapon or a star ship's laser batteries, the kid doesn't miss."

"I've seen what Val can do," Kuff said. "If he's as good as her, then yes, Chen. Give him the weapon."

Chen handed me the pouch. "Hide it deep in your boot, Ensign. Keep it in the pouch and only use it when it's truly needed, and not before. You only have four shots."

"All right everyone," Gorman said. "We all have an idea of what needs doing. Now we need to prepare. Chen, put Kizzpon to work. Extra suits we can modify for the Yakar children are a priority, though I'd also like to know of there are more than three Kalikak on the station with us. As for the rest of us let's muse over what we have, then schedule another *Granwah* game for the next shift. We can polish our plans then."

Working on the *Behemoth* was almost painful.

Not the actual work, but the horrible itch of wanting to move forward with our plans and being limited to occasional discussion when there were no Kalikak or bots about.

"Okay, let's do a full weld on this one," Ensign Rona Thorsen said. I was again on girder placement, only this time Thorsen had taken Val's place. With us was Dundor and crewman Davis Macintosh. Mac was using Valiel's swapped air module since he'd switched shifts with her as our crew had come to work so she could shadow Lieutenant Commander Boffin. He was doing his best to be helpful, but back to back fourteen hour shifts had him pretty worn out.

"Mac, you hang back," Thorsen told him. "We can do this while you nap on your feet. We'll let you know when to move."

"Aye, Ensign. Gonna lock my boots to the deck. Just need a quickie catnap."

While Dundor and I wrestled the girder into its final resting place, Rona brought up the plasma welder, a device none of us could move in standard gravity, but which in zero G could be cautiously moved by one person.

This wasn't a "special" weld, so we simply put it in place as quickly as possible. I was chafing at the whole process, but there wasn't anything any of us could do to advance our own plans at the moment. However, that suddenly changed.

"Tanner Voss, Ensign, do you read me?" a voice came through my sub-dermal transponder.

"Is... Organizer of Armadas, is that you?"

"Affirmative, Tanner Voss, Ensign."

"Organizer, you aren't with the Blah-Veht anymore. You don't need to use my full name. Just call me Tanner, okay? Why are you breaking comm protocol? The Kalikak might intercept this transmission."

"The situation has changed, Tanner Vo... Tanner. Remoras

Two, Three and Five now control communications in this area. The ones known as Kalikak are not aware of our infiltration."

"Oh... that is the best Christmas present ever! Can you you establish a network to all *Wanderer* and *Seeker* sub-dermal transponders?"

There was a moment's hesitation. "I am having Dora do that, if you do not mind. I believe that I could accomplish it, but am utterly confident that she can."

"Tanner to Lieutenant Dora, do you read?"

"I hear you, Tanner. I am reestablishing Terran Exploratory Force network communications."

"Mom, before you do that, please exclude Lieutenant Commander Boffin from the network. We have concerns about her being too cooperative with our captors. Lieutenant Kuff called it Stockholm Syndrome."

"I see. Configuring. Are you one hundred percent sure that the commander is compromised?"

"No, Dora," Ensign Thorsen said. "We're not, but we can't take a chance. Not when we need to escalate our escape plan." As we began to trudge toward the next support girder, we brought all three Remoras up to speed with the escape plan.

"Ensign Thorsen, I calculate a seventy-five percent chance that if you manage to escape, you will be recaptured or destroyed. I believe that if you all give me twelve hours, I can coordinate with Captain Yamashita to provide a very graphic distraction."

"One other thing, mom," I said. "we're going to capture the cargo sled that we're being transported on, but we need to be able to get the people on this worksite and the people on the habitat to our target ship, codenamed *Freedom*, at the same time."

A chime rang in my helmet, and I noted that Dundor was

calling me on channel five. "Yes, Dundor?"

"Uh... Tanner? I think we forgot Davis."

"Well, crap." Thorsen said. "Mac? Do you read? Mac! He's in slumberland. I'll go get him." She began to walk back to our last position.

"He probably has his radio un-attuned to any channel." Dundor said.

"Dundor, our probes are here and have control of comms. Covertly. I've been talking to them as we've been walking. I'm leaving this channel open so you can at least hear what I'm saying to them."

"Tanner, I can patch specialist Dundor into our network via his helmet comm. Specialist, do you read me? This is Dora in Remora Probe Two."

"A sentient probe? How thrilling! Were you designed especially for that assignment or..."

"Dundor," I said. "Focus, my friend. Task at hand."

"Ah, yes. Apologies."

"I am pleased to meet you, as it were, Specialist Dundor," Dora said. "Tanner, there is a second sled on your habitat station. It is rather sloppily attached to a railing on an exterior walkway opposite your regular departure bay."

"Assuming that it's working, it could be the answer to our transportation problems. Can you tell if it's functional?"

"I cannot. It has no onboard computer and appears to be utterly pilot-controlled. To call it 'quaint' is a vast understatement."

"One of us is going to have to go out an have a look, Tanner," Dundnor said. "Later, someone is going to have to circumnavigate the station on its exterior... and steal it."

"Looks like you're right," Ensign Thorsen said, leading Crewman Macintosh to our position. "But for right now, we need to get this next girder in place before we attract unwanted attention."

38

By the time we got back to the habitat, Macintosh was about done in. Thorsen double-checked his attachment to the sled as we started back for our habitat, while I stared intently at our crazy pilot's back, thinking of ways to take him out quickly and efficiently when the time came.

Back at our 'lodgings' poor Mac went straight to his bunk, and we didn't see him again until what passed for pre-work breakfast. Meanwhile, Thorsen and I subtly signaled Lieutenant Kuff to join us in the corner.

"What's new, ensigns?" he said. "I'd love to hear some good news, or something that'll move our plans forward."

"We have both, sir," Rona Thorsen told him. "We. Control. Comms."

He looked at her blankly for a moment. "The Remoras? Has Evan taken control of the Kalikak comms? Do the K know?"

We both grinned at him.

"That is outstanding," he said. "They won't be able to contact each other when we make our move."

"It gets better, sir," Thorsen told him. "We have our own comm network now. All sub-dermal transponders are now connected, *Seeker* and *Wanderer* alike. You can contact anyone except Commander Boffin."

"You actually could contact her, sir," I said. "But only through the Kalikak suit comms."

"This is a huge game changer," Kuff said. He reached up and tapped a spot just below his right ear. "Kuff to Valiel, do you copy?"

"Affirmative, Leon. Reading you five by five." Val's voice came over my transponder as well. Thorsen didn't seem to be tagged into the conversation however. She could hear us talk, but not Val's responses.

"From your lack of surprise, I assume you were made aware of our new capabilities?"

"Yes, sir. My dad clued me in," Val replied. "The Remoras are waiting for authorization to inform all TEF personnel under your command."

"Authorized. Tell them, however to be very discrete while communicating. Absolute necessity only. We don't want to give the show away by someone's facial expressions."

"Understood, Lieutenant," Evan's voice came over the feed.

"Though, to be honest," Val said. "The K don't seem to have a clue about human facial expressions."

"Or they don't care when we glare at them in hatred." Kuff said. "Val, how are you doing with your assignment?"

"I'm on the commander's work crew. Sir? We may have been wrong."

"Elaborate, please." Kuff said.

"Sir, I don't think Boffin is so much compromised as she is... just... broken. One of the other team members clued me into listening on channel four which is where the commander tends to keep her comm at. Sometimes, she forgets to close the channel, and Leon... it's just non-stop muttering. She just keeps looping; 'Can't let anyone else die. They murdered that girl. No more Garrovicks.' And she just keeps saying it over an over, unless she's interrupted."

"Damn."

"Honestly, she's not mentally well. I still wouldn't trust her to be in on our plans, but... I *deeply* regret my earlier words about..."

"Forget it, Val," Kuff said. "Keep her under observation, and try to come up with a plan to get her to *Freedom* with the rest of us. Willingly if possible. Unconscious if need be."

"Roger that, sir. I need to go. We're welding. Voss out."

"Sir, there's one more thing," I said. "We may have a solution to getting all our people to the *Freedom* at near the same time. There's a second sled..." I pointed to a section of the habitat, "roughy that way, attached to this station's exterior."

"Working?"

"That's just it, sir. If it was one of our craft, I'd be confident in saying 'yes,' but this is a Kalikak craft. You know how sloppy they can be with their equipment. It might just be a spare craft, or useless junk that they simply tied to a guardrail to get it out of the way."

"Someone will need to evaluate it in person," a voice said from above us. I looked up and saw Nutor hanging above us by a series of webbed pulleys and slings. It had been a while since I'd really looked up at the Grilzik section of our living space. The upper sections of the hull were crisscrossed with trails of webbing, and Nutor and his crew were using them as vertical 'trails' to move about the hull of the upper habitat. Nutor continued; "The only one of my people who can fit through the ducts is young Kizzpon and unfortunately, he is definitely not an engineer. He will need to be accompanied by a qualified human or Wulkin."

"Ensign Voss, as I understand, you're an engineer. You're elected. Nutor, haul him up."

"What? Now?"

"No time like the present," Kuff replied. I felt something touch my shoulder, and saw a thick strand of spider silk.

"Grab that, and I will bring you to me, young ensign," Nutor told me. "I have made it extra-sticky, but grip it tightly."

I looked at Kuff, and he just nodded. The strand was about double the thickness of a piece of old-school para-cord, and when I grabbed it tightly, it clung to my hand with an aggressiveness that duct tape couldn't match.

Using his front four leg/arms, Nutor hauled me to his position, then staying above the range of the surveillance cameras, hauled me over to the Grilzik platforms.

"Kizzpon! Come to me!" He said, and the smaller spider being rushed over to us with a speed I hadn't realized our arachnid allies possessed.

"I am here, my Captain!"

"Good. What have your forays into the duct system provided us?"

"Hello, Tanner Voss," Kizzpon waved a leg at me before giving his report. "I have found the suit room, venerable one. There are literally hundreds. More than I have been able to catalog. Also, there are store rooms that seem to be filled with un-inventoried equipment from several ships. Everything is warehoused *very* poorly!" This seemed to offend the young Grilzik deeply.

"Wait a minute," I said. "Does that include weapons?"

"Sadly, none that I could recognize, Tanner Voss. Equipment, electronics, some tools, what looks like foodstuffs and as I related earlier, various EVA suits."

"Holy... that could be...."

"Focus, young Ensign Voss," Nutor said. "Remember, you

need to make sure the sled is usable. That is your primary mission. You can sight-see with Kizzpon after, though I would caution you not to be gone too long. Our captors probably won't notice your absence, but that is not guaranteed."

"Understood, Captain Nutor," I said, but I was very much wondering if a certain piece of equipment was warehoused where it could be stolen back. "Kizzpon, we need to get to an area almost opposite the landing platform, and we need to go outside to see if a sled there is operational."

"I have my EVA suit here, Tanner Voss," Kizzpon said. "And it appears that Lieutenant Kuff has yours at The Corner."

I looked back down to where Kuff sat, seemingly tinkering on a suit as he sat on the bench. He looked up at us, and gestured at it. Nutor scurried back on the trail we'd come in on, retrieved it, and brought it to me.

Quickly dressing for success, I carried my helmet under my arm as Kizzpon unlatched a section of the ducts ten feet above us with Chen's multi-tool, and I was unceremoniously thrown over Nutor's 'shoulder' and carried up to the opening. Shortly there after, I was following Kizzpon's hairy butt through the station's duct system.

He led me past several junctions, and in the dust, I could see spidery footprints leading down most of them. Kizzpon had taken exploring the station quite seriously.

After what seemed a relatively short time, Kizzpon stopped and pointed through a large grating in the side of the duct. Below, I saw a small landing platform, similar to the one that we used to go to the job site every day. A blueish force field held atmosphere in the bay and through it, I could see the beginning of the walkway that the sled was said to be attached to. I couldn't see the sled, however.

"Hmm. I wonder why the outer door to this bay is open?

There's no one in sight," I said. "You think they have any surveillance on this bay?"

"Look at its condition, Tanner Voss. Dust everywhere. This bay is not only unused, it is neglected. It's a wonder the force field is still working. Sloppy, stupid Kalikak." Kizzpon seemed offended by the very name of our captors, and I had a feeling it was as much by their sloppiness as their barbarity. "I cannot guarantee you anything, but I would wager you my pre-shift rations that it is unmonitored."

"No need for that, Kizzpon. Can you lower me down? I want to do this as quickly and as quietly as possible."

A few moments later, the grating was hanging by one fastening, and I was standing in the bay. Kizzpon wasn't kidding. If a Kalikak happened to venture into the place, my footprints in the quarter-inch of dust would probably give the game away.

I quickly made my way to the force field, and was concerned to see it flicker for a moment, and a light poof of dust go drifting into space. I looked back and was relieved to see a tightly-latched pressure door that would keep the entire station from depressurizing. Then I looked up at the duct we'd come through, and hoped there were emergency seals on that as well.

I slowly and carefully pushed my way through the field and in a moment was outside in full vacuum. Stepping onto the walkway, I realized I hadn't brought my tether and momentarily panicked. I grabbed the walkway railing in a death grip. I didn't have a thruster pack with me.

"Is everything all right, Tanner Voss?" Kizzpon, who had remained behind in the duct, asked.

"I'm fine, but I am untethered here. Coming back into the bay to see if I can scrounge something."

I pushed my way back through, and began scavenging the

empty bay. I found a short length of electrical cabling, and with the multi-tool formed a loop in each end. Returning to the walkway, I ran the cable through the railing and through a loop to secure it. I then did the same around my waist. I was secured.

"Do you see the sled?"

"Negative. The walkway continues in both directions past the curve of the hull. Tanner to Remoras, can anyone out there see me? I need to know which way to turn to get to this sled we're trying to evaluate."

"Hang a left, son," Evan's voice came over my comm. "It's about another two hundred and fifty yards to port."

"Thanks, Dad. You all three on station?"

"Organizer and I are here. Dora jumped out to have a palaver with your captain. They're cooking up something, and you can bet these Kalikak aren't going to like it."

" Confusion to our enemies!" I said, grinning.

"Confusion indeed, Captain Jack Aubrey. You sure loved those stories."

"I sure did, Dad, and... hold on. I have visual on the sled. Wow. They just chained it to this flimsy guardrail. And only one chain."

"I told you they were sloppy, friend Tanner," Kizzpon said. "May I call you friend, Tanner Voss?"

"You better believe it, Kizzpon. We are definitely friends after this."

"I am deeply gratified. I am the youngest of my crew, and quite honestly usually feel like my seniors are patronizing toward me."

"Well, none of that from me, friend and... hold on, I've found a problem."

There was silence for a moment from my new spider friend, then in a small voice he asked, "Is it a mission-killing problem?"

"No, I don't think so," I replied. "We're lucky that Chen had this multi-tool. The K have disconnected the fuel tanks, uncharacteristically, for safety's sake, I think. I can reconnect them. The main problem, I just realized, is how to get the sled loose from this chain."

"There were tools in the warehouse I told you about. perhaps there is a cutting implement there?"

"We'll go check on the way back," I said. "In the meantime, let me hook the fuel tanks up and manually go over the systems. Then, we can go back and check."

———

There are times, on occasion, when your hopes are answered.

Kizzpon and I had back-tracked to the store room that he'd told me about, and as I dropped down into the dimly lit and cluttered space, I saw several pieces of Terran Exploratory Force gear scattered about, along with a number of unfamiliar items from other species.

The most irritating thing I found almost immediately was boxes of TEF emergency rations gathering dust. Pre-made, nutrient bars, soups, dehydrated drinks, all sitting here while we ate the slimy gruel the Kalikak fed us. I had to take a minute to get my anger under control.

"Are you finding the tools you need, Friend Tanner?"

"Not yet, Kizzpon. The light in here is very poor, give me a few minutes to look around." While the storage room wasn't nearly as dusty as the other landing bay, there was still a thin layer of the stuff on everything. *Wanderer*'s equipment had the least of it, but the room obviously was rarely visited. Evidently any reverse engineering was done on a "when we get around to it" basis.

That suited my purposes just fine.

Our EVA suits had a bank of lights just under the chin,

and they provided enough light to differentiate between all the items I was looking through. After searching a while I found a standard TEF engineer's tool box and sighed with relief. I knew what such a box contained from memory, but opened it anyway to make sure the contents were still there. They were. Rotating cutting tools, variable multi-tools, spanners, standardized electronic spares, various lubricants and even a small hand-held plasma cutter.

I tested the plasma cutter which ignited like a champ, then clipped it to my belt. I started back to the duct then stopped.

"Kizzpon, I'm bringing a whole toolbox back with me. Do you think we can get it back through the vent to our hab without making too much noise? It's a bit heavy."

"If I cannot carry it on my back, which I am sure that I can, I can make a web-net we can drag behind us. The webbing should blunt any noise."

"Okay, then. Let me get it, and I'll be right there." I turned back where I'd found the kit and bent down to dead-lift it into a position I could carry it. As my light swung toward the tool box, it swept over a pair of gigantic dust-covered feet.

"Shit!" My heart tried to punch out of my chest as I swung the lights up the front of the huge being looking down at me! My danger sense hand't warned me at all, and I was in shock for a moment before I realized what I was looking at.

"Friend Tanner! What has happened? Are you all right? What is wrong?"

It's... okay... friend Kizzpon," I gasped out between the belly laughs I was not emitting. It was an emotional release from finding out that I'd not stumbled over a new enemy.

"What have you found? Is that human laughter? I'm coming down there!"

"No, Kizzpon. Everything is all right. I was just surprised. Surprised by an old friend."

"A friend?"

"Oh yeah," I said, as I looked into the face plate of the Mark II engineering armor.

39

"Okay, I have power," I said to myself as the Heads Up Display on the inside of the suit's helmet came to life. I'd sent Kizzpon back to the sled to hide the plasma cutter on its undercarriage while I played with my new toy.

There were two Mark IIs, and I'd really had to squeeze to get between them and the wall they were against. I'd just managed to slip into the first one I'd found.

The heavily armored suit, intended for highly dangerous EVA environments, gave green lights across all its diagnostic displays, and I decided to see if it was still mobile. These suits were incredibly "tanky," but they'd been captured by an alien race. Who knows how the Kalikak might've damaged them just fiddling around.

To enable the main functionality of the suit, I just had to enter my access code, which was my TEF serial number. I punched it in; 5487117, and hit enter. Unfortunately, it wasn't going to be that easy.

The HUD lit up and told me; *AuthCode: Voss, Tanner, Cadet. Stationed TEF Academy. Not authorized personal. Prerequisites not in place. Access Denied.*

"What? I am not at..." Then it hit me. My last minute early transfer to *Seeker* and my promotion to Acting Ensign had never been logged into its software. To the armor, I was just some punk third-year academy student trying to take a joyride.

I said some very unprofessional words before finally getting myself together and actually using my brain. This was easily fixable.

"Tanner Voss to Remora Five. Dad? Do you read?"

"Five by five, son. How can I assist."

"I've found a pair of *Wanderer*'s Mark II engineering armor suits in a storage room. Unfortunately, I can't access them, since I'm still a third-year student back at the academy."

You wouldn't think AIs could laugh, but I'd found my digital parents actually both had a sharp sense of humor. Once Evan had stopped chuckling, he said, "Honestly Tanner, that's an unforgivable lapse. That suit should know that you're a fourth-year student at the academy."

"Oh, funny Dad. Really. You should take that on the road. Could you please work some of that voodoo that you do and give me access to this contraption?"

"Sorry Tanner, you should be golden on both suits now. I've updated your resumé from *Seeker*'s records, courtesy of our friend Organizer of Armadas."

"Thanks, Dad. Tanner out."

I accessed the main start-up sequence, and the huge armored suit hummed to life. I hadn't been that worried, these things were designed to be tough, as well as able to function independently for a long time.

I flicked on the flood lights that were resident on the helmet and chest and for the first time saw the entire room clearly.

"I wonder," I said to myself, "If they had these suits, is there a possibility they could've brought a Godzilla?" The heavily armored security suits straddled the line between armor and mech. If there was one of them here...

Of course, there wasn't. I almost kicked myself for forgetting that every one of *Wanderer*'s Godzilla armored suits had been accounted for, with dead SecOps people in them. They'd all died defending the ship and their suits had died with them.

I took a very slow, tentative step in my armor, putting my foot on the deck carefully. Inside a ship, these large engineering suits were moved on A-grav carts to prevent wear and tear on the ship's decks and hallways. I didn't want to wake every Kalikak on the station with a big set of 'thoom' sounds.

"Friend Tanner, I am back and...." Kizzpon's words trailed off, seeing the armored giant in front of him. "What is *that*!?"

"Friend Kizzpon," I said. "This is the answer to the guards on this station."

———

"Two suits, you say?"

"Yes, Lieutenant Kuff," Kizzpon told him. We were reporting to Kuff, Nutor, Gorman and Targus in The Corner. Behind us, on the main floor, the *Wanderer* crew was trying to teach a popular human dance to the Wulkin. The Grilzik and Yakar were spectating, as were a few of the *Wanderer*'s non-human crew members.

"Both Mark IIs are functional, sir," I said. "I tested each one. Evan provided me with access, as my own credentials still read "cadet" in its database. Not that I was miffed by that or anything."

"Yes, I can see that," Kuff said, a slight smile on his face. "When we take this habitat, which we're going to need to do to get to our escape ship, having those suits will really level the playing field against our guards."

"These armored suits are that good?" Gorman said. "Our captors may be short of stature, but they are nonetheless quite strong. As short as they are, no Wulkin could stand against a Kalikak warrior in a one-on-one confrontation without some efficient weaponry."

"Nugh. I don't know if these armors are even needed," Targus said. "We Yakar have been stealing bulkhead plating from sections of the station for our home-made shields. If we get close to these guards, their time will end quickly."

"Sir, if I may," Michael Chen had sat in as our security consultant, "Why not use all our assets. The Mark IIs will stand up to some pretty rough treatment, they even have light shielding. Rather than risk the Yakar getting shot, let's use the armor to get their attention, then have the Yakar hit them from behind while they're looking at us."

"I like this," Nutor said, shaking his eight legs. "Anything that kills Kalikak without killing us is a proper strategy to my thinking."

"As soon as we have the green light from Dora," Kuff said, "and by extension Captain Yamashita, we move. Gorman and I have an outline of our final plan..."

———

Of course, the green light came when our two shifts were in the wrong position, outlining the problem with our plan. Everyone had a job to do when the plan would be initiated, but we'd forgotten that we needed each job to have under-studies.

"Dora to TEF officers. I have returned and Captain Yamashita has put things in place to aid in your escape. I would suggest that your plan be implemented as soon as humanly possible."

The Kalikak around us went about their business, having

no idea that rebellion was being instigated. The Remoras had their comms completely blocked from any transmission we might send or receive.

"Dora, this is Kuff. We can't go until the shifts have changed and my team is back at the habitat. Seventy percent of the Yakar are here with us, and we need them to take down the Kalikak. We can't do anything until the shifts switch again."

"That is worrisome, Lieutenant. The Kalikak are, as we speak, finalizing the attachment of the last thruster assembly on the battleship. It is conceivable that they will do a ship-moving test in a fairly short time. There are too many variables to know exactly when, but if they do so, I would expect that they would remove all of the workers and bots for safety's sake."

"Any normal overseers would indeed do that," Ensign Thorsen piped in, "but the worker safety is really far down on the K's priority list."

"But sir," I said. "If we could convince them to take us off and back at the hab during the test, half our logistics problems would be solved."

"Ah, dear sweet naive Tanner," my sister's condescending voice came over the comm. "The Kalikak not only won't listen, but if you get too insistent, there's a chance they'll give you the fastball special one-way trip to the Andromeda galaxy. Mom? There's only two hours until shift change. Do you think you can infiltrate their computers? Maybe put a monkey wrench in their plans?"

"Perhaps. We have access to the Command Center and the escape vessel you've renamed *Freedom* because Lieutenant Truval provided us with backdoors into their systems. If I am detected, though, it could alert the Kalikak to the effect that we are in the area. I will probe the battleship's network for openings, but we were unable to break their encryption before without inside help."

"Perhaps, another way is possible," Lieutenant Truval's high-pitched voice warbled over my sub-dermal. "Dora, you have control of the *Wanderer*'s bots, do you not?"

"I do, but there are only six of them. The rest were left on *Wanderer* or destroyed. Using them to attack the thrusters would probably be futile."

"Too overt, that is," Truval replied. "You are thinking of digital incursion, but perhaps simply severing power feeds may be the path forward. I believe from what you have told me, these Kalikak tell the bots what to do, then ignore them. This could be a way to damage thruster control without showing the hand of poker."

"I like it," Dora said. "But eventually the sabotage will be found..."

"By that time," Kuff said, "we'll be implementing our escape, and a couple of cut power feeds will be the least of their worries."

40

Kuff had informed everyone of the plan via comms. Every TEF crew person (except Boffin), every Wulkin, Grilzik, and Yakar (even the young ones) knew what was going down.

As soon as our shift returned to the hab and our two standard guards had once again went back to whatever it was that they did while not bullying us, project *Escape* began. Everyone going off shift went to the recharge station to refill their EVA suit oxygen, and Kelley DeCosta was first in line.

Since Michael Chen and I were going to be in the Mark IIs, Kelley, a much better pilot that I, would be on sled-stealing duty. It was now her job to retrieve Valiel's shift aboard *Behemoth* and bring them to *Freedom*, all without being seen by any of the other ships in the area. Hopefully, the crews of any nearby ships were as sloppy as our guards.

Speaking of guards, Valiel's group also had guards, and quite a few more than we had on the hab. It would've been a real problem if the Remoras had been unarmed, but they were not. They were well-armed. Each of the 2.0 Remoras were equipped with a high-powered (for a probe shell) laser. The weapons were actually for cutting, but combined with super capable alien AIs, they also worked well as sniping weapons.

In other words, shift two had air support. Or I guess that would be space support.

When everyone had racked their suits, and began what looked like normal activity in the habitat, Kelley's suit, which had been smuggled to The Corner on the belly of a Grilzik named Zilzon, was smuggled up into the ducts. Ten minutes later, Kelley herself was covertly lifted into the same ducts. Kizzpon would be her guide to the sled. Twenty minutes after that, Chen and I were being hauled up to the Grilzik platforms, and from there into the same ducts.

By this time, we'd worn a trail in the dust, and I had marked every room we needed, including the warehouse room.

"Here we are, Michael," I said, looking though the loose grate to make sure the place was deserted. "The Mark IIs are right down there. A little dusty, but working just fine."

"Well, then, let's get to it. We're working on a tight time schedule here."

We dropped down into the room and were sealing up the two suits in just a few moments. As I heard the wheeze of the seal engaging, I activated my Mark II and for a moment had a flashback to Derilon. I'd spent a good portion of my time there in a Mark II, and had needed to use it in combat against an aquatic race of jerk-holes called the Ravrath. The engineering armor wasn't intended for fighting, but it sure rose to the occasion when needed.

"Chen for Kuff," I heard over the suit comms, which were pre-attuned for each other. "Add in Tanner Voss." I was now hearing him in stereo, through the suit and my sub-dermal.

"I read you, Corporal. Status?" Kuff's voice was very quiet, and I guessed that he was outside of the protection The Corner provided.

"Both Mark IIs spun up, sir. We are going to do our best to get to the door of this room quietly. I've taken a good look at its locking mechanism, and I'm very sure that our suits will make short work of it. As far as I'm concerned, we are green to go."

"Outstanding work, gentlemen. We go in thirty. People are casually drifting to the suit racks and are suiting up. The small Yakar are already suited, but still hiding in their shelters. Guys? If you hear an alarm go off, forget stealth and come in like the hammer of God. Understand?"

"Solid copy. Chen out."

We began our move to the door, taking great care to make as little noise as possible in the heavy armored suits. Just watching Chen, it was all I could do to keep from laughing. Imagine a huge armored knight tippy-toeing to get around and you'd be pretty close to the picture I was seeing.

When we reached the door, Chen reached out to grab the locking mechanism, but I stopped him. "Hold up, Michael."

"What? You think you can access the mechanism?"

"Yes. And with a little Remora support..."

"Organizer of Armadas on station," Came from my subdermal.

"Hi Organizer," I said as I extended a multi-function access cable from the back of my gauntlet. The end of the cable scanned the alien access port and reconfigured itself to fit. "I am accessing a door lock with the cabling from my Mark II engineering suit. Can you access it through my onboard computer and open the door? I'm afraid breaking the lock might be too noisy."

"Affirmative, Tanner Voss, Ensi.... Tanner. It is the pie of easiness."

"Easy as pie?"

"Yes. That's it. As easy as a large round pastry. I must confess though, in truth I do not understand the reference."

"Remind me when I'm back on *Seeker* and I'll try to explain. For now...?"

"For now, the locking mechanism is circumvented." I heard (though my exterior mic) a distinct beep, a click and the door began to open. And my danger sense went off big time.

An armed Kalikak guard stared at us in astonishment on the other side.

I don't know if he was guarding the store room or if he'd just heard the beep and investigated. It didn't matter. What mattered was the heavy "blaster" that he was raising even as we all recovered from the surprise.

Fortunately, Chen's SecOps-trained reflexes were faster than the guard's and the heavy gauntleted fist of his Mark II smashed into the Kalikak's grafitti'd faceplate. The armored helmet of our enemy was not up to the task of protecting its owner from the force of a pile driver, and teal-colored blood spewed from his mask as he flew across the corridor and slammed into the opposite wall.

"You think he's gonna get up from that?" Chen said, picking up and checking the blaster.

"Not ever," I replied. "Not unless it's in a bag. Hopefully no one heard that. These metal walls carry sound all too well. Great reflexes, by the way."

"Thanks." Chen checked the rifle he'd taken, and with the precision of a consummate professional, had it ready to fire before I'd have even known where the safety (if there was one) would be located.

We waited to see if any alarm sounded, and when none did, I called Organizer of Armadas. "Organizer, do you detect anything to indicate that the Kalikak have detected us?"

"Negative, Tanner. No alarms or attempted communication from the station you are on. Do you and Corporal Chen require a map to get back to your sleeping area?"

"That would be great, Organizer," Chen said. "On that map, can you indicate life forms, and designate species for us?"

"Easily. I can also designate TEF personnel by name if you like."

"Perfect. Please do so."

On my HUD, a corner of the view now had a transparent map with a green line for the best path forward. Several dots then appeared. In our shelter area, it was filled with green and blue dots. TEF crew persons were green, our allies blue. And in several areas in the rest of the station, their brightness based on what deck they were on, were red dots. Our enemies.

And there were about three times as many as we'd planned for.

"How many?"

"Lieutenant, according to the maps on our HUDs," Chen told Kuff, "We've got nineteen living Kalikak on this station. Almost all are in a central area, except for five which are patrolling the corridors."

"Corporal, we are go in less than fifteen minutes. That many Kalikak... that's a lot of firepower for our Yakar allies to charge at. We're going to take heavy casualties, if we can fight to the sled at all."

"Yes, sir. We need a plan."

"Christ, Chen. I was a navigation officer. I've had the basic academy courses on guerrilla warfare, but..."

"Sir? This is Voss. I have an idea," I don't know how the idea jumped into my head, but it seemed like a personal battle-muse had suddenly slipped it into my brain.

"Ensign, at this point, any idea would be welcome," Kuff said. "Hit me with it."

"Sir, we need a big distraction. Or more accurately, two big distractions. I believe that Chen and I can pull the Kalikak away from the landing bay. We're having to be very careful to move quietly, and I'm thinking, what if we went to the abandoned landing bay... and stopped being quiet."

"Hell yeah," Chen said. "Sir, we can make some serious ruckus in theses suits."

"I like where this is going, except for one thing," Kuff said. "Two of my people facing a horde of Kalikak and effectively sacrificing themselves."

"Needs of the many," Chen said.

"Actually, sir. Sacrificing ourselves wasn't part of the plan. Our Mark IIs are built for space. All we need to do is throw ourselves out through the force field, angling away from the door so we can't be shot in the back as we're going through space. We've seen that the Kalikak armor acts as an EVA suit, but they have to put on their combo oxygen/thruster packs to be space-worthy. That takes them a few minutes to get in order."

"And you're betting that they won't take the time to put their oxygen/thruster packs on in a station emergency. That's some serious best case scenario thinking there, Ensign."

"I believe that I have an idea," A new voice came over our comm. "Pardon me for monitoring your comms, but under the circumstances..."

"Dora? We'll be glad for *any* extra help," Kuff said.

"Then, Sir, I believe this is what we should do..."

———

Chen and I were getting near the secondary landing bay when we met the second guard. This one had even slower reactions than the one Chen had taken out earlier. This Kalikak died slightly slower also. Having an engineering suit's plasma cutter jammed through your faceplate, though quickly fatal, probably gave the guard a few seconds to regret his life choices.

"Damn, Tanner," Chen said. "Remind me never to piss you off when you're in one of these suits."

"Yeah. That was pretty gruesome, sorry. I'm just carrying a lot of pent-up anger at these freaks."

"Oh, that was not in any way criticism, my friend. I wish I was more familiar with these engineering suits, or I might've used that plasma thingie myself. Anyway, now we both have a blaster."

We weren't even trying to be quiet at this point. In fact, we were trying to be as loud as we could. Before we even reached the secondary bay, a loud blaring alarm began sounding thought the dusty corridors.

As we went through the main bay hatch, Chen turned and looked at the door mechanism.

"Should we break this and make them cut their way in? It'd take them extra time to get in, keep them away from everyone else."

"No," I said. "Best if we get them all in here. Hopefully the door will shut behind them. With the state this habitat is in, we can't be sure of the state of the emergency bulkheads. We might prematurely decompress the entire station."

"If all our people are suited up, that might not be such a bad thing... Oh wait. The front-line Yakar won't have their suits on if they have to fight. Can't afford a ruined EVA suit."

"That's right. I think our time would be better suited to making a barricade in the bay to hide in. I don't know how many hits our armor can take, shielding or no. Considering the way they melted *Wanderer*'s Godzilla suits, I don't really want to find out."

We began hauling every loose piece of machinery to a spot near the flickering environmental field enclosing the bay. With the heavy suits, we were able to haul crates, machinery (most of which I didn't recognize), and assorted flotsam to make a wall to hide behind.

Looking at my HUD, I saw that the Kalikak were spread out across the corridors and decks in what could only be a search pattern. It was time to concentrate them in one place.

"Michael, I think it's time to make some noise. Tanner Voss to Ensign DeCosta. Kelley? You ready to roll?"

"Yes. I've got the sled loose and I've been sending it though some gentle maneuvers near the station to get the feel of it. I'm as ready as I'm going to get."

"Okay, then. I suggest you edge your way around the station toward the *Behemoth* side. Or at least get away from this bay. Things are about to get very hot in here."

"Affirmative. Moving away. Tanner, Michael, may God go with you. May we all raise a glass back on *Seeker*."

"We'll see you there, Lieutenant," Chen said. "Tanner, let's get this show on the road. Lieutenant Kuff? We're in position, sir. Ready to attract some attention."

"All right, Corporal. All hands. We are green. You all know what to do. Let's give 'em hell."

42

A space station is one huge interconnected mass of metal parts and conduits. Metal conducts sound very well inside the station, which was why we had to be so careful in the air ducts.

If I'd still had my personal padd, I'd have put my favorite playlist through the exterior suit speakers, but as it was, Chen and I had to do things the old-fashioned way.

Like a pair of half-ton chimpanzees.

We began by pounding on the walls of the bay, and I had to mute the sound my exterior microphones were picking up, or risk damaging my ear drums. Stomping on the deck, we left several dents that weren't going to buff out. One of our pieces of junk looked like the frame of a small space sled, and we supplemented our noise-making by throwing the bent frame around the bay.

"I think we have their attention," Chen said. Glancing at my HUD, I saw almost all of the red dots were now on the same deck (ours) and were converging on our position. "Maybe we better get behind the barricade."

His words were punctuated by a wildly fired plasma bolt

going right between us and out through the forcefield into space. We scrambled to our fall-back position.

"Chen for Kuff, we have engaged the enemy. Our HUDs indicate that three Kalikak are still in your area, and are moving toward you on the main corridor. Good luck, sir."

"You too, Corporal. We are making our move. Kuff out."

Chen had shown me how the Kalikak rifles worked, but as I started to rise to return fire, Chen stopped me.

"No, Ensign. Let them all get in the bay first. I want them confident we're unarmed."

Blasts began slamming into our barricade, and I got a first-hand look at the power of the Kalikak weapons. Our heavy barricade was jumping and shifting with each hit.

"Definitely want to take one of these weapons back to *Seeker,*" Chen commented. "Pretty sure none of our SecOps weapons pack this much of a punch, not even with the Blah-Veht upgrades."

"They're great if you want to decompress the ship," I noted. "The Kaliakak've punched a couple holes in the hull of this station already. The bay's starting to decompress. And this barricade we're behind is starting to glow. That can't be a good sign."

"It's a good sign that we need to get the flip outta here," Chen replied. "On my signal, we dash for the force field. Once we're through, hit your thruster pack hard to port, that's the closest edge of the opening. We want to get out of the line of fire as quick as we can."

"Roger that. Mom? Do you copy?"

"I'm here and ready, Tanner."

"We are ready to evacuate. As soon as we're clear..."

"I know what to do. You worry about not getting shot, young man."

"Tanner!" Chen yelled. "Go! Go! Go!"

He didn't have to tell me twice. I was up from my

kneeling position and sprinting for the edge of the station, doing my best to keep the barricade between myself and our enemies. Bolts of energy followed alongside me, but none actually hit me.

I barely noticed the resistance of the force field as I went through it, and seconds out from the station, I hit the Mark II's built-in thrusters to port. A few seconds later, I was out of the line of fire. Turning, I saw Chen following, but a bolt hit him in the back, sending he and his suit flipping end over end for deep space.

"Michael! Do you read me?"

His static-laden voice replied. "Wow! That was a kick in the ass! Obliterated my shielding and I think it damaged my thruster pack. Other suit systems are operational, but I'm having trouble slowing my spin."

"You're clear of the entrance," I said. "I see them coming up to the force field, Mom. If you're gonna do something..."

"Done," was all she said.

The blue force field in between us and our captors, the field that was doing its best to hold the oxygen in the bay, simply blinked out. Pressurized oxygen did what it does when introduced to a vacuum. It burst from the bay into space in explosive decompression, taking the Kalikak out into the universe in a dusty cloud.

My theory about our enemies not wanting to walk around inside with oxygen and thrusters on their back the whole time proved to be true. Almost the entire complement of K went tumbling off into space, most of them losing their holds on their weapons as their suits sealed in the small amount of oxygen within them. Panic was the order of the day as the brutes tried to stop their tumbling and find some way back to safety.

In every group though, there is always an over-achiever. One of the Kalikak had been wandering around inside with his full load-out of gear, including a thruster pack. He had the chance to at least save some of his nearby slowly-asphyxiating comrades. In typical Kalikak fashion, he didn't bother.

Instead, it seemed he was only interested in making his prey pay.

I realized I was in trouble when I saw the flare from his thrusters as he came around and toward me in hot pursuit. He was farther out from the station, having been forcefully ejected by the decompression. I went to full burn back toward the now decompressed bay. He took a shot at me but trying to hit a target while in EVA under full thrust was beyond his capabilities.

I realized I was panicking, and did my best to calm my mind. Once my mind was clear, I did what I did best. I raised my rifle almost randomly, and when the feeling was there, I fired. He took the high-powered bolt right through his unshielded faceplate.

I spun myself end-to-end and touched down on the side of the station. His corpse bulls-eyed right into the open bay, and slammed to the deck when he hit the still-functioning artificial gravity.

"Mom? Are you there?"

"Affirmative, Tanner. I've been occupied with retrieval of Corporal Chen. I monitored your situation."

"How is he?"

"S'all good here, kiddo," Chen's said, his comm still having static issues. "Thrusters need work, but I'm whole, hale and hearty. I think it's time we join the others."

———

Dora towed the two of us around to the main bay of the station and dropped us off. "Tanner, Michael, when the sled is ready to leave, I will tow you both to the escape ship. I can get you there shortly before everyone else, and we can work together to over-ride the entrance hatch."

"Roger that, Dora," Chen said. "Right now, I want to see if our comrades need any help with the remaining Kalikak."

We moved through the forcefield and lumbered into the gravity of the main bay. Everyone was clambering on to the sled and it looked as if the remaining Kalikak hadn't been a problem. That's what I thought until I saw a suited figure being carried to the sled. Closer inspection showed a burned hole through their mid-section.

"Who's down," Chen demanded. "How many casualties. Someone report!"

"Corporal, It... it was Kuff," Rona Thorsen said, her voice sounding broken."

"Has anyone notified the next in command?"

"N-no. I don't think so. It was so unexpected... Targus has taken charge."

"The Kalikak are neutralized, Corporal," A Yakar approached, and I saw it was Targus. "I deeply regret the loss of Kuff, he was a good sentient."

"Are you taking Command, sir?" I asked. Targus looked over at Gorman and Nutor, both signaled assent in their way.

"I am. Ensign Thorsen, let's get everyone on the sled. We cannot delay and risk being discovered. We need to get to the *Freedom* with all possible haste."

"Chen to Valiel Voss," Chen said. "Do you read, Lieutenant?"

"Voss here. We can see DeCosta approaching with the sled."

"Ma'am. There's been a casualty here. Lieutenant Kuff is dead. Valiel, you have to take command of all TEF personnel."

There was silence for a moment. "I... well... shit."

"Val, you've got to do this," I said. "What's the situation with Lieutenant Commander Boffin?"

"She's with us, and coming along, but she's in no condition to command anyone. She's damn near had a full breakdown, so I guess it's me. Status, Ensign Voss?"

There was no bother and sister now. Only two officers desperately invested in saving their crew members.

"Val, We're about five minutes from having everyone loaded. Five minutes after that, we'll be on our way. Targus has taken command in Kuff's absence. He's got everyone organized over here."

"Tanner and I, in our Mark II suits, are about to ferry to *Freedom* with Dora," Chen reported. "We'll have an ingress point ready by the time everyone gets to the ship."

"All right. I need to get everyone here sorted. The sled's docked, and all our nearby guards are neutralized. See you there."

Chen and I turned back toward the atmosphere field. As we left, I turned and took a last look at Kuff as they attached his body to the sled. He'd taken on caring for all these people without hesitation and without him this whole plan might've never come to pass.

Dead or not, he was escaping with us.

43

We sailed the space ways.

Michael and I clung one of Dora's manipulator arms, both of us facing so that we could see the ship that, hopefully, would take us out of here.

"To Tanner Voss, I must speak," A voice came over my sub-dermal.

"Lieutenant Truval? This is Voss, sir."

"Greetings young one. AI Evan has kept me apprised of this situation, and am ready to assist. What is your status?"

"Corporal Chen and I are being ferried to the ship you're on by Dora," I told him. "We plan on entering through a hatch near the midsection, but two sleds full of our comrades will be not far behind us."

I noticed a change in my HUD, and saw that the schematic of the station had been replaced by a tiny wire-frame of the ship we were approaching. A flashing dot appeared near the center of the ship, and I realized it was over a hatch.

"See you the best spot to enter, Ensign?" Truval said. "I

will force the airlock open, while forcing the inner door to also stay open. There are Kalikak sitting in a mess room very near the airlock. I hope to catch them unaware."

"That would be very helpful, sir. Chen and I are going in to distract any defenders. It'll take some time to get all of our people through that hatch."

"I have a plan there, as well, Ensign." A purple rectangle appeared on the ship schematic. "This is a cargo bay. When you are on board, I will open the bay doors and drop the force field. While I cannot decompress the entire ship, I can empty certain sections. I am hoping to catch several of the enemy off guard and reduce the number you have to contend with."

"I'll be happy for any help we can get. Until we can get the Yakar shock troops aboard, it's just going to be Chen and I. Not really liking that part of the plan."

"Understood. May the universe guide you, Tanner. Truval out."

"Michael, you catch all that?" I asked.

"Five by five. Hey, once we get on board, let me take the lead. No offense, but I'm a little better trained for this situation. Master Chief Kurakin made sure her people were well-trained in ship boarding."

"You ever wonder if maybe she was a pirate in a former life?"

"If so," Chen replied, "My money is on a viking raider."

"That scans. I think if..."

"Gentlemen," Dora interrupted, "we are close enough, and your two suits present a challenge for me. Too much inertia. Tanner, since you have functioning thrusters, please jump and blast. Michael, I'll do my best to slow you down, but you'll also need to jump just before we reach the hull. I can't have my own hull slam against that ship."

"Understood," Chen said. "Ready for your signal to jump, Dora." As he said it, I kicked free of the Remora hull and flipped around to orient my feet toward *Freedom*. I activated my thrusters just enough to begin slowing my approach, and I saw Michael carry on toward the ship. I could make out a vague outline of my mom's vessel as she ferried him closer to the enemy's hull.

Moments later, I saw him kick loose, and lost visual on Dora's Remora immediately. Chen pivoted with the grace of a true space professional and hit the ship feet first. While I couldn't hear anything in the vacuum, I was sure from the slight denting of the hull that everyone onboard knew something had hit their vessel.

A few seconds later, I was making my much softer thruster-assisted landing.

"Chen to Truval, we are in position."

There was no reply, but a moment later, the indicator light above the hatch we'd landed next to switched from blue to purple. Shortly thereafter, the hatch flew open. Instead of the normal semi-slow opening I'd seen on all the hatches around the area, this one snapped open so fast that I could've lost a finger if I'd been touching it. Atmosphere exploded out of the doorway so fast that it looked like a thruster jet. Chairs, food trays, trash and guns flew out, spinning off into the abyss and were followed by one, two, three Kalikak. None of them had on thruster/oxygen packs. The last one didn't even have his helmet on.

He was the only one who managed to slow the inevitable. For a few moments, he caught the edge of the hatch and I saw the panic on his flattened brute face. His tiny black marble eyes began to bulge as he clawed at the door, trying to get a grip with both hands. The terror on his face was clear, and part of me wanted to help him...

But this was war.

In a few minutes, his grip slackened and the lessening rush of atmosphere nonetheless carried his limp body away into the depths. I felt sick to my stomach.

"Pull it together, Voss," Chen's voice came over subdermal. The friendly guy that had become my friend was gone. In his place was a no-nonsense, hard-as-nails warrior. "Guns ready, let's go."

We slipped into the hatch, one after the other, and came into a standard airlock, it's only oddity being that the inner door hadn't automatically locked down. We carefully emerged into the ship proper and encountered our first actual resistance. A fourth Kalikak had managed to get to his oxygen pack and was trying to communicate with his bridge through a wall comm.

Seeing us, instead of grabbing for his sidearm, he dove at us. He could've been screaming a battle roar or reciting Kalikak poetry, but in the vacuum we couldn't hear which. Chen shot him in mid-leap, sending his burning corpse slamming into a bulkhead.

"Chen for Truval. Sir? We're in and have momentarily neutralized resistance in this area. Ready for part two."

"Opening cargo bay doors," Truval replied. "Dora? Evan? Please guide sleds of our comrades into the bay once decompression is complete."

"C'mon, Tanner," Chen said. "We need to work our way aft. Schematic says engineering is back that way, and we need to control that area."

Back on *Seeker*, Master Chief Kurakin had been in charge of taking a still wet-behind-the-ears cadet and turning him into a useful officer. Aside from making sure I passed all my academy graduation exams, for physical training, she made me train with her security team.

This often included battle exercises. I was by no means as

skilled as my SecOps compatriots, but I knew the basics. Chen and I emerged into a corridor just as the gravity plating turned off. Our Mark IIs automatically magnetized to the deck as we began to leap-frog each other from position to position down the hallway. Chen moved up, found cover and then signaled me to move up and pass him until I found cover. Then he passed me, and so on.

We were moving as quietly as our armor and lack of atmospheric sound would allow. It was slow going. Our magnetized boots didn't really allow for quick movement.

We were nearing engineering, and encountered only one Kalikak on the way. This one was floating in corridor helmetless, eyes bulged out and his grayish skin looking even grayer from asphyxiation. Chen pushed him out of the way.

At the main entrance to Engineering, I put my hand up to stop Chen from moving forward.

"What's up, Ensign?"

"My danger sense is tingling. Definitely some live ones ahead, and they're on high alert. How're we gonna dig these ticks out without damaging the ship?"

"Chen for Truval. Sir? How's the boarding going?"

"Our peoples are on board. When the ship decompressed, most of the crew between the bay and the bridge without supplemental oxygen were caught and are... dead. Our people are now trying to take the bridge, which is sealed."

"Understood. Lieutenant, how absolute is your control over the gravity plating?"

"It is complete. I can override at will," Truval answered. "How can I assist?"

"Can you activate the gravity plating in Engineering only? Then, can you reverse it?"

"Ah. Yes. A good plan indeed. Prepare. I cannot guarantee the control I have regarding zone size."

"Lock down, Tanner. We're good, sir. Proceed at your discretion."

I felt myself sink down into my suit as gravity returned to our section, and a moment later, my head bumped the top of my helmet as the gravity abruptly reversed itself.

The gravity reversed again, and felt as if it was a couple more gravities more than Earth standard. From the room ahead, I felt, rather than heard, heavy impacts through the plating of the deck. This alteration of gravity direction happened three more times, and I could feel the threat level decrease with each switch.

"That's good, Michael," I said. "The threat level has dropped dramatically."

"Lieutenant Truval," Chen said. "Tanner says that's all we need. Normal gravity, if you please."

"Affirmative, Corporal Chen."

We peeked around the hatchway and looked in at a chaotic scene. The consoles for the controlling the ship's functions seemed to all be intact, but loose equipment was strewn everywhere.

As were three Kalikak. One had an obviously broken neck, and the other two were unmoving. One of these had a pool of teal-colored blood leaking from his helmet. The other twitched but didn't move.

"We've got a live one. I'll keep an eye on him, while you see if you can make heads or tails of this equipment."

"Lieutenant Voss for Corporal Chen," Valiel's voice came from our suit speakers. "SitRep?"

'We've taken engineering, Lieutenant. One surviving Kalikak who's in poor shape. If you have any engineering experts from any of our species, the ensign can use all the help he can get. Do we control the ship?"

"Affirmative. One survivor up here also. The Captain, a Kalikak female. Fortunately, this ship has a prisoner section.

Targus says that a lot of this ship's systems are based on Yakar designs. He's sending some of his people to take over down there. They'll also move that prisoner to the cells. When they get there, I want you both on the bridge."

"Understood. We'll see you there."

44

We arrived at the bridge expecting pandemonium.

Much to our surprise, everyone was at a station, and Valiel sat calmly in the short Captain's chair. Much of the equipment was unfamiliar, but the practice of having the command seat dead center in the bridge seemed to translate across species.

There were also several blood smears of a distinctly purple-teal-ish color. The same color we'd seen leaking out of the Kalikak's helmet in engineering.

"Tanner, you and I are on guns," Valiel said as we entered. "Chen, you're on security for this room. Captain Targus, are you ready to fire up the engines, sir?"

"We are, however, flying this strange vessel is going to take all my concentration. I must request that you take command, Lieutenant." Targus sitting at one of the forward consoles gestured at the command chair. "I insist."

Val took a moment to take in the gravity of the situation, and I couldn't pass up the chance to comment. "First command, sis. Let's hope it's not a short one." She grimaced and then took charge.

"Targus, let's get this ship moving. Maximum light speed plus as quickly as we can accelerate. Mother? We're in, we're powering up, we could sure use that distraction you kept alluding to."

"Understood," Dora replied. You'll know exactly when to go, I assure you. Just watch out your forward port."

"Engines are ready," Targus said. "We can go on command and... what is that!?"

Everyone on the bridge saw the flash of light ten degrees off our port bow. All the TEF personnel knew exactly what had just happened.

The *E.S.S. Seeker* had just jumped in, and the Kalikak were caught flat-footed.

Seeker began firing on ships that had their shields down, and I saw the tell-tale flash of the Sallan-designed FTL missiles launching. There was no discernible time between the flash and a Kalikak cruiser exploding at its mid-section and breaking in half.

"Targus! Maximum speed!" Valiel shouted.

Freedom leapt forward, aiming between two of the enemy cruisers. My heart went to my throat as we cleared one by less than a hundred yards. I looked down at the unfamiliar weapon console, for a moment feeling stymied. Then, almost of its own accord, my hand reached down and I was aiming the Kalikak ship's lasers. My talent could only do so much with the unfamiliar equipment, and instead of pin-point striking, we raked the enemy vessel as we went past. Damage was done, but it was still a threat.

I could see that if *Seeker* didn't jump out soon, there was going to be trouble. The Kalikak may have been surprised, but they were hardened warriors, and had bounced back fast. Shields were coming up, which meant that weapons were charging.

A moment later, Captain Yamashita jumped out. *Freedom*

was still in the process of reaching light speed. We were on our own. Or so I thought.

We'd cleared the area perimeter when the Kalikak command station began firing on the ships surrounding it and two of their vessels were heavily damaged. That was the last I saw before spatial dilation prevented further viewing. A few seconds later, we were moving faster than light, and continuing to accelerate.

"Thanks for the assist, Remoras," Val said.

One of the Yakar, at what could only be the sensor station, began calling out what was going on behind us. "They're in disarray! I think we might get away clean... wait... no.. I misspoke. Three light cruisers and one heavy cruiser are in pursuit." The turtle-like alien turned toward Valiel. "I think we can keep ahead of the light cruisers, but the heavy will eventually catch *our* light cruiser."

"Captain," another Yakar said, "In coming message from... *E.S.S. Seeker?*"

"That's the ship that helped us, Krovin," Val replied. "Message?"

"We've been sent coordinates. They request that we move to them so that they can help us."

"That'll be a hellacious fight," Chen said, "even for *Seeker*'s double shields."

"I hope Captain Yamashita isn't biting off more than she can chew," I said.

"Our captain knows what she's doing," Emily said from behind my chair. "Have faith, Tanner."

"Helm, make for the attached coordinates," Valiel said. "And if you have specific deities, I suggest you pray to them. This is gonna be close."

45

We were all sweating by the time we reached the coordinates. The heavy cruiser in pursuit had outstripped its lighter companions, and was only a few minutes behind us. Needless to say, the next communication we received was a surprise.

"Vessel *Freedom*, go sub-light at these coordinates. Make sure your shields and weapons are ready."

"I'm not reading anything at those coordinates, Captain," the sensor officer reported. "There's nothing there. The enemy battle cruiser will be on us in moments if we go sub-light."

"Have faith," Valiel said, echoing what Emily had said to me a short time earlier. "Targus, prepare to decelerate on my mark. And... MARK!"

The darkness at the forward viewport was instantly replaced with a comparatively brighter star field and energy streamers flew ahead of us as we dropped back into normal space-time.

"Shields to maximum. Evasive maneuvers, now!" Val called out. "Tanner, they're probably going to come out right on top of us. See if you can hit them as they emerge."

Emerge the enemy did, and it was a big ship. Twice the length of our light cruiser, it carried at least fifty-percent more firepower. I was hitting them with missiles and laser bolts before the flare of their emergence had even dissipated.

They began to return the favor almost immediately.

Freedom shook and people standing lost their ability to do so. Emily fell to the deck, and as much as I wanted to extend a helping hand, I had my hands very full.

Normally, my talent tells me where an opponent's weak spots are, but I was struggling to find one. We were seriously out-matched.

"Whatever *Seeker* has planned," Chen said, picking himself up off the deck, "I wish they'd do it soon! We can't take much of this!"

And Captain Yamashita granted his wish. *Seeker* appeared out of Nth space, unleashing three FTL missiles from less than half a mile distance. The yield on the Sallan missiles was exceptional, but the Kalikak ship had exceptionally strong shields. It also had a crap-ton of weapons, all of which now turned to Yamashita's ship.

On the screen above the weapon console, I could see *Seeker*'s shields literally glow from the hits she was taking. Our layered shielding was good, but it wasn't going to hold up to that much firepower for long.

Turned out, it didn't need to.

"Multiple vessels coming in at high light speed," the sensor officer said.

"Who is it?" Val yelled. Her answer came less than a moment later.

"Those are Yakar ships!," Targus said. "And Wulkin! Grilziks! Drovens! Kanthars! These are all confederation ships!"

"They'll be torn apart without shields," Krovin cried out, "Even that many can't fight a shielded Kalikak ship that big!"

Even as he spoke, the confederated ships emerged and engaged the enemy battle cruiser as *Seeker* jumped away. The Kalikak battle cruiser immediately swung its weapons toward the nearest emerging ship and opened fire. Fortunately, things didn't go the way Krovin had thought. The first ship took several hits, but didn't explode, catching the enemy fire on what was obviously strong shielding. The alien ship fired a huge amount of missiles, then veered off, making way for the ships behind it. These also fired barrages of missiles and veered away like old-time torpedo bombers.

"They've got shields! Our ships have shields!" Targus cried out. Valiel looked at me and raised an eyebrow. I simply nodded.

More ships were converging from different locations, and the battle cruiser could no longer concentrate firepower in one direction. Barrage after barrage of high-powered missiles slammed into its shields, while its firepower was diluted across several vectors.

"Enemy vessel is powering up its faster than light drive," Krovin said. "Their shields are buckling! They're taking damage."

The Kalikak ship began speeding up, running up to FTL speed, when *Seeker* appeared again, this time right behind them. They sent a a salvo of FTL missiles right up the K ship's "tail pipe" and their weakened shields did little to protect the enemy. I've mentioned the high yield of the Sallan weapons, and in this case, the aft quarter of the battle cruiser simply blew apart. The heavy Kalikak ship was done for, but several of the confederated ships continued to pound the remainder to wildly-spinning slag.

Payback is, indeed, a bitch.

"Captain, the enemy light cruisers have reversed course," the sensor officer told Val. "They're running. Incoming message from the Earther ship."

"Let's hear it."

Captain Yamashita's visage appeared on several monitors across the bridge. "This is Megumi Yamashita, Captain *E.S.S. Seeker*. We are very happy to see you, Captain...?"

"Lieutenant Valiel Voss, ma'am. Acting captain of the prize ship *Freedom*. I cannot even express how glad we are to see you. I have ex-prisoners and refugees aboard, and am awaiting your orders... Commodore."

At Val's name, Yamashita smiled. "I am very glad to meet you, Captain Voss. Your brother was very worried about you. Status?"

"Forty-six surviving crew from *Wanderer*, four, no.. make that five, from *Seeker*. Lieutenant Kuff was in charge, but was lost during our escape. Lieutenant Commander Boffin is aboard, but..."

"But?"

"The Commander has had mental health issues that precluded her from command. Our captivity was... hard on her. Thus, ma'am, I am in command." Val said. "We also have numerous, Wulkin, Grilzik and Yakar on board, including Yakar juveniles. Awaiting orders."

As they spoke, Lieutenant Truval emerged out of a ventilation hatch and ambled his exo-suit in my direction. He raised a clawed hand and I high-fived my superior.

"Well, Captain Voss," Yamashita said. "Here's what I want you to do. I need my five people back on *Seeker* ASAP, then the fleet and I are going to go pound that Kalikak shipyard into pieces. You, in the meantime, will take your captured ship to these coordinates. Evan will accompany you, broadcasting "friend" transmissions so you aren't shot to pieces at the space station I'm sending you to. At that station, you will transfer back to *E.S.S. Wanderer*, ceding command of *Freedom* to your confederation comrades. At that point, you will meet with Captain Moton for further instructions."

"Understood, Captain," Val replied. "We'll see you when you return. Good hunting."

46

The transfer to *Seeker* was quick. A shuttle flew over, landed in the same bay as the sleds, and in a few moments we were ready to go.

Val had accompanied the *Seeker* crew-people to the bay, and before we boarded, stopped me and gave me a hug.

"No getting killed," she said with mock sternness.

"Nope. Or God forbid, captured," I said. "Don't worry Val. We're going in there hot, and when we're done, there will be no *Behemoth*, and the Kalikak will be very sorry for their transgressions."

"This is the first time in over a century that I've had all my original family in one place," Val replied. "Well, except Krizon, and I'm not broken up about that. Just make sure you all come back."

"Scout's honor," I said, feeling awkward at the emotions pushing up from my chest. "See you back at *Wanderer*." We looked at each other a moment, unsure of what else to say, then Val simply turned and left for her bridge.

The flight to our ship was brief, and looking out a side port, I could see all the Confederation ships forming up on

Seeker. When we landed in the port-side bay, Master Chief Kurakin was waiting for us. When we stepped down the ramp, the look of concern on her face told us that we all probably looked almost as bad as the *Wanderer* crew did when we first picked them up from the gas giant.

"Missed a few meals, have we?" she asked. "Get settled in you lot, then get some food. You, Tanner, on the other hand need to shower, put on a new uniform, grab a snack, then get to the bridge as fast as you can. Captain Yamashita wants to hit the Kalikak as soon as we can. Can't have them preparing for us, can we?"

The water at the prison station had all been room temperature, in fact, often cold, so the hot shower I stepped into felt like heaven. It was brief, due to time constraints, but it underlined how good it was to be back home.

I arrived on the bridge ten minutes later, hair still wet and with a few crumbs from a ration pack on my lapel, but ready for action.

"Acting Ensign Voss, reporting for duty, Captain," I said, saluting the command chair.

"I am glad and relieved to have you all back, Ensign," The Captain replied. "Take your station, and we'll get this show on the road."

I sat at the tactical station, nodding to Lieutenant Forbes, and configured my console. I realized a moment later, that not only had Captain Yamashita been waiting for my appearance, but so had every ship in this makeshift fleet.

"Mr. Kolara, set course for the enemy stronghold," The captain said. She switched on the all decks intercom and continued; "All hands. Return to Condition One. We are about to jump into the heart of the enemy shipyard. We will be distracting the Kalikak while our allies sneak up them at maximum FTL. The enemy will be expecting us, though they haven't had much time to prepare. Nonetheless, this is going to be rough, people. Man your stations, stay frosty and we will prevail."

"Captain, the fleet is signaling ready," Lieutenant Sedgewick reported.

"Tell them to move to our objective at maximum speed, and to be ready for a hard fight." Yamashita replied. "Lieutenant Kolara, spin up the Jump Drive. Lieutenant Forbes, Ensign Voss, prepare to layer shields on emergence. And gentlemen? On emergence, weapons are free. Hit them hard in the most appropriate places."

"We're ready, Captain," Forbes said.

"Kolara, jump us."

47

The Kalikak hadn't had much time to prepare, and possibly hadn't expected our single vessel to return. The two light cruisers that had fled the battle hadn't made it home yet, but they'd definitely sent word ahead.

Even without much time to get ready, the enemy knew trouble was coming.

Fortunately for us, we had an idea of what to expect when we arrived. Organizer of Armadas had remained behind when we fled the shipyard, concealed in his Remora shell's stealth field. The distance that our escape ship, *Freedom*, had traveled before being intercepted was not far on a stellar scale. Organizer was able to keep *Seeker* updated on the Kalikak's activities almost in real time.

We emerged well away from the remaining heavy battle-cruiser, amid a tight formation trio of light cruisers and opened fire immediately. The advantage of *Seeker*'s jump drive was self evident. Ships approaching at FTL speeds, even the high speeds used by everyone else in this neighborhood, were still detectable. *Seeker* simply appeared amongst them with no warning whatsoever, and we capitalized on that with gusto.

"Targeting nearest cruiser," I called out as I used the new, focuser-enhanced "ruby" plasma cannons.

"I'm hitting them with our point defense lasers, too," Forbes called out. "We are damn close!"

"Kolara, prepare to jump out on my command," the captain said.

The nearest light cruiser did not take the criticism provided by our plasma cannons well. One beam was deflected on their shields but still managed to damage their outer hull, but its twin arrowed in and pierced the cruiser right where my talent directed it, into their main reactor. The containment breach was so fast that our captain barely had time to give the order to jump out before the enemy ship went nova.

We emerged less than two light hours away, and Organizer updated us on the fruits of our labors immediately.

"Captain," Sedgewick reported, "tactical update from Remora Three. Routing to science."

"Enemy light cruiser obliterated," Commander Torvald said. "The resulting explosion damaged both of the other Kalikak cruisers in its proximity. One is heavily damaged and likely out of the fight."

"Nice Three-fer, Tanner," Commander M'Buku said from the executive officer's station.

"Organizer reports that the Kalikak are putting distance between their ships," Torvald said. "Fast learners."

"Perhaps," Captain Yamashita replied. "But now they can't overlap their fields of fire as well. Torvald, send inquiry to Remora Three. Are we still able to co-opt the weaponry of the enemy command station?"

"Organizer replies that is unlikely. As you noted, the Kalikak are fast learners, Captain. Evidently, they've already found and plugged the holes in that system. However, the station has a lot less firepower at the moment."

"Oh?"

"Yes, Ma'am. When we subverted their weapons system earlier and had that station fire on their own ships, the cruisers surrounding the station did *not* take it well." Torvald said. "They hit their own Command and Control station pretty hard. They didn't destroy it, but it has almost no defenses."

Yamashita's expression shifted to a sly grin. "Indeed? That's a pretty sizable station."

"Good cover," M'Buku said. "If they have to shoot through their own command center to hit us…"

"My thoughts exactly, Commander. Shoot and duck. However, it is awfully close to that mega-battleship."

"Captain, if I may?" Emily said. I hadn't realized that she'd come onto the bridge during the battle.

"Yes, Ensign?"

"Ma'am, if we can goad them into trying to move the *Behemoth* to get to us, I think the Kalikak will get a very nasty surprise." Emily then described the hidden sabotage that we and the other slaves had engaged in while working on the gigantic vessel.

"I like the idea, Ensign Darkfeather, but that damn ship has a *lot* of heavy firepower. Commander Torvald, what is the ETA of our fleet to the enemy shipyard?"

"Fourteen minutes."

The captain drummed her fingers on the command chair. "If we can take that thing off the board, our allies will have a much better chance of victory. Right now, even stationary it's a big threat. That much firepower…"

"Captain, if we threaten it, then slip behind the enemy station…" M'Buku said. Our executive officer was a cautious man, but if even he was on board, Captain Yamashita might bite.

"All right, it's big risk," she said, "but the reward is a much better chance of complete victory. Mr. Kolara, on my mark, jump us to these coordinates, and be prepared to dive behind that station. Mr. Voss, you'll likely only get one shot before we have to save our asses. FTL missiles, full spread. Make them count, Ensign."

"Ready for your command, Captain," Kolara said from the helm.

"Torvald, I want a countdown to the earliest possible time the Kalikak will detect our fleet coming in. This time, they can be a diversion for us."

———

Eleven minutes later, *Seeker* jumped back into the frying pan.

We emerged less than twenty five miles from the Behemoth, and unfortunately we did not catch them flat-footed.

"FTL missiles away!" I reported.

"Mister Kolara, get us behind that station," the captain ordered.

Seeker rocked as heavy mega-laser fire hit our shields, and a breach alarm sounded. A beam from the behemoth had slipped past both our shield layers.

"Mr. Voss, did you get a hit with that barrage?" the captain asked.

"Negative, Captain. It was on target, but the heavy laser fire took them all out before they got close."

Suddenly, the rocking and blast impacts ceased as if someone had turned off a thunderstorm at a moment's notice. Looking at my tactical scanners, I saw that we were behind the station, almost hugging its hull. As much as I wanted to attribute brute stupidity to our enemies, I saw that the weapons pods on the command station had previously been taken out with surgical precision, leaving the entire structure, for the most part, intact.

"Any movement on that battleship, Dora?" Yamashita asked.

"Not as such, Captain," Dora's blue hologram appeared next to her. "However, the heavy cruiser is now moving our way. May I suggest we peek out again and "incentivize" the *Behemoth* into action."

"Shield status?"

"Fully reformed, captain," Forbes said from the station next to me.

"Time to fleet arrival, Mr. M'Buku?"

"One minute. The Kalikak have to know they've going to to get hit from both sides now. Light cruisers are moving to intercept, and... the heavy cruiser is turning with them. Two light cruisers are still coming our way."

"Mr. Voss, prepare FTL missile tubes one through three. We may not get a hit through all that laser fire from the battleship, but maybe we can get them to do something stupid."

"All weapons ready, Captain," I said.

"Kolara, make a quick loop out and back. Let's piss them off."

Seeker blasted out of our hiding place like a racehorse with the gate open. My firing solution presented itself almost immediately, but I was not getting much help from my talent. I felt that the missiles were not going to get to their target almost before I launched all three of them.

The ship rocked with several hits, and the engineer on the bridge called out. "Hull breach, shuttle bay one!"

"Two missiles destroyed," Dora reported. "Missile three made it through, but was stopped by what is apparently a very powerful shield generator."

A minute later, we were hiding behind the control station again.

"Report!" The captain said.

"My scans show that the Kalikak have invested a great deal of time into that ship's shielding," Dora said. "Though the back third of the ship is incomplete, the shielding covers the vessel's entirety. It will be very difficult to..."

"What is it, Dora?"

"I believe that our plan is working, Captain. Putting camera feeds from Remoras Two and Three on screen."

Looking at the forward screen, I saw that the gigantic thruster packs on the *Behemoth* were firing. Evidently, they had grown weary of our game of hide-and-seek.

I had to look away for a moment and send my reloaded FTL missiles at one of the light cruisers who was getting too close for comfort. I knew that they'd hit home before they ever got there.

When I looked back toward the fate of the *Behemoth*, I saw that our weeks and months of sabotage had paid off.

The huge battleship was now misshapen, with the bow no longer aligned with the stern. As I watched, the disparity of angles increased, and I saw one section of the aft start swinging away from the front. It only got worse from there, and in a few moments, the front section of the Behemoth was spiraling away from its back half. Explosions began appearing across both sections, and one of the huge thrusters blew and went spinning off into the abyss.

"Their shielding has collapsed, Captain," Dora reported. "Time for a *coup de grace*, perhaps?"

"Indeed," Yamashita replied. "Mr. Voss, two FTL missiles for the fore section, one for the back. Mr. Kolara, give Mr. Voss an attack vector, please."

"Captain," Dora interrupted, "I am getting indications of a Jump Drive on the aft section. It is not functioning, but it appears that the Kalikak were engaged on mounting it on the *Behemoth*, though I'm quite sure that it could not have powered a ship that size."

"*Wanderer*'s people gave the K a lot of misinformation, Ma'am," Emily said. "The Kalikak, from everything we were told and observed, don't really understand the specifications for that drive."

"We could still scavenge it, Megumi," M'Buku said. "Save *Wanderer* the time of rebuilding one from scratch to get home."

Captain Yamashita looked at the ruined battleship for a moment, but shook her head. "No. We could still lose this battle, and as far as I'm concerned, our main objective is keeping jump technology out of the Kalikak's hands. Mr. Voss, change of plans. All three missiles are to go to the aft section. Specifically, into that Jump Drive. Am I clear?"

"Aye, Captain," I said. "Scratch the drive with everything we've got."

"Kolara, go!"

Seeker rounded the control station, and without having a wall of laser fire headed our way, I realized just how close we'd jumped in to the Behemoth. The front half of the huge vessel was on a collision course with the command and control station (and us!) Kolara had to curve around its tumbling mass to get past it.

The aft section of the vessel, was moving away much more slowly, and I took the time to feel in my mind for *Wanderer*'s drive. I delicately hit the missile-fire section of my touch screen and sent nuclear destruction to our wayward technology.

The Jump Drive and most of *Behemoth*'s unprotected aft section were annihilated. A few moments later, The Kalikak battleship's fore section slammed into the space station, utterly destroying both.

Even if we died in the remaining battle, our missions were accomplished.

"Dora, how goes the battle?" Yamashita asked.

"Confederation and Kalikak forces are engaged. The superior numbers of our allies are taking a heavy toll on the lighter Kalikak cruisers, but the enemy heavy cruiser is inflicting a great deal of damage to our allies as well."

"Mr. Kolara, plot a course. I want to jump right in on top of that bastard." The captain tapped away at the controls on her command chair. "I want to emerge at these coordinates."

Kolara looked at the screen on his console and I saw his eyes widen. He looked back at Captain Yamashita, his eyes questioning. She nodded. Our helmsman took a deep breath, adapted his coordinates and signified we were ready to jump.

"Jump!" the captain said.

———

At the short distance we had to travel, our emergence seemed almost instantaneous, and I saw why Kolara had looked alarmed.

Proximity alerts began blaring as *Seeker* appeared so close to the enemy battlecruiser that our shields overlapped. *Seeker*'s ventral shield grid went down immediately in the huge release of energy caused by this collision, but so did the battle cruisers's dorsal shields.

"Hit them!" the captain practically screamed.

I realized that my hands were already doing her bidding before my brain had registered the command. We were at an awkward angle to hit their power systems, being far forward, but I'd fired the plasma cannons without consciously knowing where I was aiming.

"Direct hit on their bridge!" Torvald said.

"Helm! Jump us back to our previous location. Now!"

Kolara jumped *Seeker* back to the remains of the *Behemoth*, which at this point was an expanding cloud of scrap.

"Captain, our allies are capitalizing on our attack on the

battle cruiser," Dora reported. She raised a tactical display on the main viewer. Several of the Yakar ships, along with a Wulkin vessel were attacking the area of the enemy ship where we'd decimated their shields. Barrages of missiles impacted the unprotected areas of the enemy craft, heavily damaging large sections of its hull.

Dora spoke to our comm system; "Confederation ships. This is *Seeker*. Distance yourself from that battle cruiser. We're reading an exceptional power spike from their aft section. They are either losing containment, or self destructing. Protect yourselves."

Her hologram turned toward the captain with a perfectly sculpted expression of contrition. "I beg your pardon, Captain, for speaking to our allies out of turn, but the situations was..."

She was interrupted by the icon for the enemy battle-cruiser erupting in a simulation of a FTL drive containment breach. A moment later, only the very front of the ship was still intact, though spinning away with no indication of power. None of our allies had been caught in the blast.

"No apologies needed, Lieutenant Dora. Good work all around."

"Captain, they're running," Lieutenant Commander Torvald reported. "All remaining light cruisers just went to maximum FTL. The Confederacy ships are following."

"Do we go after them too, Ma'am?" Kolara asked.

"We've done our part," Yamashita replied. "Our allies outnumber the remaining Kalikak, and I think we'll let them decide how far they want to take this. We are, after all, still guests in their space."

"Aye, Captain."

"Commander M'Buku, we took some hits on this endeavor. Ship's status?"

"Damage to dorsal hull plating from the shield collision.

Our bottom Laldoralin shielding is at twenty-three percent and climbing. However, the dorsal magna-shielding is not reforming. I think we blew out the shield emitters in that section."

"We took a hit in a shuttle bay, did we not?"

"Yes Ma'am, breach has been temp patched."

"Casualties?"

M'Buku was silent a moment. "Yes, Captain. Two crewman severely injured.. And one fatality. It was... Corporal Chen."

48

No one ever figured out exactly why Michael Chen had been in shuttle bay one when he should've been sacked out in his bunk, but we all guessed that the burly Sec-Ops corporal had been trying to help. He'd always been a fire-eater, a bit of an overachiever, and I guessed that he couldn't've just sat in his quarters while *Seeker* was at battle stations.

Seeker's crew, as well as most of *Wanderer*'s stood at attention in *Wanderer*'s largest shuttle bay, which now sat empty except for the crews... and several sleek coffins.

Captain Yamashita made an inspiring speech, much of which I barely heard. My mind was occupied remembering all the times that Michael had encouraged a gangly cadet during brutal physical SecOps training, how he and his comrades had come to our rescue on Derilon, how he'd kept the crew safe on Salla. Mostly though, I thought about the last couple of months living and working with him while we all tried to subvert the Kalikak.

Somewhere, in all that, we'd become friends, brothers in arms, and the heavy grief at his loss threatened to explode out of my chest. It was like having your heart filled with lead.

As the captain spoke, I felt a warm hand take my own, and looked over at Emily. Her face was wet and my own eyes began to brim over with tears. I wiped them away, and noted the number of crying faces in *Wanderer*'s crew. It had been some very difficult months for most of us. We'd all taken losses. We were all hurting.

When the ceremony was over, several float-bots began to take the coffins, one-by-one to cold-storage. There would be none of the "launch them into a star" business that seemed to permeate popular fiction. Our people were going home with *Wanderer*, even those who were only represented by an empty coffin.

They'd be interred where their families could visit them.

————

Exactly forty-three days later, *Wanderer* began her journey home. Before she left, her Remoras, deployed from *Seeker* had thoroughly mapped and scanned the as-yet-unnamed uninhabited world where our sister ship had run afoul of the Kalikak.

With the blessings of the Unity Confederation, the planet was claimed as a colony world of Earth. And with that, a sliver of the Laldoralin Hegemony was now extant in this quadrant. Even if no one lived there yet.

Seeker stayed on station, as we had no new orders. We spent our time exploring and gathering data on the new world, giving it the fine-toothed comb treatment and making very sure that there was no sign of alien civilization there, present or past.

The Confederation, now that they had improved shielding and weapons, went on the offensive to find the Kalikak. They'd also built the first stages of a confederation fleet built solely for the purpose of battle, the Unity Defense Space Force.

While we could see the reason that it was formed, to say Captain Yamashita was uncomfortable with the whole thing would be an understatement. There was no denying that *Seeker* had been instrumental in its inception.

We'd expected that our next contact with Earth would be through the new long-range transceiver that sat dormant in our comms array, but that was not the case.

We were all surprised when we were joined in orbit by no less than a Laldoralin heavy frigate and an unidentified Earth ship.

49

"She's like *Seeker* on steroids," I said, watching the unknown ship move into orbit near us.

"Definitely a warship," Commander M'Buku said. "I don't see a single extendable science section anywhere on her." The unknown ship was a third bigger than our own, and was heavily armed with plasma cannon emplacements.

"Plenty of weapon pods, though," Captain Yamashita noted.

"They're hailing us, Captain," Sedgewick reported.

"The Earth ship? Not the Laldoralin?"

"Yes, Ma'am, the Earth ship."

"On the forward screen, please, Lieutenant."

The main viewer switched from view of the planet below to the bridge of the other ship. Standing near the screen was a tall shaven-headed man, with a very fancy black mustache, carefully curled on the ends. His piercing blue eyes looked into the camera with an almost raptor-like gaze.

"Greetings, Captain Yamashita and the crew of the *Seeker*," he said. "I'm Richard O'Brian, Captain of the *E.D.S. Defender*."

"Welcome to the neighborhood, Captain," Yamashita said. "Not that I'm not happy for the support, but I wasn't aware that Earth was building... well... warships."

"*Defender* is intended as part of an Earth security force, Captain Yamashita. She's not intended for aggressive offense, and, to be honest, *Seeker*'s reports convinced EarthGov that our new colonies would likely need protection."

"Color me surprised."

"Yes, like the the Explorer Initiative, three ships were commissioned in the Defender Initiative, but we can discuss this over coffee. We have much to discuss, and I'd appreciate it if you and your senior officers would be so good as to shuttle over for a meeting. Also, if I could impose, would you also bring Acting Ensign Tanner Voss. There's someone here I think he'd like to see."

O'Brian stepped aside and a lieutenant stepped up beside him. My jaw nearly hit the floor when I saw who it was.

"Val? You're on Defender?" I said.

"Well, that's kinda obvious, little brother. I'll tell you what's what when you come to visit."

"What time would you like to meet, Captain O'Brian?" Yamashita said.

"We've got 0900 ship's time, here, how about 1100 hours?"

"We'll be there."

———

The *Defender* still had that new ship smell.

Her corridors were wider, but she was laid out along similar lines as *Seeker*. It's just that everything felt... roomier. This was amplified when our people were escorted to a conference room twice the size of our own. It was big enough that each spot at the table had a small microphone.

"Tanner!" Valiel said, appearing from a side corridor. "Hang back a moment."

I let all the officers pass me as they continued into the conference room.

"Val, I thought you were still on Earth. You should be resting. Everyone who was captured by the Kalikak…"

"Or spent weeks hiding out in a shuttle," Val said. "Yeah, I know, but I barely had a week at dad's house before I was given new orders to report to *Defender*. You'll note the new rank?"

I hadn't noticed, but her collar told me that my Lieutenant Junior Grade sister was now a Lieutenant Senior Grade. She looked better than she had in our prison, but my sister still looked thin, her cheekbones standing out on her face.

"I see. So, how's life on this ship?"

"Honestly, a little tense," she said. "O'Brian's command style is a lot different that Captain Kilmer's was. He's very demanding, and very by-the-book."

"Bit of a martinet?"

"Your words, not mine, Tanner. I just wanted to warn you, that he's going to try to filch you from…"

"Lieutenant Voss, Ensign Voss," a lieutenant commander wearing Defender's black and dark gray uniform motioned to us. "You're holding up the show. You can catch up on your own time."

"Aye, Commander," Val said.

We both entered, and being an ensign, I found myself at the farthest end of the table from the senior officers. To my surprise, Captain O'Brian wasn't at the head of the table, he sat to one side. In that place was the Captain of the Laldoralin ship.

"Captain Yamashita," O'Brian said, "Welcome to *Defender*.

May I introduce Orexar, Captain of the Laldoralin heavy frigate *Inspiration*."

"I greet you, Captain Yamashita," Orexar said. "I am here to mediate a treaty between the Hegemony and the Unity Confederation. As you are the one who made contact with these races, I would appreciate your help in facilitating a meeting, and sitting with me in negotiations."

"I would be honored, venerable Captain," Yamashita said. "Perhaps after our meeting, our vessels can translocate to Drexul station, My contacts there can contact their council of leaders to organize such a meeting."

"That would be most acceptable, Captain Yamashita. While the Laldoralin Hegemony is not an expansionist group, we are open to new members. As the world below us extends Hegemony influence to this area of the galaxy, we intend to become trading partners with the Confederation and perhaps later invite them to become part of our greater whole."

"Excellent. I will assume *Seeker* will be on detached service to you, Captain Orexar."

"*Seeker*'s orders from EarthGov are as follows," O'Brian said, looking at a viewer on the desk in front of him. "*E.S.S. Seeker* will indeed detach to help the Laldoralin representative. Upon completion of that task, you will be 'exploring' our, hopefully, new partners section of the galaxy. Our leaders want to know as much about these new neighbors as possible. Your little ship will be engaged in diplomatic visits, showing the flag, much more than exploring, I expect." O'Brian's tone was dismissive.

"Meeting new races is exploring in its own way," Yamashita said. Her face was expressionless, which, having been on the wrong end of her displeasure before, I knew was a sign of her irritation.

"The second half of your orders are to make yourself available as support to *E.D.S. Defender* should our vessel need help," O'Brian continued. "A very unlikely scenario with the defensive capabilities this ship has, as well as our luck charm." He gestured toward Valiel.

Val nodded to Captain Yamashita, who nodded back.

"Which, by the way, brings me to a question I'd like to pose, Megumi." Whatever the question was, I doubted using our captain's first name without being well known to her was a path to a positive response.

"What is that, *Captain* O'Brian?" Yamashita said, a cool tone in her voice.

"As you're going to be tied up glad-handing with the Confederation, I'd like to propose a trade. I hear you're short a SecOps person. I'd gladly trade one of mine for young Ensign Voss here. With two such hybrid luck charms at tactical, I'm pretty sure that these Kalikak, should we run across them, would be taught the error of their ways in short order."

I'd heard the phase "silence so thick you could cut it" before, but had never really understood the term. I did now.

"An interesting proposition," Captain Yamashita finally said, "but *Seeker* needs its 'luck charm' as much as *Defender* does hers. If there's one thing I've learned in the past year, it's that nothing is certain. I like having Tanner aboard. I must unfortunately decline."

"*Defender*'s services are going to be offered to the Confederation as support for their ongoing efforts against the Kalikak, to keep this area of space stable. Surely the boy would be better used on the front line," O'Brian said, a little heat coming into his own voice.

"You have Lieutenant Valiel Voss on board. She is an extremely competent young woman. I have no doubt that she can handle the challenge of your tactical needs."

"But..." O'Brian started.

"I believe that concludes this meeting," Orexar interrupted. "Captain Yamashita, if you would return to your ship and escort us to the station you spoke of..."

"Immediately, Captain Orexar," Yamashita said, rising. The rest of *Seeker*'s people were less than a half step behind as she exited the room. I winked at Val as I exited and began the walk back to our shuttle. It was going to be interesting having *Defender* around, and it would be nice to have Val in the neighborhood. Hopefully we could visit on occasion.

But... I decided it would be better if she came to *Seeker* to visit me.

As you might've expected, the Unity Confederation was eager to become trading partners with Earth, and by extension the entire Laldoralin Hegemony.

There were a few rough patches, as there are in any negotiations. Our new neighbors really wanted access to Jump Drive technology and our Laldoralin emissary just as adamantly refused to give it to them. I understood why. Our relationship was new, and we were still getting to know each other.

However, there was a great deal of goodwill towards us, what with us giving them shield technology and better sensor systems. I never heard whether our Laldoralin Captain gave Captain Yamashita any grief over sharing that tech, but as she's still our captain, it seems it actually *was* easier to get forgiveness than permission.

Defender left a few days after our meeting to join the Unity Defense Space Force in their efforts to find the Kalikak homeworld or base. I was very surprised when Emily told me that *Defender* didn't have the magnetic shield layering that *Seeker* does.

"What the... So they don't even have the generators on their hull?" I asked.

"Nope. My guess is she was sent out here before the science folk back on Earth had confirmed our designs," Emily said. She had her head on my shoulder and sat with her feet under her as we gazed out of the large ports in the forward lounge.

"Oh boy," I said. "Not really liking that. Maybe they have bigger everything, but if a fleet of K ships go after them, I'd feel better if they had all the advantages they can get."

"I doubt they had time to update their plasma cannons either," Emily said. "We sent those schematics back with *Wanderer*, and it sounds like they left Earth orbit less than two weeks after *Wanderer* returned."

"If they have the schematics, hopefully their engineering team can rebuild their weapons as they go."

"Maybe," Emily said. "But it's another reason I'm glad that the Captain kept you here. I wouldn't want my investment threatened."

"So I'm an investment now, am I?"

She looked up at me and batted very long lashes at me in a caricature of innocence. "Yes, but you're a very good investment." Emily had a very wide grin.

"All hands," the intercom blared, "prepare to unmoor. We will be jumping to the Yakar homeworld in ten minutes."

Emily and I were off duty, and were able to watch as *Seeker* rolled away from the station and toward her jump point, following our Laldoralin ally. As we held each other, sitting in the comfortable crew lounge chairs, I realized it was the nicest moment we'd had together since we were captured.

And we intended to make the most of it.

END

OTHER BOOKS BY CLINT HOLLINGSWORTH

––––––

Clint's Amazon Page

Voyages of the Seeker

- Seeker One
- Seeker Two
- Seeker Three
- Seeker Four

––––––

The Mac Crow Thrillers

- The Sage Wind Blows Cold
- Death in the High Lonesome
- The Deep Blue Crush
- Dying to Win
- Rise of the Fury

––––––

The Wandering Ones graphic novels

- The Die Off (prequel)
- The After Time
- The Mad Scout
- The Mission
- The Road Home

- Turf War
- Mind games
- Scout Trial (standalone)

———

Standalone books

- The Road Sharks (Prose, Wandering Ones Prequel)
- Wolves in Street Clothing (Non-fiction with Kris Wilder)
- Wilderness Survival Knives: Tips for Choosing and Using
- Shin Kagé: Duel at the Derelict (graphic novel)
- Tales of the Timewalker (graphic novel)
- Melpomené (Graphic novel with Jamie Robertson)
- Nature Scout Emily (graphic novel/coloring book)